THE WITCH IS BACK

WICKED WITCHES OF THE MIDWEST BOOK 17

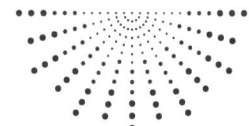

AMANDA M. LEE

WINCHESTERSHAW PUBLICATIONS

Copyright © 2020 by Amanda M. Lee

All rights reserved.

No part of this book may be reproduced in any form or by any electronic or mechanical means, including information storage and retrieval systems, without written permission from the author, except for the use of brief quotations in a book review.

❦ Created with Vellum

PROLOGUE

FIFTEEN YEARS AGO

"You're doing it wrong."

Tillie Winchester grabbed the container of wasp wings from her great-niece Thistle's hand and fixed the girl with a hard look. They had a tempestuous relationship on the best of days and it was obvious a fight was brewing.

Thistle was at that age — you know the one, where childhood sweetness meets teenage angst — and her attitude was on full display. "You said we were making up this spell as we went along," she challenged. "How do you know I'm doing it wrong?"

"Because I know." Tillie lifted the container to survey the contents. "You used at least ten of them. I told you to throw five in there."

Thistle rolled her eyes. "I did throw in five."

"Five pairs," Clove corrected, tucking a strand of dark hair behind her ear. She loved learning new spells, especially if she thought they might benefit her later in life, and when Tillie announced that they were going to be taking on a fearsome enemy, all three of her great-nieces jumped at the chance to be part of the potion-making team. "That's different than five wings."

"Oh, thank you for the math lesson, Clove," Thistle drawled, her hair pulled back in a messy bun. She'd been making noise about cutting it all off but, so far at least, her mother had managed to talk her out of it. Thistle wasn't one to be dissuaded, though, and it was only a matter of time before she went with her impulses and turned her hair into a work of art, much like the sculptures she'd been messing with in the basement the past few weeks.

Clove's happy expression didn't diminish. "You're welcome."

Her bright response only served to dampen Thistle's already dour mood. "Suck-up."

"I'm not a suck-up," Clove protested. "I'm simply pointing out that you made a mistake and Aunt Tillie, the brightest and most beautiful witch in all the land, is right."

"Manipulative suck-up," Thistle hissed.

Tillie extended a warning finger in Thistle's direction. "I happen to like a suck-up under the right circumstances. Don't give her grief."

Clove preened.

"And don't get full of yourself," Tillie warned her dark-haired great-niece. "Sucking up is only fun for a few minutes, and then it turns cloying. Nobody likes that."

Clove's smile faded. "What does cloying mean?"

The third junior witch, the blond Bay, lifted her head from the book she was reading. It was one of Tillie's dark spell books, and whenever the older witch deigned to allow the younger generation access to them, Bay was the first to dig deep and learn as much as she could in a short amount of time. "Cloying means to gross somebody out by being too sweet."

Tillie smiled as Clove's eyes narrowed. "No one can ever say you don't have the best vocabulary of this lot, Bay. You should pay attention to the spell instead of the book, though."

"And watch your back," Clove warned in a low voice. "I'm going to make you eat dirt later because you're mean."

"She's not being mean," Thistle argued. "She's just being honest. You're cloying. I like that word. It reminds me of clowns."

"They're not spelled the same way," Bay argued.

"Don't make me help Clove wrestle you down, Bay," Thistle snapped. "I want to be on your side, but you're being difficult."

"You're all being difficult," Tillie said. "In fact, I'm considering taking a photo of you and sending it to one of those groups that think children are monsters and nobody should have them."

"Those types of groups don't exist," Clove supplied. "Everybody wants kids. They're awesome."

Tillie arched a dubious eyebrow. "Who told you that?"

"My mom."

"Was she drunk at the time?"

"Maybe." Clove had a manipulative streak that she wasn't afraid to showcase in the oddest of times, like now. "She was drinking wine. I bet you want to know where she got that wine."

Since Tillie made her own wine — and kept it under lock and key so her nieces, the girls' mothers, couldn't get their hands on it — that was a foregone conclusion. The Winchester matriarch wasn't about to be shaken down by a thirteen-year-old, though. "I'm sure I already know where she got the wine."

"Yes, but I know how she got by your wards," Clove said. "I saw her doing it."

"It was probably only a momentary lapse. I must've forgotten to draw them properly after the last time I was down there."

"Or they've found a way around your wards."

Tillie worked her jaw, debating. Clove was smarter than anybody — including Tillie — gave her credit for. She knew exactly how to get what she wanted out of life. Sometimes she had good information. Other times she only thought she did.

"She's messing with you," Thistle volunteered. "She doesn't know anything. She just wants to get on your good side."

"That's not true." Clove employed the patented whine that continuously had Tillie's teeth on edge. "I know things. I'm smart." She tapped the side of her head for emphasis. "Who are you going to trust? I mean ... there's me, your favorite great-niece, or there's Thistle, the girl everybody wants to lock in a shed and forget about."

"That did it!" Thistle slapped her hands on the workbench and stood. "I think we should take this outside."

"That is where the dirt is," Bay agreed, flipping a page. "Why do all these spells talk about revenge? I didn't think we were supposed to seek people out to hurt them. Isn't karma supposed to be our equalizer?"

At almost fifteen, Bay was a student of the English language. She loved writing and reading, and she spoke at a level Tillie often found uncomfortable. The attention she was showing the spell book now only heightened that emotion.

"Don't worry about that book," Tillie snapped. "That book is none of your business. You shouldn't be reading it."

"Then you shouldn't have it out," Thistle said. "You know Bay has never met a book she doesn't want to read. This is really your fault."

"Keep it up, Mouth," Tillie warned. "You're on my last nerve. If it snaps, it'll be like a rubber band and smack you in the face."

"You're all talk."

"We'll see." Tillie went back to the cauldron and stared at the contents. "Ten wasp wings really are too many. This could blow up if we're not careful."

"Not literally, right?" Bay raised her eyes until they connected with Tillie's annoyed glare. "If you blow up the house, Mom will really be angry."

"Don't worry about the house."

"Aunt Tillie has it under control," Clove reassured her cousins. "She's the strongest and bravest witch in our family for a reason."

"Okay, that will be enough of that." Tillie planted her hands on her hips and glared. "You really are being a suck-up today. What do you want?"

Clove was suddenly the picture of innocence. "What makes you think I want anything? Can't I just love you without being accused of terrible things?"

"Oh, good gravy." Tillie lifted her eyes to the ceiling, as if praying to an invisible goddess to give her strength, and then forced her attention back to the cauldron. "Whatever you're selling today, Clove, I'm not buying it. I'm warning you now."

"I'm not selling anything."

"Good."

"I'm not."

"Great."

Clove stared at Tillie for a long time and then extended her lower lip. "You're going to make my eyes leak if you keep being suspicious of me. I saw a show on television — it's damaging to a teenager's self-esteem when adults don't trust them."

"I can't hear you," Tillie sang out. The girls might've been the children, but she was more than willing to give them a run for their money when it came to immaturity. "Your voice is nothing but the droning wind."

Thistle stuck her tongue out at Clove, obviously amused. What was supposed to be a simple potion-making adventure had turned into mayhem, as usual. Thankfully, all the Winchesters thrived on mayhem ... at least to some degree.

"How to make a harlot cry," Bay read aloud from the book. "How to make a knife in the back transfer to the person who planted it. Seriously, these spells are about revenge and we're supposed to be above that."

Tillie's patience had been tissue-thin before Bay decided to take on the mantle of morality police. "They're not revenge spells. They're simply ... something I like to have in my pocket just in case."

"Just in case you want revenge?"

"Just in case the world ends and I need them."

"What's a harlot?" Clove asked, studying her fingernails. "I've heard the word before but I can't remember what it means."

"A harlot is a promiscuous woman," Bay explained.

"Someone who goes after wives and boyfriends," Thistle added. "If you ask me, that's not a revenge spell. It's just a way of helping karma work faster than it might under normal circumstances."

Tillie shot the girl an appraising look. "You might not be a lost cause just yet."

Bay shook her head. "You can call them whatever you want, but these are bad spells. This one here, for example, allows you to turn a man's ... you know ... green if he cheats on you."

Tillie's expression never changed. "So?"

"So, that's a revenge spell. If you were following karma's guidelines, you would just let his misdeeds catch up to him."

"Only a kvetch would think that."

Clove, who had looked to be deep in thought for several seconds, stirred. "Why would you want to turn it green?"

"Because green is the color of death," Thistle replied.

"Black is the color of death," Bay corrected. "Green is the color of sickness. If you turn it green, anybody who sees it will think it's diseased."

"The Hulk is green," Clove argued. "I bet his thing is green too. Nobody would think it's diseased if he whipped it out."

"No, but they might think it's broken because it's so big," Thistle said. "He is the Hulk, after all. You know that thing has to be ... ." She didn't finish, instead holding her hands more than a foot apart.

"See," Tillie said. "Green isn't the color of disease. It's simply a different color."

"I think it would be cool to see one that was purple," Clove offered. "That's my favorite color this week."

"Why don't you wait until you're older and see a regular one before you ask for them to do tricks," Tillie suggested.

"I've seen a normal one."

Tillie straightened, her eyes turning to slits as she regarded the perky brunette. "When have you seen a normal one? Wait ... did Roger Feldman flash you at the lake last week? He flashed me, which was bad enough, but you're a minor."

"He wasn't flashing people," Thistle countered. "He just had an ice pop in his pants and thought it was funny to wave it around."

"Oh, is that what that was?" Tillie's forehead creased. "I thought it was awfully small." She shook her head. "Seriously, though, where have you seen a normal one?"

Clove looked taken aback. "Um ... ."

"Tell me," Tillie insisted.

Perhaps sensing she was in trouble, Clove demurely lowered her eyes. "I forget."

"She's been watching *28 Days Later*," Bay volunteered, still flipping through the book. "There's full-frontal nudity in the opening shot. I caught her freezing the DVD and getting really close to the television to get a better look the other day."

Tillie's eyebrows hopped. "I didn't know that movie had male nudity. I thought it was just fast-moving zombies, which defies the laws of man, by the way. Zombies can't run fast."

"They're not zombies," Thistle countered. "They're humans infected by rage."

"Do they eat people?"

"Kind of."

"Then they're zombies."

"But they're not."

"I say they're zombies."

"Who cares about that?" Clove exploded. "The only good thing about that movie is the naked guy."

"I'm going to have to watch it again to prove that," Tillie said dryly.

Bay, who had only half an ear on the conversation, straightened. "Here's a spell to make your enemy develop a rash whenever eating cake." She lifted her accusatory eyes to her great-aunt. "That's just mean."

"It is." Tillie's smile was evil. "I've only used it once and it was well worth it."

"Who did you use it against?" Clove queried.

"Mrs. Little," Thistle replied, naming Tillie's arch nemesis without missing a beat. "There's only one person Aunt Tillie hates enough to use that spell on."

"She had it coming," Tillie said. "She tried to get my plow confiscated because she said I wasn't licensed as a service provider. Well, I showed her. I made it so she can't eat that chocolate cake she loves so much at the diner. That will teach her to move against me."

"Except she doesn't know you did it to her," Bay pointed out. "We can't tell people about our magic. Mrs. Little thinks she developed a sudden allergy or something. She's probably spending a bunch of money at the doctor to figure out what's going on."

"That's just an added benefit." Tillie grabbed a handful of goober dust and threw it in the cauldron. "I don't know why you're feeling sorry for her. It's not as if she's ever nice to you. In fact, she once told me that I should lock you in the basement and throw away the key."

"Was that after you made us do something to her?" Bay asked. "Like, I don't know, turn her snow yellow."

"She also had that coming." Tillie wasn't in the mood to have her methods called into question. "Seriously, why are you being like this? You're usually the first to jump in and help me with a plan."

"I believe you're confusing her with me," Thistle corrected.

Tillie made a face. "No, you only volunteer your services if you're bored. Usually you complain nonstop."

"Yeah, Thistle," Clove intoned.

"And you're usually sucking up," Tillie added. "Together, you're a nightmare of complaints and fake sugar. That's the reason Bay is my preferred sidekick."

"That's the meanest thing you've ever said to me." Clove folded her arms over her chest. "I'm supposed to be your preferred sidekick. I'm the easiest to get along with."

"Only in your head." Tillie's gaze was penetrating when it landed on Bay. "What is up with you? I would appreciate a little enthusiasm with the revenge plotting today. I don't think that's too much to ask."

Bay shrugged, noncommittal. "I've just been thinking. Haven't you ever wondered if the world would be a better place if everybody just got along?"

Tillie's mouth dropped open. "Who has been teaching you this nonsense?"

"It's just something I've been thinking about."

"Well, stop. The world isn't all cookies and rainbows."

"Ooh, cookies," Clove whispered.

Tillie ignored her and barreled forward. "You can be the best person in the world, but it won't get you anywhere because there are rotten people at every turn. You can be a good person without being a doormat, and I certainly didn't raise you to be a doormat."

"I don't want to be a doormat," Bay reassured her. "I just think it would be nice if we weren't always fighting."

"That sounds like a Hallmark movie, and you know how I feel about those," Tillie snapped.

"Yes, they're only good if Tori Spelling dies," Thistle supplied.

Tillie nodded. "Exactly. Life will never be easy, not for us or anybody else.

If you want something, you'll have to fight for it. Letting other people walk all over you is a surefire way to be unhappy forever.

"You need to be strong, Bay, and when an enemy comes after you it's your job to take them down," she continued. "I'm not saying to go after someone just to go after them."

"Tell that to Mrs. Little," Thistle interjected.

"Shut up, Mouth!" Tillie jabbed a finger at Thistle but kept her eyes on Bay. "You need to be careful. Not everybody has a good heart like you. Not everybody will always tell the truth. It's up to you to make sure that you're protected, and if somebody comes after you, make them wish they'd never been born."

Bay pursed her lips. "So ... revenge is okay in moderation. That's what you're saying."

"No. Revenge is awesome no matter how heavily you dish it out. I'm saying that allowing someone else to hurt you isn't okay. Payback should never be limited."

"Huh." Bay flicked her eyes to the cauldron. "And what sort of payback are we dishing out to Mrs. Little today?"

"She looked at me funny when I was downtown. She has it coming."

"Oh, well, at least you have a reason to go after her."

"That's what I was saying." Tillie stood directly in front of Bay. "You can't allow bad people to get a foothold in your life, because they'll never cede that territory once they have it. You have to be willing to get down and dirty. That's the only way to thrive."

"But who gets to decide who is in the right?"

"Me."

Thistle snorted. "Who didn't see that coming?"

"If you're ever in doubt, ask me," Tillie pressed. "I'll always steer you in the right direction."

Bay knew that was bunk but she was in no mood to fight. "Okay, but if Mrs. Little cries again this time, I'm not providing her with the Kleenex."

"Fair enough. We'll make Clove do it."

"I can live with that."

ONE

PRESENT DAY

"Give me a kiss."

Landon Michaels, a cheeky grin taking over his handsome face, leaned in and invaded my personal space. He was attractive, almost painfully so, and I often wondered if the Goddess got a glimpse of him somehow — perhaps through a magical hourglass — and guided the ancient Greeks when it came time to chisel a masterpiece in his image. I didn't mention that to him, of course, because his ego was already big enough to suck the air out of a castle, but I often thought it.

"I'm eating," I responded, holding up my elephant ear for proof.

"I don't care."

"I need my nourishment."

"You could just live on love."

It was a cocky statement — he was full of them — but there was also something earnest about the way he looked at me. "Fine." I leaned in and gave him a closed-lip peck. "Happy?"

"No." His frowned. "That was not a kiss. That was a slap in the face more than anything else."

I looked around to see if anyone was watching us. Our spot on a blanket at the edge of the Hemlock Cove fairgrounds provided prime real estate to watch varying degrees of shenanigans. Nobody appeared to care what we were doing.

"Fine." This time when I kissed him, I put some effort behind it. We both were both breathless when we separated. "Are you happy?"

His grin was lightning quick. "Ecstatic. Now give me some of that thing." He inclined his head toward the elephant ear.

"No way." I clutched the box tray the treat rested in closer to my chest. "You can have my virtue but not my sugar."

That had him laughing as he leaned back on his elbows and looked up at the blue sky. "I see how it is."

"The food cart is right over there. You can get your own."

"We're supposed to share."

I made a face. In the Winchester household, sharing was something of a touchy subject. When we were growing up, Aunt Tillie often told us it was a dirty word, much to our mothers' chagrin. I'd learned quickly at a young age that I had to hold on to what I valued most. Landon now topped that list. "Why are we supposed to share when there's enough for both of us to have our own?"

"Because we're getting married."

It had been a few weeks since we'd gotten engaged, and the statement still sent chills down my spine. "We are getting married," I agreed, hating the way my cheeks burned. I'd turned into a total sap. In addition to being a badass witch, I, Bay Winchester, was also going to be someone's wife. It still felt alien to me. "Do you want to talk about that?"

He lifted an eyebrow and cast me an unreadable look. "Not if you're going to suck the fun out of the afternoon."

"What makes you think I'm going to suck the fun out of the afternoon?"

"You have your serious face on."

"I just made out with you in public. If I had my serious face on, I wouldn't have done that."

He chuckled. "Bay, I love you more than life itself."

"I love you too."

"What's not to love?" He winked at me before sobering. "You tend to dwell on things, and I don't want that. We're at a festival. We should be having fun."

"I didn't realize we weren't." Miffed, I turned my full attention to my snack. "I'll just sit over here and commiserate about how boring I am with my elephant ear. If you'll excuse me, please."

"Oh, don't even." He wagged a warning finger. "I'm not in the mood for an argument, fake or otherwise. I never said you were boring. In fact, you're the most interesting woman I've ever met. That's why I proposed ... and in the most romantic way possible."

I had to fight the urge to laugh, mostly because it would only encourage him. I barely managed to tamp down my mirth. "It was a pretty good proposal," I conceded, momentarily holding up my left hand to study the ring he'd given me. It was beautiful, simple and yet elegant. The stone seemed huge on my finger, and not for the first time, I wondered how I'd gotten lucky enough to have him in my life.

He swooped in and gave me a kiss, jerking me out of my reverie. "See, you have your serious face on," he whispered, not moving his mouth away from mine. "It's the Fourth of July Festival, Bay. You should be focused on me, fun, and food ... in that order."

That made me laugh and I obligingly broke off a piece of my elephant ear and shoved it in his mouth. "In that order, huh?"

He chewed and nodded, the glint in his eyes causing my stomach to churn, although not in an unpleasant manner.

He waited until after he'd swallowed to speak again. "It's the time of fireworks, sweetie. I thought we could ignite some of our own while waiting for the town's display."

He had a deep charming streak — and he knew it — and it nudged a resigned sigh out of me. "Okay, we don't have to talk about the wedding."

He shook his head. "That's not what I want." He was firm. "I would love to talk about the wedding, as long as you don't get too serious about things. I want to have fun with this. I don't want you constantly worrying about whether or not your mother will be happy with our choices. I just want you to be happy."

Could he know that was exactly what I wanted to hear? Probably. He was good that way, and nobody knew me better than him. "Okay, let's do the easy stuff first. When do you want to get married?"

"Today."

I snickered. "That's not much lead time."

"Bay, the only thing I want is to be able to call you my wife. Well, and bacon. If you could have your wedding dress made of bacon, by the way, that's pretty much my dream event."

"I'll take it under advisement," I said dryly. "But I don't think I can make a wedding happen today, especially if you want a bacon dress."

"Fair enough. When do you want to get married?"

"I was thinking about August."

He sat up straighter and regarded me with an expression of surprise and hope. "Really?"

"Um, yeah. Why are you so surprised?"

"I don't know. I thought maybe you would want to drag it out longer. I mean ... Clove got to be the center of attention for much longer than two months when planning her wedding."

"I know, but ... I don't know that I need to be the center of attention."

He shook his head. "I want you to be the center of attention. You deserve it."

"Being the center of attention comes with a whole lot of baggage."

"Like what?"

"Like constant visits from Mom and the aunts for planning sessions. They'll invade the guesthouse regularly."

Landon's forehead furrowed. Obviously he hadn't considered that.

"They don't knock either, as you're well aware."

"Well ... we'll change the locks."

"They're witches. That won't work on them."

"Good point." He leaned in and brushed his lips against my cheek. "I want you to get everything you've ever dreamed about from the day. We're only doing this once so it's important that you not cede your wishes to anyone."

"I don't plan on ceding my wishes. I already know what I want."

"Tell me and I'll make it happen."

I knew that was true, and it warmed me all over. "I want to get married on the bluff, right where you proposed."

He didn't look surprised at the declaration. "I figured."

"We live in Michigan. If we want an outdoor wedding, it has to be in the summer. I don't want to wait until next year, do you?"

"No." He rubbed his chin, considering. "I hadn't thought about that."

"Are you okay with getting married so soon?" A niggling doubt invaded the back of my mind. "I mean, if it's too quick ... ."

He grabbed my hand and squeezed. "I just told you that I wanted to marry you today. August is perfect. Can you get the dress you want in that amount of time?"

"I'm sure I can."

"Well, then August it is." He grinned as he brushed a strand of hair from my face. "Can we have bacon cheeseburgers as the entree?"

His bacon love, while cute, was overpowering at times. "I was thinking we could make mini bacon cheeseburgers for appetizers."

"Seriously?"

"It's your wedding too."

"If I didn't love you before." He grabbed me around the waist and started tickling, rolling until he was on top and his lips were on mine. He'd been in a perfectly wonderful frame of mind since proposing — as if planning for the romantic gesture had taken all of his energy for weeks and now he could relax — and he was constantly in the mood for petting and snuggles.

"Oh, don't make me get the hose," a dour voice announced from somewhere to our left.

I strained my neck to look up, ignoring Landon's growling, and fixed Chief Terry Bradshaw with a huge smile. "Hi."

"Don't 'hi' me." Chief Terry had been a fixture in my life since I was a kid. He'd gone out of his way to spend time with Thistle, Clove, and me during our youth — probably because we were bereft of paternal influence at the time — and he'd stood as our godfather ever since. In addition to being chief of police, he was Landon's constant companion in law enforcement. They worked through a thorny relationship of their own.

"Why are you bugging us?" Landon complained as he rolled off me, his whine reminding me of a petulant teenager.

"You're making spectacles of yourselves," Chief Terry said, folding his arms over his chest. "I've had numerous complaints about the ... stroking ... that appears to be taking place here."

Landon propped himself on an elbow. "Stroking?"

"That's what I said."

"Nobody has been stroking anybody. We're not animals."

"I'm kind of an animal," I countered.

"Oh, yeah? What animal?" Landon looked interested. "I've always fancied myself a wolf."

"You've got the look," I agreed. "I either want to be a bat or a cat."

He wrinkled his nose. "Why those?"

I shrugged. "I think they're cute."

"You're definitely cute." He gave me a kiss, probably because he knew it would agitate Chief Terry, and rubbed his nose against mine. "You're more of a bunny. You do that nose twitching thing."

"I will get the hose," Chief Terry warned.

"Then I'll arrest you for attacking an FBI agent," Landon countered.

"I'm not afraid of you." Chief Terry's gaze moved to me. "I expected better from you, young lady. Public displays of affection are ... so gross."

"You're only saying that because in your head I still have pigtails and beg for ice cream."

"We should totally have an ice cream sundae bar at the wedding," Landon noted. "Who doesn't love hot fudge?"

"We can do that."

He slid his gaze to me. "Are you going to actually let me plan things with you?"

"Why wouldn't I?"

"Because movies and television have taught me that I should let you plan everything. Letting you have your way is imperative to marital harmony."

"I want you to be involved."

"Does that mean the bacon dress is possible?"

I hesitated. Giving him false hope probably wasn't a good idea. "No, but there might be some way to do something with bacon lingerie for our wedding night. I'm going to have to do some research, so don't get your hopes up just yet."

"Sold." He gave me another kiss, this one chaste, and then fixed Chief Terry with an annoyed look. "We're celebrating our engagement, and we're not near anybody else. We're fully clothed and I've kept my hands from wandering."

I shot him a dubious look.

"Mostly," he added. "Why are you ruining our celebratory blanket fun?"

"You're in public," Chief Terry snapped. "You're not supposed to have blanket fun anywhere but in the privacy of your own bedroom." As if realizing what he'd said too late to take it back, he barreled forward. "And she's still my little girl, so you shouldn't be having blanket fun with her anywhere."

Love for him welled up. "Would you like an ice cream bar at the wedding? It sounds kind of neat."

The look Chief Terry shot me was equal parts exasperation and adoration. "You should have whatever you want, sweetheart. As long as it doesn't involve public lewdness, I want you to be happy."

"Nobody is being lewd," Landon argued. "We're minding our own business."

"Then why have eight people complained about tongues?"

"Tongues?" I cocked my head, confused. "There hasn't been any tongue action."

"That doesn't change the fact that people are complaining. As the chief of police, it's my job to make sure the residents and guests of Hemlock Cove are comfortable. You're grossing everybody out with the schmaltz ... and the filthy thoughts."

"I *have* been having filthy thoughts," Landon conceded, grinning. "But you need to suck it up. We're being good."

"I want to know who has been complaining," I interjected. "If it's Mrs. Little, she shouldn't count. She'll never be happy."

"Which is why I ignored her the first two times she approached me," Chief Terry replied. "Then other people started complaining."

"Have you considered that Mrs. Little paid them to complain?" Landon asked. "I mean ... she is still angry about that whole pirate treasure thing out by the lake. She's vowed revenge."

"Of course she's responsible for some of the complaints. But she's not responsible for all of them."

Landon refused to back down. "How do you really know that? She's wily. It would be just like her to pay people to complain. If we want to defeat the evil — and she's all kinds of evil — we should do the opposite of what she demands." As if to prove he was serious, Landon slid closer to me. "You should go over there and tell her you did your best, and we'll continue stroking each other in public."

I shot him a dirty look. "Don't say stroking like that. We weren't stroking each other. That's really gross when you think about it."

"Oh, man." Landon rolled to his back. "Now you're going to go all prudish on me. I blame Mrs. Little for this."

"Welcome to my world," Chief Terry groused. "I want to blame her for everything, but she has a point this time. You two are making people uncomfortable. If you don't stop, I'm going to give the fire department the okay to hose you down."

Landon was quiet for a moment, as if really contemplating the situation, and then shook his head. "I want to see these complainers with my own eyes. I don't believe they exist."

"Think again, Sparky," Aunt Tillie announced, appearing on the other side of the blanket. Where she'd come from, I couldn't say, but she was altogether sneaky for a woman of her age. Landon often joked about tying a bell around her neck so we would always know where she was. I was starting to think it was a good idea. "I'm one of the people who complained. You guys are officially disgusting. If I wanted a porn show, I would order it on Pay-Per-View."

Now it was my turn to make a face. "Since when are you into porn?"

"There's some really good stuff out there these days. What you guys are doing is just nasty."

"Fine." Landon threw up his hands. "I will not touch my wife-to-be in public for the rest of the day. Will that make you both happy?"

"If you extended the timeframe for the rest of your lives, I would be thrilled," Chief Terry responded.

"Yeah, that's not going to happen. But in the interest of spending time alone with my fiancée, I'm willing to refrain from stroking her in public if it means you two will go away."

This time my stomach twisted at the suspect word. "You can't say stroking like that. It's giving me a sour stomach."

"This is your fault," Landon muttered darkly, his gaze on Chief Terry. "We were having a perfectly nice afternoon, making plans for an August wedding, and now you two have ruined everything. I knew we should've locked ourselves in the guesthouse for a month to celebrate in private."

"You could definitely stroke there without anybody complaining," Aunt Tillie agreed.

"Stop saying that word," I insisted. "It's grossing me out. In fact ... ." I broke off, a whisper of distress rolling over me and causing the hair on the back of my neck to stand on end.

"What is it?" Landon was in tune with my moods of late, almost to a distressing degree. He recognized the moment the merriment had fled my body.

"I ... don't ... know." I rolled to a sitting position and glanced around, reaching out with my senses. Even though I had no proof, I recognized something very bad was about to happen.

"This is what happens when you stroke each other in public," Aunt Tillie muttered. "You've turned her into a paranoid mess. I hope you're happy."

Landon snapped. "We were both extremely happy until you interrupted our day. Now she's upset ... and the elephant ear is cold. This just bites."

The whisper returned, this time louder, and when I looked to the left it was as if some magic force parted the crowd. There, standing together as if they didn't have a care in the world, evil took human form ... and it was recognizable.

"Son of a ... !" Aunt Tillie let loose an explosive curse when she realized who I was focused on.

"Is that ... ?" Landon squinted to better make out the two figures.

"Rosemary and Willa," I replied, resigned. "They're here."

"And I finally have a chance to kill them," Aunt Tillie said, a dark glint in her eye. "The stars have aligned. It's time for Armageddon."

She started in their direction, and the Winchester world officially shifted on its axis.

2

TWO

"It's the end times," Chief Terry intoned as he watched Aunt Tillie stalk toward her sister.

I had to bite the inside of my cheek to keep from laughing as I stood — honestly, very little about this situation was funny — and fought to keep it together as I brushed the seat of my shorts. "Aunt Willa isn't that bad."

Chief Terry shot me a withering look. "I've been around longer than you. In fact, I'm fairly certain that I know her better than you despite the familial bond. She's terrible."

"I guess the public stroking wasn't so bad in hindsight, huh?" Landon challenged as he moved to my side, his eyes narrowed in shrewd disbelief. "I thought you guys ran her out of town."

I elbowed his stomach to get his attention. "Stop saying 'stroking.' It really is grossing me out."

He offered up a soft smile and kissed the tip of my nose. "You'll live. Tell me about them." He inclined his head toward Willa and Rosemary, who looked perfectly at home among the other tourists. "Didn't they swear to never return?"

"I think they swore that they would rather die than ever come back," I replied, thinking back to their last visit. It hadn't been pleasant. Aunt Willa wanted a piece of the Winchester business pie and threatened to sue the family if they didn't hand over a stake in the family land. Aunt Tillie came through in the end with documentation that proved Aunt Willa was only a half sibling — our great-grandfather apparently liked to sleep around — and because the land came through our great-grandmother, who was not her biological mother, she had no claim on the property. It had been an ugly scene and I was glad when they left.

"And yet here they are," Chief Terry said. "How much do you want to bet they're up to something?"

"Only a fool would take that bet," I muttered, sliding between him and Landon. "I'd better corral Aunt Tillie before she smites them in public."

"And there go my picnic snuggles," Landon complained. "This really is your fault, Terry. We were having a perfectly pleasant afternoon talking about bacon lingerie and ice cream sundae bars. Now look what's happened."

Chief Terry's eyes were slits of distaste when they landed on Landon. "I'll thump you, son. I know we're supposed to have professional courtesy and all that, but I really will smack the crap out of you if you don't quit putting filthy images about my sweetheart in my head."

"*My* sweetheart," Landon corrected. "We're getting married."

"Not if I find a shallow grave to dump you in."

I ignored their banter — they both got off on messing with each other — and hurried to catch up with Aunt Tillie. I'd lost her in the crowd. If she got to Aunt Willa and Rosemary first it would turn into a scene from *Goodfellas* ... and Aunt Tillie would be channeling Joe Pesci for the takedown.

"You know what I just realized?" I asked Landon. "Aunt Tillie is kind of like the female Joe Pesci."

His eyes were incredulous when they locked with mine. "That's what you were thinking?"

"Kind of."

"It's a good thing I'm already a goner where you're concerned, because otherwise the twisted turns your mind takes might freak me out."

"Luckily you don't scare easily."

"There is that." He linked his fingers with mine and took the lead, cutting a path through the crowd and not stopping until we were directly in front of Aunt Willa and Rosemary. They didn't look particularly surprised to see me, but Landon's appearance was another story.

"Well, hello." Aunt Willa straightened and flashed Landon a smile that could be described as almost friendly.

Almost.

"Hello," Landon replied, his expression placid. "It's nice to see you again. We saw you from across the way." He pointed toward the blanket we'd abandoned. "We had to get a closer look because we couldn't be sure it was really you."

"It's really us." Aunt Willa's smile was less welcoming when she turned it to me. "And how are you, Bay?"

"Confused," I replied, opting for honesty. "What are you doing here?"

"Walkerville is my home. I visit from time to time."

"Hemlock Cove," I corrected. I'd grown up in Walkerville too. I should've been attached to the town's original name. However, it felt like a distant memory, and not an altogether pleasant one. Hemlock Cove fit our town's needs, and it felt right.

"It doesn't matter what it's called now," Aunt Willa said primly. "It will always be Walkerville in my heart."

"Uh-huh." She was definitely up to something. Even if I didn't know her — and Chief Terry was right, I had little familiarity with the woman — I ascertained rather quickly that it wasn't altruism or a yearning for home that had brought her here. "Where are you staying?"

"We've checked into an inn," Rosemary volunteered. She was a cousin ... kind of. She was the same age as us. Her mother was the same age as our mothers. But we rarely saw her. I knew Rosemary and Willa best, and everything I knew about them pointed toward an apocalypse.

"That's ... weird," I said. "I thought you guys had decided that you didn't want to be here any longer."

"No, we decided we didn't want to be around you any longer," Aunt Willa clarified. "The town has done nothing to us."

It didn't take a genius to read between the lines of that statement. "But you think we have done something to you."

"You specifically? Not as much as your older counterparts. Speaking of, where is my sister?"

Aunt Tillie had started in our direction as if she had murder on her mind, but then conveniently disappeared. I should've been relieved that she hadn't caused a scene or picked a fight. I knew better than to feel relief about anything regarding Aunt Tillie, though.

"She's around," Landon replied, his hand moving to the back of my neck to send a silent message of support. We were in this together. All of it. We were a unit, and even though the enemies we'd been fighting of late had been of the supernatural variety, I couldn't help but wonder if Aunt Willa and Rosemary were more dangerous.

"Did Mom know you were coming?" I asked.

The way Aunt Willa rolled her eyes told me it was a stupid question. "I am not in contact with your mother. In fact, I'm not in contact with any members of your family. You shouldn't feel obliged to carry on a conversation with me."

For some reason, I found the statement amusing. "Well, that's just ... great." I glanced at Landon and found a muscle working in his jaw. He hated it when he felt I was being disrespected. "Well, if you're not here to see us, I guess that means we can go."

"That would be preferable," Aunt Willa agreed.

I glanced between her and Rosemary one more time and then took a step back. I shrugged in answer to Landon's silent question and then headed back in the direction we'd come from, moving a full twenty steps before slowing my pace.

"Well, they're definitely up to something," Landon noted as he scanned the people moving past us.

"Oh, you think?" My anxiety level had quadrupled in less than five minutes. "What was your first clue?"

"I don't think I deserve the sarcasm, Bay. I was just making an observation."

I squeezed his hand. "I'm sorry. They just caught me off guard. I don't know what they're doing here."

He slid his hand over the back of my head, a comforting move, and pulled me close. "It doesn't matter why they're here. They can't hurt us."

I wasn't entirely certain that was true. "They know."

"Know what?"

"The big secret. They know we're witches."

Instead of joining in my concern, he barked out a laugh. "Oh, you're so cute." He pulled me tighter against him. "Baby, everybody in this town knows the big secret. Heck, people in the neighboring town know the big secret. Hemlock Cove is full of witches."

"It's a town full of normal people pretending to be witches with one family at the center of things who might actually be able to perform magic. If the truth gets out ... ." I left it hanging. He knew as well as I did that things could get ugly for all of us if the wrong people figured out the truth.

"Bay, everybody knows. Even those who don't *know* know somehow know. They at least suspect. Even if Willa and Rosemary broadcast it from one end of town to the other, it won't matter."

In my head, I knew he was right, but my heart was putting up a fight. "I just don't want anything to ruin us ... or our wedding plans ... or anything else."

The amusement never left his face. "Nothing can ruin us," he promised.

"We're going to be together forever. Nothing can ever take me away from you. I won't let it."

He shouldn't have to reassure me this way, I realized. This insecurity — something I was working hard to eradicate — was a bigger issue than Aunt Willa and her sniveling granddaughter. "You're right." I rested my head on his shoulder. "We can't let them get to us."

"I have no intention of letting them get to me." He was firm. "I'm not afraid of them. You shouldn't be either. But they should be afraid of Aunt Tillie. Why not just let her handle this? She'll have them crying and begging for mercy in twenty-four hours."

He had a point. "Where did she go?" I craned my neck to find her in the crowd. "One second she was here and the next she was gone."

"I'm sure she's planning something terrible."

I chewed my bottom lip. "If Aunt Tillie murders Aunt Willa, will you be able to look the other way?"

His chuckle warmed me. "I'll deal with it."

"Okay."

"Does that mean you're willing to return to the blanket with me? I need some vigorous stroking."

"Landon!"

"You're so easy." He slid his arm around my waist. "Come on. We'll get fresh snacks along the way. I'm thinking nachos and churros."

"I want cinnamon rolls, too."

"Good idea."

"And hot dogs."

"An even better idea."

"And maybe some tacos."

"Everything on the menu it is. I ... ." He pulled up short when Rosemary skirted around Jenna Bigelow, a local who fancied herself a festival chaperone when it came to the younger children, and placed herself directly in front of us. Thankfully she was sans Aunt Willa, but that didn't offer me much hope for a pleasant interlude.

"What do you want?" Landon whined. "You're ruining my picnic blanket day."

Rosemary's expression was blank, which wasn't all that different from her everyday expression. "I don't want to take up much of your time," she said, clearly uncomfortable.

"It's fine," I interjected, figuring the quicker we let her speak, the faster she would retreat. "Is there something you want?"

She held up her hands in a placating manner. "I want to apologize for my grandmother's reaction to you. She promised she wouldn't be aggressive toward your family — that's the only reason I agreed to come back here with you — but obviously she's having trouble keeping her word.

"I just want you to know that we're not here to cause trouble for you," she continued. "Grandmother has been feeling nostalgic for home. I think it's a side effect of getting older. I'm sure you see it in Tillie."

"Yes, Aunt Tillie is often nostalgic," I agreed. "Usually she wants to revisit some horrible thing she did to another person."

Rosemary ignored my sarcasm. "We don't want to get in your way. We also don't want you getting in our way. I think it's best if we simply ignore one another."

"I'm all for that."

"Great." Rosemary flashed a smile that somehow felt more genuine than any other emotion she'd ever experienced in my presence. "So, um ... I guess that's it."

"Totally." I held up my hand to wave goodbye. "Have a nice life."

Her eyes moved to the ring on my finger. "You're engaged."

It wasn't a question, but I nodded all the same. "I am."

Rosemary's eyes flicked to Landon and all traces of warmth, whether fake or otherwise, disappeared. "To you, I assume."

"No." Landon shook his head. "Here in Hemlock Cove we just go around holding hands with random people."

"Well ... that's nice." Her bland smile was back. This time it made me uncomfortable. "So, um, I should go. I don't want to leave Grandmother on her own for too long."

"That's probably wise," I agreed. "Aunt Tillie knows she's here. She won't ignore Aunt Willa's presence for long."

She grimaced. "Well, then I should definitely get back. It was nice to see you ... I guess. Good luck with your wedding."

"Yeah. Thanks." I pressed my lips together and turned to Landon when she was gone. "Weird, right?"

"Yup. She's definitely up to something."

"Absolutely."

POTENTIAL MAYHEM WASN'T ENOUGH TO keep us from eating our weight in bad food. We had a regular feast spread out on the blanket when the bank owner, Jackson Douglas Washington, appeared before us.

"Bay, I've been looking for you," he announced.

"Oh, hey." I used the back of my hand to check for nacho cheese at the corners of my mouth. "What's up, JD?"

Landon's smirk was obvious and I had to force myself not to react. "I've never loved you more," he said in a low voice.

I pretended I didn't hear him. "Did you need something, JD?" I dealt with the man regularly because he ran ads in my newspaper every week. He was a familiar face, and I was mostly comfortable with him ... at least when I didn't look as if I was trying to bury myself in junk food.

"I just wanted to make sure we're still on for the full-page ad this week," he said. "The last one brought me ten new accounts. I'm hoping the next one does the same."

"We're running it," I confirmed. "It's the same ad as last week."

"That's fine." He shot Landon an agreeable smile. "By the way, I'm not certain if I've congratulated either one of you yet, but I heard the big news. I'm very happy for you."

"Thank you."

Landon's hand moved to my back. "We're excited," he agreed. "In fact, I want to get together with you to open a joint account. Right now we have separate accounts, but with the property out by the lake and everything, we need to consolidate."

I glanced at him, surprised. "You want joint accounts?"

"We are getting married."

"Yeah, but ... you make way more money than me."

He let loose a sigh of exasperation. "We make money together. My money is going to be your money. We need joint accounts."

It seemed a big step and yet I was glad he was so adamant. Grownups have joint accounts. I'd never really felt like an adult, even though I obviously was, and this was a big step. "A joint account sounds nice."

"Good." He poked my side. "We'll come in after the holiday weekend."

"No problem." JD looked unbelievably pleased. "I'll be happy to help you. Between your new accounts and the one your great-aunt just opened, I'm bursting at the seams with Winchester money."

I froze, taking a moment to absorb his words. I looked to Landon to make sure I hadn't misheard. He looked equally as perplexed. "Aunt Willa opened an account?" I asked, hoping my tone wouldn't betray my surprise.

"She did. She seems like a nice woman, although she absolutely hates your aunt Tillie. I don't know what's up with that. They're sisters, right?"

"You've met Aunt Tillie," I replied dumbly. "Imagine growing up with her."

JD made a face. "Well, either way, I appreciate the business. Call and make an appointment for your accounts. I'll handle it myself."

Landon waved at him as we walked away and then switched his gaze to me. There was a question there, but he didn't ask it.

"If Aunt Willa was just feeling nostalgic, why is she opening accounts here?" I asked for him.

"That's a very good question." Landon leaned closer and rested his chin on my shoulder. "It could be nothing."

"When is it ever nothing with my family?"

"Good point." He tapped my chin to get me to look at him. "If you promise not to let this derail our day, I'll do some digging."

"Isn't that illegal?"

"So is covering for a witch."

A smile, unbidden, curved my lips. "Thank you."

"You're welcome. Now, give me some nachos before you eat them all."

"Again, we could've gotten two orders."

"Or you could learn to share. In fact ... ." He broke off when an ear-splitting scream tore through the air, causing everybody milling about the festival to look in a million different directions. The scream cut off almost as quickly, followed by another.

"There goes your blanket day again," I lamented.

"It's always something," he agreed, pushing himself to a standing position. "I have to check it out."

"I'm going with you."

"That's the way I prefer it."

3
THREE

Even though Landon outdistanced me, I was determined to follow. I kept my eyes on him as he chased the source of the screams. The thick crowd parted for him — he had an air of authority that caused people to take notice — but they started milling together in his wake and I had to push through them. By the time I reached the other side of the crowd, I'd lost him.

And then I heard the scream again. This time I was certain it came from behind the petting zoo barn, which happened to be near where my cousin Thistle and her boyfriend Marcus lived.

Dread overwhelmed me as I kicked in and rounded the corner, pulling up short when the scene came into focus. It was hard to pick out who was screaming because three teenage girls stood in a half-circle, all looking borderline hysterical. The body on the ground was more concerning.

All I saw were legs and feet. I was relieved when I registered that the shoes were far too large to belong to Thistle. Then another possibility hit me and I was breathless when I skirted the bush cutting off my view.

There, face down on the ground, was Marcus. I would've recognized his shoulder-length blond hair anywhere. He didn't move, not as much as a muscle twitch, and I thought my heart might explode as I watched Landon kneel next to the man who had become something of a brother to him and press his fingers to Marcus's neck.

After a few seconds, Landon lifted his eyes and found me. He managed a nod, although the charming grin he'd worn all day was long gone. "He's alive."

I let out a breath, some of the fear that had been threatening to overwhelm me lessening, and then a new set of questions bubbled to the surface. "What happened?"

"I don't know." Landon looked toward the girls, whispering together in a gaggle. One of them, a willowy blonde, opened her mouth and let loose an earth-shattering scream that caused my bones to chill. "Knock that off," he ordered gruffly, causing the girl's head to snap in his direction.

"He's dead," she said, her lower lip trembling. "I'm traumatized. I'm allowed to scream."

It seemed an odd thing to say, but I let it go. Instead, I moved closer to Landon to offer whatever help he needed. "What do you want me to do?"

"Come over here." Landon gestured toward the spot near Marcus' head and I dropped to my knees. "Monitor his pulse. It seems even, but ... just do it. I'm going to call for an ambulance."

I nodded and did as he asked, my fingers trembling as I placed them on Marcus' neck. He was a good guy. That's all I kept thinking as I tracked his heartbeat. Landon said his pulse was steady, and it was, but it also felt faint. Of course, as a Winchester, I was prone to embracing the worst-case scenario, so I couldn't help but wonder if the light beating would suddenly cease.

"We should find Thistle," I murmured, more to myself than him. "She should know."

Landon kept his eyes on me but didn't respond, instead barking orders into the phone when the 911 operator picked up. It didn't take him long to convey the information, and once he disconnected he turned to me. "Everything okay?"

The questioned bothered me on multiple levels. "Does this look okay to you?"

He was used to Winchesters, so his expression never changed. "Just keep doing what you're doing."

"What are you going to do?"

He inclined his head toward the teenagers. "I need to find out what happened."

My first thought was that Marcus had fallen and struck his head. That seemed ridiculous on the surface. He was athletic — even more so than Landon — and I'd never seen him as much as teeter when working around the barn. "You don't think they did this, do you?" I blurted without thinking.

"Of course not," he replied, aiming a smile toward the girls. They were all blond, likely from a bottle, and they were dressed in capris and matching floral sandals. He had a way with women — and teenage girls — and his charm was on full display as he approached them. "Can you ladies tell me what happened?"

"He's dead," the first girl wailed, bursting into tears. "I can't believe we saw someone die."

Professional that he was, Landon's expression never changed. I, however, couldn't keep from rolling my eyes. There was little I detested more than teenagers. I was also familiar with these girls. They were the type to give teenagers the world over a bad name.

"He's not dead," Landon reassured the girl. "An ambulance is on the way. He'll be fine."

The words soothed me, even though I knew he couldn't promise anything of the sort. Marcus would be fine. He had to be. He was too good to die. Besides that, he was the only one in our family who could control Thistle. Without him, it would be mayhem.

Even as I thought it, I hated myself. My heart ached for Thistle. She needed to be informed, and it was with determination that I removed my fingers from Marcus' neck and pulled my phone from my pocket. Landon, focused on the girls, didn't notice.

"Let's start with your names," Landon prodded.

"This is the worst thing that's ever happened," one of the other girls intoned. "I'm going to be scarred for life."

"Yes, it's all about you," I muttered as I typed. Sending a text that Marcus was injured seemed somehow callous, but I couldn't waste time on a call when I had to monitor his vitals.

Landon's gaze was quizzical when he looked down at me. "What are you doing?"

"Texting Thistle."

"Do you think that's wise?"

He couldn't be serious. "She's his girlfriend."

"I'm well aware."

"If it was me, wouldn't you want Thistle to text you?"

He worked his jaw, debating.

"If it was you, I would expect someone to inform me. I can't not tell her."

"Fine." Landon held up his hands in defeat. "Ask her not to tell the others. The last thing I need is a gaggle of Winchesters mucking up a potential crime scene."

I furrowed my brow and glanced around. I was familiar with the property

— Thistle lived one barn over, so I visited often — but nothing looked any different. "How do you know it's a crime scene?"

He ignored me and turned back to the girls. "Names?"

"I'm Paisley Gilmore," the tallest girl announced. She seemed the most stoic of the group.

"Paisley?" Landon rubbed his chin. "Like ... the pattern?"

"Like Paisley Park. My parents were big fans of some rock star."

"Prince," I volunteered. "His music is great."

Paisley didn't appear impressed. "He's dead ... and he was really short."

"That doesn't change the fact that he was the greatest musician of his time," I countered, gently moving my hands over the back of Marcus's head.

"Bay, don't do anything weird," Landon ordered when he saw what I was doing.

I pretended not to hear him. "To save time, I'll help you," I offered. "Paisley is the tall one. The one who keeps screaming is Sophia Johnson. The other one is Emma Graham. They're all going into their senior year this fall."

Landon blinked several times, as if absorbing what I said, and then nodded. "Right. Okay. Paisley, Sophia, and Emma. Those are great names, girls. In fact, you could start your own band with those names."

Paisley's glare was withering. "Only losers join bands."

"Well ... ." Landon glanced at me, as if begging for help.

"Oh, you don't want me getting involved," I warned. "These are the types of girls I avoided when I was that age. I'm certain they're much more your speed."

He made a face. "What's that supposed to mean?"

"Just that you had a type in high school." My gaze was pointed when it landed on him. "I saw one of them during that ... um ... trip we took." The trip in question was actually a curse that allowed us to magically see the past. I obviously couldn't mention that in mixed company.

"Right." Landon flashed an empty smile. "Let's go back to you, girls. Can you tell me what happened?"

Paisley focused on me. She seemed intrigued, but in that superior way only teenagers can muster. I did my best to ignore her. I'd found a bump on Marcus' head; it seemed to be doubling in size by the moment.

"You're the woman who runs the newspaper," Paisley noted. "Your family runs that inn out on the bluff."

"And you have that wacky old lady living in your house," Sophia added. "She rides a scooter and wears really gross leggings. Somebody should tell her she's too old for leggings."

"You should tell her that," I fired back. "She loves it when people tell her what to do, especially teenagers. I think she'll want to plan future outfits with your needs in mind if you approach her the right way."

Sophia appeared intrigued by the suggestion. "What's the right way?"

"Make sure to tell her that she's too old for leggings. Open with that. She should be in a great frame of mind for the rest of it. Oh, and use the whiniest voice you have. She responds well to that."

Landon shot me a dirty look and shook his head before flashing another smile for the girls' benefit. "Don't worry about Aunt Tillie. I need you to tell me what happened."

"It was the worst thing I've ever seen," Sophia said. "The absolute worst. I think I'll need therapy."

Paisley rolled her eyes. "Talk about dramatic."

"Why don't you tell me what happened?" Landon prodded Paisley. "You seem ... on top of things."

"I am," she agreed, gracing him with a pretty smile. "Are you really an FBI agent?"

"Yes."

"You don't look like an FBI agent."

"Well, I am."

Paisley put her hands on her hips. "Let's see your badge. I mean ... you could be lying."

"Why would I lie about being an FBI agent?" Landon demanded, digging in his back pocket. He removed his badge, which he always carried, and held it up. "Satisfied?"

Paisley leaned closer and studied the plastic-covered credentials for a long time. "What's an FBI agent doing here?"

"This is my home now," he replied. "I live with Bay."

"She's a witch," Emma hissed, causing Landon to dart his eyes toward her.

"She doesn't mean anything by it," Sophia offered hurriedly. "Everyone in town is a witch, of course. There are rumors about Ms. Winchester's family. A lot of people are afraid of Miss Tillie."

"As well you should be," I muttered, my eyes drifting to the sidewalk in front of Hypnotic. It was as if I sensed Thistle exiting the shop, and my heart stuttered when I caught sight of her ashen face.

Landon followed my gaze, frowning. He understood that things were about to get loud ... and maybe even a little bit mean. Thistle didn't handle the big things well. Heck, she didn't handle the little things well. Marcus was the most important thing in her life, which meant she was going to explode.

"I don't think we should be talking about Aunt Tillie," Landon admonished. He was trying to exert control over the conversation, but given who the girls were, I decided to help.

"Did Marcus fall?" I demanded, drawing three sets of eyes to me. "Was he tripped? Did something else happen?"

"The man did it," Sophia replied solemnly. "He killed him when Marcus tried to stop him."

"Stop him from what?" Landon asked, straightening.

"Bay?" Thistle stopped twenty feet away, as if frozen in place. Her eyes were fearful when they locked with mine. "Is he ... ?"

"He's alive," I reassured her, ignoring the petulant look on Paisley's face. She obviously didn't like it when someone else grabbed the center of attention. "He's unconscious, but he has a pulse. I found a bump on his head."

"From what?" Thistle moved forward, and when she dropped down on the other side of Marcus I saw her hands shaking.

"I think these girls were just about to tell us," Landon said, his hand moving to Thistle's shoulder to offer her a bit of his strength. "He's going to be okay."

"Of course he is." Thistle mustered a watery smile, purely for show. "He can't leave me. I'll have to do my own laundry, and nobody wants that."

Laundry was the least of her worries. She loved Marcus with her whole heart. The prospect of losing him was more than she could bear. She had to put on a show. That's who she was.

"He won't leave any of us," Landon promised. "I need him too. He's the only sane one in the family. Without him, it will just be me, and I'm not sure I can live up to the pressure."

Rather than laugh, Thistle simply nodded. "Where is the ambulance?"

"It's coming," he reassured her, turning back to the girls. "Okay, girls, enough is enough. We need to know what happened, and we need to know right now."

"I don't know what we can tell you," Paisley said. "I mean ... it's all a blur."

Emma stepped forward. She shot a brief eye roll toward Paisley's back and then held Landon's gaze. "We were all just hanging around having a good time, like we always do. The three of us and Amelia. We were minding our own business, laughing at the fat girls and their elephant ears, when this guy came out of nowhere and started making a scene."

"Amelia?" I looked around. I was familiar with only one Amelia — Amelia Hart. "Where is she?"

"He took her. The man, he was big and had a gut like this." She held her hands in front of her to demonstrate. "He's like those guys on the beer commercials who have the stomachs big enough to balance pizza boxes on."

"I'm aware of the sort of gut you're talking about," Landon said dryly. "I need to know what happened."

"He came out of nowhere and grabbed Amelia by the arm," Emma replied. "He pulled really hard and made her cry. She tried to get away, but he wouldn't let her go. We started yelling at him to stop, and Paisley even hit him with her purse. That's when Marcus showed up."

"He heard the noise from inside the barn," Paisley explained. "He seemed confused when he came out but he jumped in to help. The other man tried to fight him off, called him names and told him to mind his own business. When Marcus refused, the dude hit him like this." She lashed out with her fist, using it as she would a hammer.

"Marcus fell down," Emma volunteered. "He didn't get back up. The man dragged Amelia away after that. He put her in a car and took off."

Landon's mouth dropped open. "Wait ... ."

"Amelia Hart has been kidnapped?" I asked, equally shocked.

"She's gone." Paisley shrugged. "That guy took her and left. I bet he's a pervert. Guys who look like that are always perverts."

Landon reached for his phone. "What was he driving?"

"I ... don't know. It looked like a regular black SUV."

"What make?"

"Um ... I don't know what that means." Paisley's expression was blank.

"Was it a Ford? A Chevy maybe?"

Paisley knit her eyebrows and shrugged. "I don't know."

Landon looked to the other girls but they shook their heads. "Which direction did he head?" Landon demanded.

"That way." Paisley pointed east. "I don't think he was a local. I would've recognized him. I bet he was one of the loser tourists. You'll never find him."

"Oh, I'll find him." Landon was determined as he stood, his eyes connecting with mine. "I'm calling the state police for a roadblock. Find Terry."

I nodded and rose. "Then what?"

He glanced at Thistle, who remained next to Marcus. She almost looked as if she was in a trance. "Stay with your family," he instructed. "I'll let you know when I have something."

He strode away with that swagger that told me he was loaded for bear. I knew him better than most. If the kidnapper was still in the vicinity, Landon would find him, and if he'd done something to Amelia, there was no rock big enough to hide under.

4

FOUR

I rode with Thistle in the ambulance. The paramedics didn't bother arguing when I insisted on attaching myself to my cousin. As I climbed in, I caught Clove's gaze from across the road. She stood in front of Hypnotic, horrified, and I thought for a second she would try to join us. Thankfully she didn't, instead turning to return to the store. I assumed she would wait there for word.

I was wrong.

By the time we reached the hospital, which was one town over — Hemlock Cove had only a very rudimentary urgent care center — the rest of the family had already arrived. Aunt Tillie looked as if she was about to set the world ablaze.

"What happened?" she demanded, her gaze on me rather than Thistle.

To my utter surprise, my stalwart cousin — who refused to lean on anybody — was already in her mother's arms. Twila, often the most scattered of my aunts, was completely focused on her daughter. She whispered soothing words as she led Thistle to a couch in the waiting room. I couldn't hear what was being said, but Thistle's tears chilled me to the bone.

"We're not exactly sure," I replied, forcing my attention to Aunt Tillie. The fire in her eyes told me she was looking for vengeance. "It sounds like Marcus intervened when a man tried to grab a local girl."

Mom's hand flew to her mouth. "Oh, no. Did she get away?"

I shook my head. "It was Amelia Hart. Her friends saw what happened, but they didn't recognize the man who took her."

"It was probably a pervert," Aunt Tillie muttered, rubbing her chin. "There are too many perverts these days. I blame the Kardashians."

I hated the Kardashians as much as the next person, but I had trouble connecting the two. "You think the Kardashians caused an increase in perverts?"

"Yes."

"Why?"

"You've seen them. They put too much emphasis on looks. That always leads to destruction."

I partially agreed, so I decided to let it go. "Landon called for backup from the state police. They're looking for Amelia right now. I'm sure Chief Terry is with him, although I haven't seen him since right after we realized Aunt Willa and Rosemary were here."

Slowly, as if trapped in a horror movie revolving around murderous androids, every face turned in my direction.

"Aunt Willa is here?" Mom finally asked.

"And Rosemary?" Clove made a face as she rubbed her pregnant belly.

"Why would they be here?" Marnie asked. "Why now?"

"I'll tell you why." Aunt Tillie fiercely clenched her hands into fists. "It's the end times, people. I've been warning you for years that it was coming, and we're finally here."

"Oh, geez." Mom looked to the ceiling and pinched the bridge of her nose. "We're not talking about the end times right now."

"We have to." Aunt Tillie was firm. "The Rapture is upon us."

I cocked my head. "Isn't the Rapture a Christian thing?"

"So?"

"We're not Christian. We're Wiccan."

"So?"

"So ... we can't believe in the Rapture."

"We don't believe in the Christian Rapture," Aunt Tillie replied in her best "well, duh" voice. The looked she pinned me with said she thought I was a moron. "We believe in the Wiccan Rapture."

"What's the difference?" Clove asked.

"In our Rapture, evil witches try to take over. They confound men with spells to make them do perverted things. They bring enemies to your doorstep." She leaned close. "They train dolphins to deliver bombs to underwater communities."

She'd always said crazy things. It was just something we got used to. Despite that, I had always been thankful that she remained spry and sharp given her age. Now I wasn't so sure. "What underwater communities?"

"You know."

"I don't."

"Of course you do." Aunt Tillie shook her head. "That's not important right now ... other than the fact that I read in the newspaper that they were training dolphins to deliver explosives to terrorists, which is the first step to Armageddon."

"What newspaper carried that story?" I demanded.

"I forget which one." She averted her gaze. "It doesn't matter. All the signs are coalescing. The end times are upon us."

I could only deal with so much, and this was beyond my pay grade. "You're full of it, and if you've been reading the National Enquirer again we're going to have issues. I've told you that thing is nonsense."

"Just because you don't want to believe there's an army of monkey babies trying to infiltrate hospital nurseries by pretending to be babies and take down all our hospitals in a coordinated attack doesn't mean I can't be prepared." She raised her fist. "It will be over my cold, dead body that monkeys rule the Earth. We already have enough of them in politics."

I pressed my lips together, debating, and then opted to focus on my mother. "Landon said he would call when they have information. I don't expect to hear from him anytime soon. There are a lot of rural roads out there to cover and only so many bodies to do it."

"Is there anything we can do?" Marnie asked. "We could use a locator spell and go searching."

I'd considered the possibility but discarded it. "I don't think that's smart. If we get caught out there — which seems likely given the number of state troopers they're calling in — we'd have a hard time explaining ourselves."

"Will that matter if we find Amelia?" Mom challenged. "It might be worth it."

"The thing is, the girls who were with Marcus when we found him were scattered, jumping all over the place. I don't know that I believe their story."

Thistle stirred. "Do you think they did something to him?"

"That's unlikely," I answered after a few moments of thought. "I think something close to what they related happened. But they're scattered. I don't understand why they were hanging around behind the barn in the first place."

Thistle smiled as she leaned back in her seat and stretched out her legs. "I can answer that one for you. Paisley — the tall one — has a crush on

Marcus. She's been showing up everywhere he is trying to get his attention."

"I didn't realize."

"All the girls think he's hot. There's something about a guy and a horse."

"Or a guy holding a kitten ... or petting a cow ... or delivering chocolate," Clove added. "Speaking of chocolate ... ." She glanced toward the vending machine.

Marnie, her mother, was already on her feet. "What do you want?"

Thistle made a disgusted sound in the back of her throat. "You shouldn't give in to her every whim. She'll be as big as a house in another month if she doesn't try to control her sweets intake."

Clove's brown eyes went wide and glassy. "That's the meanest thing you've ever said to me."

"It's the truth," Thistle snapped. "You've been eating enough for five lately."

"Why do you care?" Marnie challenged. "If she wants to indulge a bit, that's her decision."

"I'm the one who will have to listen to her whine when it comes time to drop the weight. She doesn't need a candy bar. Get her a salad or something."

"Oh, no way!" Clove vehemently shook her head. "I was wrong. *That's* the meanest thing you've ever said to me."

Sensing the conversation was about to spiral out of control, I decided to drag my family — every nutty one of them — back to reality. "While I don't want to indulge Aunt Tillie's Wiccan Rapture fantasies ... ."

"It's totally a thing," Aunt Tillie groused, her eyes hot. "Just wait. You're not allowed to be on my Rapture team if you don't believe."

"Somehow I think we'll survive," I shot back. "We need to talk about Aunt Willa and Rosemary. I don't know why they're here. I talked to them briefly, and Aunt Willa was as surly as ever. She said that she felt a yearning for home."

"What a load of elephant dookie," Aunt Tillie said. "She has never cared about this place. Well, other than when she thought she deserved a piece of the family land. She would've tried to force us to sell the property so she could make some money and never looked back once she got her payout."

I rubbed my forehead. I could feel a headache coming on. "Rosemary followed Landon and me afterward. She claimed that Aunt Willa was telling the truth. She said that they didn't want anything to do with us — good or bad — and she hoped we could stay away from one another."

"I'm fine with that," Twila said. "I've always thought they were jerks. If they're only here for a few days, we'll ignore them."

"Yes, well, I don't think they're telling the truth." I told them about running into JD and what he let slip. "If she opened an account at the local branch, she has other plans."

"I agree with Bay," Mom offered. "It's a bad sign."

"It's the end times," Aunt Tillie whispered. "I've always believed Willa would serve as the Devil's minion when the forces of good and evil gathered for the final battle."

Mom made an exaggerated face. "What have you been watching?"

"CBS All Access has the remake of *The Stand*," Aunt Tillie replied. "It's really well done."

"Well, great." Mom's eyes flicked to me. "What do you think they want?"

"I don't know them well enough to figure out what they're doing. Landon said he would run a few checks but ... that was before all this." I watched Thistle as she stared at the double doors that led to the hospital interior. She was obviously in agony waiting for word on Marcus.

"Well, even though I know you don't respect me enough to join my Rapture team, I have news, too," Aunt Tillie announced, forcing all eyes to her. "I did some digging on Willa and Rosemary this afternoon."

"I wondered where you disappeared to," I said. "I thought you would attack from the front."

"A wise warrior attacks from behind."

She contradicted herself left and right. "When we were kids, you told us that only weaklings attacked from the back," I reminded her. "What changed?"

"I never told you that."

"You did."

"I did not."

I turned to my mother for backup. "You heard her, right?"

Mom looked to be over the conversation. She rubbed her forehead — perhaps the same headache threatening me was making a go at her — and refused to make eye contact. "I can't recall. On top of that, I don't care."

"That's because you haven't heard my news," Aunt Tillie persisted. "When you do, you'll be on my side."

"Then tell us your news," Marnie barked as she handed Clove her candy bar. "This conversation is lasting longer than any of our marriages."

"Speak for yourself," Clove said, happily ripping at the candy bar wrapping. "I'm going to be married forever."

Aunt Tillie made a face that I would've found funny under different circumstances. However, I shot her a warning look when it appeared as if she was going to pick a fight. "Fine." Aunt Tillie threw up her hands, ceding defeat. "Never mind what I heard. I thought it was big news. Obviously you guys don't care that Rosemary is engaged."

I almost fell over. "What?"

"Who would marry her?" Thistle asked, horrified. "I'm serious. What moron would marry her? It's not as if she has a good personality or face."

"Whereas I'm blessed with both," Aunt Tillie said. "I don't know who she's marrying. I only know what I heard when I was eavesdropping. They're in town because Rosemary is engaged. And they have some plan to take over the world with the help of her husband."

Annoyed, I flicked her shoulder and earned a dark glare. "You had me right up until you mentioned taking over the world. This has nothing to do with the Rapture, Wiccan or otherwise."

"But ... it does."

"It doesn't."

"It does."

"It doesn't!" My voice echoed through the lobby, and when I realized everyone else had gone silent, I looked over my shoulder and found Dr. Stuart Hubbard watching the scene with overt amusement.

"Hello." He glanced between faces, sympathy replacing amusement when he got to Thistle. "I'm treating Marcus."

Thistle hopped to her feet, not stopping until she was directly in front of him. "Is he okay?" Her voice was thick with emotion. "Please tell me he's going to be okay."

Hubbard's hand went to Thistle's shoulder. "We're hopeful. He has a concussion. We believe he was struck over the head with something, but we're not certain what."

I frowned. "Witnesses said he was hit with a fist. They didn't mention a weapon."

"That's possible. He suffered a mighty blow. I'll leave that part of it up to the police."

"Is he awake?" Thistle asked hopefully.

Hubbard shook his head. "Not yet. We don't expect him to wake until tomorrow morning. If everything goes as it should, he should open his eyes with the sun tomorrow and be perfectly fine."

I could read between the lines of that statement. "And what if he doesn't?"

Hubbard hesitated and then forced a smile. "Then we'll take it from there. We'll monitor him through the night and see where we are in the morning."

And just like that, thoughts of the Wiccan Rapture and Aunt Willa's machinations went out the window. There were more important things, and

Marcus was one of them. Once we were sure he was out of the woods, we could focus on Aunt Willa and Rosemary.

I STAYED AT THE HOSPITAL WITH THISTLE.

Clove wanted to — she was the nurturing sort, after all — but there was no way she could sleep in one of the hospital's lumpy chairs and be comfortable. That left me, though Twila was also keen for the job. I didn't want Thistle arrested for murdering her mother while waiting for Marcus to wake, so I insisted I was the only one who could be trusted with Thistle's mental health. By the time everyone left, and it was just the two of us sitting in chairs next to his bed, she was an overwrought mess. It was almost a relief when she drifted off.

I thought sleep would be impossible, but my body believed otherwise. I fought slipping under twice, but ultimately succumbed. It wasn't some pleasant dreamscape I landed in when sleep claimed me. Nor was it a horrific landscape of Wiccan Rapture proportions. No, the space I found myself in was familiar, though hardly comfortable.

"The cemetery? Really?" I was disgusted as I looked around. "Why couldn't I dream of a tropical beach or something? Just once. That's not too much to ask."

A warm chuckle from behind caused me to swivel, and turning, I found my dead grandmother. Ginger Winchester had been a beauty in her time, which ended long before I appeared on the Winchester scene. She died when her daughters were teenagers, so she now appeared to look younger than her children.

"What are you doing here?" I blurted out, surprised.

"I needed to talk to you," she replied, a kind smile on her face. This wasn't the first time we'd interacted. For some reason, she found it easy to slip into my mind when she had a message she needed to send. "Bad things are coming, Bay."

"Oh, well, great." I threw my hands in the air and growled. "That is just lovely. I can't tell you how happy I am to hear that, especially now."

Her smile widened. "You have so much of Tillie in you."

I thought my eyes might bulge out of my head. "If you weren't already a ghost, I would totally make you eat dirt over that comment."

She chuckled, the sound light and airy. "You're definitely like her. Thistle is too. Even Clove has a bit of her to lay claim to. But you remind me of her the most."

I wanted to cry. "That is such a weird way to kick me when I'm down."

"There's no need to be down," she reassured me, moving closer to one of the tombstones. It was only then that I realized we were standing at the grave of Chief Terry's mother. "I hear congratulations are in order. I knew you and Landon would get your happily ever after."

"You just told me bad things are coming," I reminded her. "How happy are we going to be if the world ends?" Something occurred to me. "Wait ... it's not the Wiccan Rapture, is it?"

She laughed again. "No, and tell Tillie to give it up. That's never going to be a thing." She sobered after a moment. "Danger is circling. There are dark shadows lurking on the edges of your reality. You have to be prepared to beat them back."

"With what?"

"Magic. Heart. Love."

"Great. That doesn't sound weird or anything."

"You'll figure it out." She sounded certain. "I just wanted you to be aware that trouble was coming. You have to band together with your cousins, with your mothers, and with Tillie to make sure the evil that's on your doorstep doesn't gain a foothold."

"What kind of evil are we talking about?"

"That I can't say. But it feels dangerous. You've taken down numerous foes, some extremely strong. You need to be wary."

"Is it coming for me?"

"It's coming for all of you."

I would've been more comfortable if I was the only target. "So, what do we do?"

"Work together."

I waited for her to continue. When she didn't, I scowled. "Don't you have better advice to offer?"

"I would tell you if I knew what to do. I don't. I can only warn you so you're ready."

"Except I don't know what to be ready for."

"That is life."

"Yeah, yeah, yeah." I rolled my neck and heaved out a sigh. "How about the next time you drop in for a visit you give me actionable information? I don't want to ask too much — you are a ghost after all — but that would be helpful."

Her enigmatic smile was back. "You've grown so strong. I always knew you would. You're not done growing yet. You're not invincible. Make sure you're ready."

"I'll be ready."

"Good." Briefly, her eyes turned sad. "Take care of your cousins."

A lump formed in my throat. "Is something bad going to happen to one of them? Is Marcus going to be okay?"

She disappeared before answering, which only served to fuel my terror.

"Thanks for stopping by," I yelled into the ether. "Come back and say something cryptic again soon. I freaking love it when you do that!"

It didn't matter. She was gone, and all I was left with was trepidation. What was coming for us now?

5
FIVE

Thistle and I had been alone when we fell asleep next to Marcus's bed. Landon was with us when I woke.

He'd moved an uncomfortable plastic chair into the room from the hallway as we slept and positioned himself on it. It should've been impossible for him to sleep in the position he was in, and yet his eyes were closed and he snored lightly.

"Hey." I rubbed my thumb over his cheek as he opened his eyes.

He smiled. And then he said my name, just my name on a breathy whisper before leaning forward to kiss me.

"What are you doing here?" I whispered. "I thought you went home to get some sleep."

"Believe it or not, I don't want to sleep in our bed without you."

"No?"

"I need my Bay next to me to sleep." He rested his forehead against mine, his hand moving to my back to rub at the kinks there. "How is he?"

"He's supposed to come around this morning. If he doesn't ... ." I couldn't finish the sentence.

"He will," Landon reassured me. "There's no way out of this family. It'll be okay." He moved his lips to my forehead and then peered around my shoulder.

When he didn't look back, I turned in my chair to check on Thistle and found her watching us. "Are you okay?"

"Yeah." Her voice was dull and she gripped Marcus's hand tighter. As far as I knew, she hadn't released it the entire night. "You guys are really gross. Has anybody ever told you that?"

I smirked. "Everybody tells us that. Chief Terry even accused us of being inappropriate in public yesterday."

"He accused us of stroking one another," Landon corrected.

Thistle snorted and then caught herself, her eyes drifting to Marcus's face. "He's not awake." Her voice cracked and it almost broke my heart.

"He will be." I refused to believe otherwise, even if we had to use magic to ensure the optimal outcome. "He'll wake up, and the first thing he'll ask about is Amelia." I shifted my eyes to Landon. "Did you find her?"

He looked pained. "No, sweetie, we didn't."

My stomach constricted. "But ... ."

"I'm sorry." He moved his hand over the back of my head and sighed. "We had all the roads shut down. We issued an Amber Alert even though we didn't have enough information. She's just ... gone."

"It's likely that this guy, whoever he is, drove straight out of town," Thistle said as she rubbed her thumb over the top of Marcus' hand. "They were probably gone before the roadblocks were up."

"Probably," Landon agreed, though he didn't look happy at the suggestion. "We're not done looking by any stretch. We just need to adjust how we approach it."

"I can help." I was earnest. "I have magic ... and ghosts ... and Aunt Tillie. I can totally help."

He hesitated and then shrugged. "We'll talk about that when we know that Marcus is okay. Until then, you should stick close to Thistle."

The statement was enough to have Thistle's eyes firing. "I'm not fragile," she snapped.

"I didn't say you were." Landon didn't as much as blink in the face of her fury. "Even the strongest people — and I would include you in that group, Thistle — need support. Bay is your support."

I didn't like that he was right, especially because it felt as if he was shutting me out of the search and using my family as a cudgel to do it. I considered pushing him further, and then Marcus stirred.

"Did you see that?" Thistle was on her feet, her eyes wide.

I nodded as I stared at his moving hand.

"I'll get the doctor." Landon stood, a smile on his lips as Marcus opened his eyes.

"Marcus?" Thistle looked as if she was about to burst into tears as she leaned closer to him.

I found I was holding my breath as I waited for him to speak.

"Hey." Marcus' hand went to Thistle's head as the tears began flowing and she threw her arms around him. He looked shocked at the show of emotion, wrapping his arms around her and holding tight as she practically crawled on top of him. "What's this?" He appeared genuinely bewildered.

"I think it's a woman who loves you," Landon replied, squeezing my hand before moving toward the door. "I'll get the doctor. Then I have a few questions for you about what happened yesterday."

Marcus' forehead wrinkled, causing him to groan. "Why does my head hurt?" He reached toward the back of his head, but Thistle grabbed his wrist.

"Don't." Her lashes were thick with tears. "You'll hurt yourself."

"I don't understand." Marcus cupped her face. "Why are you crying? What am I doing here? Did something happen?"

Landon hesitated, exchanging a quick look with me. "What do you remember?"

"I was at the festival. I was going to get some chicken feed because I was out and the kids wanted to feed them. I headed toward the barn and then ... that's it. I don't remember anything after that."

Landon's expression displayed disappointment, but he quickly recovered. "I'll be right back."

Dr. Hubbard was all smiles when he joined us, and after what felt like a really long time — during which he flashed a light in Marcus' eyes and asked him a series of questions — he declared our favorite animal wrangler well on his way to recovery. Thistle was so relieved she crawled into bed with him. They were wrapped around one another, whispering, when Landon and I left the room.

"Another happy ending," Landon teased when we were safely away from prying ears.

A night spent having to be strong for Thistle had worn me down, and before I knew what was happening, I slipped my arms around his neck and buried my face into his chest. "Don't ever die on me."

He ran his hands over my back and rested his cheek on my forehead. I expected him to tease me for my emotional outburst. "Don't you ever die on me either."

I was quiet for a second, collecting myself. "You know that means we have to live forever, right?"

"Sounds perfect."

. . .

WE STOPPED AT THE GUESTHOUSE LONG ENOUGH to shower and change clothes before heading to the inn for breakfast. As much as I wanted a nap — sleeping in a chair had left me more drained than if I hadn't gotten any shuteye — I needed nourishment more. Amelia was still out there, and now that Marcus was safe I was determined to help find her ... even if I had to fight with Landon to clear the way.

"We just heard the news," Mom announced when we entered the dining room. "We're so relieved."

Landon, who had been disappointed to find the kitchen empty upon passing through, immediately went to his regular seat and surveyed the platter in the middle of the table. "Nobody ate my bacon, did they?"

Beneath the table, Peg the pig snorted.

"Sorry, baby," he called out to the pig. "I love you, but I love my bacon too. You'll have to look the other way."

I didn't know whether to laugh or cry, so I shook my head and focused on Mom. "He seems good, if a little shaky. He can't remember what happened to him."

"He has a head injury," Mom pointed out. "If the only thing wrong with him is a bit of memory loss, we can live with that."

"Definitely," Twila agreed. "How was Thistle when you left her?"

I thought back to the way Thistle and Marcus had burrowed under the blanket, shutting out the rest of the world. "She's a little shaken, but she'll be okay. A good night's sleep and a few days doting on Marcus will have her back to her snarky self."

"She definitely can't be on my team in the Wiccan Rapture," Aunt Tillie volunteered out of nowhere. "If she's going to fall apart like a total baby, then she's not right for the Tillie Brigade of Doom."

Landon impatiently drew out my chair so I could sit and then plopped down next to me. He reached for the bacon platter, ignoring everything else. He'd obviously been listening to the conversation, though, because he dove right in. "What's the Wiccan Rapture?"

"It's the end times," Aunt Tillie replied gravely.

I grabbed the bowl of scrambled eggs and dished out two heaping servings before doing the same with the hash browns. I wanted to put an end to the discussion, but that didn't seem likely given who had gathered around the table. "Ignore her," I suggested.

"No, don't ignore me," Aunt Tillie snapped. "I'm the only one talking sense here. The Wiccan Rapture is upon us. Those who want to survive have to be on my team. Thistle has already been cut." Her gaze was speculative when it landed on Landon. "You're a possibility. How would you like to be on the winning team?"

Landon's face remained blank. "For what?"

"The Rapture, you ninny." Aunt Tillie's eyes narrowed. "If you're going to act stupid, you can't be on my team."

"That's okay." Landon accepted the hash browns from me. "I want to be on Bay's team."

"Yes, but she doesn't believe in the Rapture so she's going to lose." Aunt Tillie planted both hands on either side of her plate and stared directly into Landon's eyes. "Think of it like *The Walking Dead*. Do you want to be on Daryl's team or Andrea's team?"

"Weren't they on the same team?"

"Barely."

He slid his eyes to me. "Explain what's happening. And I prefer short words and a wrap-up. I'm too tired for any nonsense."

"You're joining the wrong family for that," Chief Terry noted.

"Aunt Tillie thinks there are too many signs to ignore and that we're about to engage in a final battle," I replied. "She's making it up as she goes along. Although ... ." A vision of Grandma Ginger flashed in my head. "I did have a weird dream last night."

"Oh, man." Landon's expression twisted. "I don't like it when you have weird dreams that aren't about us rolling around in a field together. Can't you stop yourself from doing that?"

Amusement, however faint, caused me to laugh. "I'll do my best. Grandma Ginger was in the dream. She warned me that something bad was about to happen."

Landon straightened. "Did she tell you what form this bad thing was going to take?"

"No. And I dug pretty hard for answers. She said she doesn't know who or what it is, but we all need to be on the lookout. She said we'll have to fight it together."

"That's because it's the Rapture," Aunt Tillie intoned. "I told you. No one listens to me, but I told you." She snapped her fingers close to Landon's face. "There's still time to earn a spot on my team. I just need a résumé and cover letter, and I'll let you know in three business days if you've made the cut."

Weariness lined Landon's face. "Yeah, I'm going to stick with Bay."

"I'm stronger than Bay."

"She can control ghosts now. If a bunch of people are dying in the Rapture, that's going to be pretty helpful. What do you have that can beat that?"

"Um, everything." Aunt Tillie's eyes were wild as she glared at me. "Can you believe this? Tell him he's a moron. My team will wipe the floor with your team."

"I didn't realize we were on separate teams," I said dryly, mixing my eggs with the hash browns. I was starving, but every muscle in my body hurt from sleeping in an upright position. "Why can't we all be on the same team?"

"You know why." Her eyes darted to the side of the table where Marnie and Twila sat and then she leaned closer. "We all know that Twila will drag us down. She'll try to talk to the zombies instead of stabbing them in the head."

"Oh, now there are zombies?" It was hard to keep up with her fanciful imagination. "I don't know what to say. Can I think about it?"

"No."

"Just agree to be on her team," Landon snapped. "This conversation will never end if we don't sign up." He broke a piece of bacon in half and stared at her. "I'm not providing a résumé, though."

"Then you can't be on the team."

"Maybe we'll form our own team."

"That will be the losing team."

I hadn't eaten anything yet and the conversation was giving me indigestion. "Can we talk about more serious things?" I demanded. "Marcus is on the mend, but Thistle will be out of commission for a few days. Amelia Hart is still missing. The team I'm going to join is this one." I waggled my fingers at Landon and Chief Terry. "All other team discussions can wait until after we find Amelia."

Landon's mouth was full of food when I dropped my suggestion, which was probably a good thing. But Chief Terry was prepared to take me on, firmly shaking his head.

"You're not part of the team."

I told myself to remain calm as I regarded him. "No?"

"No."

"You need to find Amelia."

"That doesn't mean you need to be involved."

"But how are you going to find her? She could be anywhere."

"It's called good old-fashioned police work. I'm a big fan of it."

I risked a glance at Landon and found him staring at his plate. He obviously didn't want to be dragged into the conversation. If Chief Terry was willing to be the bad guy, Landon was ready to let him bear the brunt of my disgruntlement. There was no way I was going to let that happen, though.

"Where are you going to start looking?"

"We haven't decided yet." Chief Terry refused to meet my gaze. "We'll decide that after breakfast. I thought we might talk about it last night, but Landon wanted to check on you."

"That's because I love you," Landon offered. "More than anything ... even bacon."

Snort. Snort. Peg shifted under the table.

"I love you, too," Landon called out. "I can't show you how much until after I'm done with breakfast. It's too mean to eat in front of you."

I rolled my eyes and focused on Chief Terry. "If that guy isn't on camera — and I'm willing to bet you checked — then you have absolutely no way of knowing where he went, which means you have no solid leads with which to trace Amelia."

"We'll figure it out."

"I have magic."

Chief Terry cleared his throat. "I'm well aware."

"I can make the ghosts start a search, or cast a locator spell. If I'm with you when I do, I don't have to worry about the state police locking me up for acting like a loon."

"You don't need to get involved."

His refusal to look me in the eye had my blood boiling. "Landon." I glared at my fiancé. "You know I'm right. I need to be part of this."

His eyes were conflicted when he looked up. "Sweetie, you didn't sleep last night. I'm not sure I want you involved in this."

"Because I might be tired?"

"Because ... we don't know what we're dealing with." He was calm, his tone measured. "What if Aunt Tillie was right and some sort of pervert took her? The reason behind that kidnapping could be more than you're prepared to deal with."

On the surface, I understood that. I also felt, deep in my bones, that he needed me. "Finding her is more important than my comfort."

He opened his mouth but didn't say anything. I could practically hear the gears in his mind working. I recognized I'd already won the battle when he squeezed my knee under the table. Then my mother decided to insert herself into the conversation.

"I think it's a good idea," she said.

"You do?" Chief Terry and I asked in unison.

THE WITCH IS BACK

She nodded. "Bay is powerful, and you need a powerful friend, Terry. I also think I'm going to join this little adventure, just to make sure nothing gets out of hand."

I was officially horrified and desperately searching for a way to backtrack. "That's not necessary."

Landon joined in. "It's not that I wouldn't want to work with you or anything — you are going to be my favorite mother-in-law, after all — but you don't usually enjoy working with law enforcement."

Mom tilted her head. "Really? When have I ever worked with law enforcement?"

"Well ... ." Landon swallowed hard and waved his fingers at Chief Terry. "I think I'll leave this one for you."

"Thanks," Chief Terry muttered, sarcasm on full display. When he fixed his smile on Mom, he almost looked to be begging. "This isn't going to be your cup of tea. Maybe you should stay here and — I don't know — bake a pie or something. I love a good pie."

Landon sucked in a breath as I pressed my lips together and tried not to laugh. There were so many things wrong with Chief Terry's rescue attempt that I didn't know where to start.

"Well, I'm not in the mood to bake a pie," Mom said, her voice as cold as the ice cubes in my water glass. "I want to see what you do when working a case, so that's what I'm going to do."

"Oh, Winnie." Chief Terry whined, something I couldn't ever remember seeing. "You won't like what happens out there. It's a different world."

"I guess it's good that I'm adventurous, then. Otherwise, there might never be pie for anyone ever again."

I turned my face into Landon's shoulder to hide my laughter. He rested his cheek on my forehead and popped another slice of bacon into his mouth, swallowing before speaking.

"I think it's a great idea," he said.

"You do not." Chief Terry looked as if he wanted to throttle Landon. "You're only saying that so I'll be the bad guy."

"No, I really mean it." Landon's expression was serious. "My future mother-in-law is the smartest woman I know. Why wouldn't I want her with me?"

I propped my chin on his shoulder as Chief Terry and Mom continued to snap at one another. "That was really sneaky," I whispered.

"I'm not an idiot." He kissed the tip of my nose. "When this explodes —

and it will — Terry will be the one in the doghouse. I'll be at a safe minimum distance from the explosion."

"You know I'm going with you, right? It won't just be her."

"I know. I'm actually all for it."

I narrowed my eyes, suspicious. "Oh?"

"Your mother will keep you in line. She'll make sure you don't do anything stupid."

"It's going to be a long day."

"Yup. At least we have bacon to fuel us up."

Snort. Snort.

"Oh, Peg, it's going to be okay. I've got kisses for you before I go. I've got enough love to spread around."

6
SIX

Normally when I went to work with Landon and Chief Terry, I hopped in the back seat and left the official law enforcement representatives to talk things over in the front. This was not a normal day.

"Um ... ." Landon opened the rear passenger door for me and then glanced to his right as Mom skirted around him and opened the front door for herself. She looked excited as she climbed in, sending Chief Terry a little wink while reaching for her seatbelt.

Chief Terry looked pained as he glanced in the rearview mirror from the driver's seat and caught my eye. If he was expecting me to say anything to her, he would be massively disappointed.

"All set." Landon made a big show of fastening my seatbelt — and giving me a kiss — before crossing to the other side and hopping in next to me. He steadfastly avoided Chief Terry's glare and collected my hand once he was settled.

"Unbelievable," Chief Terry muttered as he jabbed the key into the ignition. "Un-freaking-believable."

I forced my lips together and looked out the window rather than at Landon. I knew if we made eye contact we would start laughing, and once we started, we would never stop.

"Did you say something, Terry?" Mom asked from her seat in front of me. The way she cocked her head told me she was practically daring him to pick a fight. Chief Terry had known her long enough to recognize her expressions. He had not been in the dating game long enough to learn the pitfalls of opening his mouth yet, though.

"I didn't say anything," he muttered, slamming the vehicle into reverse and dropping his foot onto the accelerator with a little bit too much gusto.

"Watch the gravel," Mom chided as it churned and hit the side of the truck. "It's a pain to rake."

I couldn't look at Chief Terry. I was too afraid. Instead, I stared at the way Landon's hand melded with mine, my mind working. "So, I was thinking," I started.

"That's always a terrifying possibility," he teased.

I ignored him. "Do you want to go on a honeymoon?"

"Is that a trick question?"

"No, but ... you didn't mention anything about a honeymoon."

"Bay, as far as I'm concerned, the honeymoon is the reward I deserve for putting up with your family poking and prodding me over wedding plans for two months."

"Do you know where you want to go?"

"Where do you want to go?"

I shrugged. "I haven't really thought about it."

"I haven't either. How about we both do some research and then approach each other in a couple of days with our top three destinations? That will limit us to six places to argue about."

"That sounds fun."

I saw suspicion lurking in his eyes. "But?"

"How do you know there's a 'but?'"

"Because I've met you. That's your 'but' face."

"Oh, really?"

He laughed. "You know what I mean. What's going through that busy brain of yours?"

"I was wondering if we could go anywhere."

"Sure."

"No, I mean anywhere. There have to be some sort of limitations. Money will be an issue."

"Don't worry about money," Mom admonished from the front seat. She'd pulled a pair of sunglasses from her purse and was affixing a froufrou scarf over her hair to keep it from falling into her face. "I already talked to your father. While nothing is set in stone, he mentioned wanting to pay for something when I said we would handle the wedding. I'm sure he'd be willing to fund your honeymoon."

It was a nice sentiment and yet it made me uncomfortable. "Shouldn't we pay for that?" I looked to Landon for an answer. "I mean ... we're adults. Shouldn't that be our job?"

He shrugged. "I don't know the rules of marriage planning. I don't want to step on your father's toes. The man barely tolerates me as it is."

"I understand, but ... it feels weird."

"Then we'll pay for it ourselves." Landon was blasé. "Tell me what you want and I'll make it happen. I don't care if I have to take out a loan."

"I don't want you to take out a loan." I meant it. "We can pick something reasonable."

He shot me an exasperated look. "Bay, it's a honeymoon. It's not supposed to be reasonable. It's supposed to be decadent. Where do you want to go?"

"I've always wanted to visit Savannah. It's supposed to be one of the most haunted cities in the country."

He made a face. "Oh, I love you more than life itself, but I don't want to go ghost hunting on our honeymoon. Let's save Savannah for a different trip."

"Okay. What about New Orleans?"

"I've always wanted to see New Orleans, too, but it doesn't sound fun for a honeymoon. I was thinking someplace more tropical, like Hawaii ... or the Caribbean."

"You only want to see if you can talk me into a coconut bra."

He grinned. "See, you know me well too."

It had a nice ring to it. Not the coconut bra. White sand beaches and piña coladas sounded heavenly. "I heard about an island off the coast of Florida. Moonstone Bay."

He hiked an eyebrow. "Never heard of it. I don't want to go to a tiny island that doesn't have proper amenities. I need a resort, plenty of bar choices — and kitschy souvenir shops."

"You need kitschy souvenir shops?" He cracked me up. "I'm pretty sure Moonstone Bay has all that. I'll do some research and bring my findings to you in a few days."

"Sounds awesome." He squeezed my hand. "Let's talk about what's going to happen at the Harts. I think you two should wait in the vehicle."

Mom and I made the same squawking sound.

"That's not going to happen." Mom was firm. "We're a team. Teams don't split up when investigating."

"How do you know that?" Chief Terry challenged, speaking for the first time since he'd peeled out of the gravel parking lot.

"I know things." If Mom was bothered by his tone, she didn't show it. "We're not dogs. You can't leave us in the car while you go inside."

"Actually, you can't leave dogs in the car either," I pointed out. "It's against the law."

"See." Mom held out her hands for Chief Terry's benefit, and when his eyes sought — and found — mine in the mirror, I knew he would demand retribution for my big mouth. "It's against the law to leave us in the car."

"I stand corrected," Chief Terry growled.

"We have to think of an excuse," Landon noted. "The parents will demand to know why we have a reporter and inn owner with us."

"Ooh, I know." Mom's eyes sparkled, telling me she was about to suggest something goofy. "Tell them we're a traveling psychic duo and we have strong feelings about Amelia but we need to touch her belongings to get a feel for what might've happened to her. Then, when we get inside, Bay and I will go to her room. You two can distract the parents while Bay calls on her ghost friends for answers."

I blinked several times in rapid succession, dumbfounded. "Psychics?"

"Distractions?" Chief Terry looked livid. "I am not a distraction. I'm the chief of police."

"And the bureau has hard-and-fast rules about using psychics," Landon added. "That lie could come back to bite us."

"Oh, geez." Mom rolled her eyes. "You guys don't understand how to investigate a case at all. You really need to watch *Blue Bloods* for inspiration."

"I'll consider that," Landon said. "That doesn't change the fact that you can't say you're psychics."

He was right. I knew Tina and Felix Hart fairly well. They wouldn't be happy with the idea of psychics. We had to come up with something else.

"I still think it will work," Mom insisted. "What family doesn't want to utilize every opportunity to find a missing child? This is a great idea."

"Tina and Felix know us," I reminded her. "They might be suspicious if we suddenly claimed to be psychic."

"Ha!" Chief Terry jabbed a finger at Mom, realizing after the fact that it was probably a mistake. "I mean ... well done, Bay." He carefully bobbed his head. "That could've been a disaster."

Landon shook his head. He seemed to be enjoying himself. "What if we say you're with us because we want to be able to get into the head of a teenager? Bay was a teenager not so long ago."

I frowned. "I'm almost thirty." I hated saying it out loud.

"At least you're getting married," Mom said. "Things would be worse if you hit thirty without getting married."

"How is that a thing?" Landon asked.

"It just is." Mom contorted to look over her shoulder at him. "It's a good thing you got your head out of your behind when you did and proposed. If you'd waited much longer, Bay's ring finger would've grown moldy and fallen off."

Landon's expression was difficult to read. "It's weird, but I never saw Aunt Tillie in any of you until just now. It's ... enlightening."

Mom's scowl was pronounced. "Are you trying to tick me off? I can curse you to smell like something worse than rancid pickles if you're not careful."

"If you make Bay smell like a bacon McGriddle, I'll be your son-in-law slave forever."

"I'll look into it." Mom was prim as she rested her hands in her lap. "I'm fine with whatever lie you want to spin. I just want to be part of the action."

I was afraid of that. "You need to be careful," I warned. "Tina and Felix will be upset. They won't want to hear anything except what Landon and Chief Terry are going to do to find Amelia. If we play our cards right, we won't have to explain our presence at all."

"Good point." Landon flipped my hand over and traced the lines of my palm. He seemed lost in thought.

"Do you have an idea?" I asked hopefully.

"Yeah. I was thinking that you could use that double-sided tape to make sure the coconut bra cups don't give you splinters. That's probably our best bet."

My mouth dropped open. "That's what you're thinking?"

The grin he flashed was devastating. "That's how much I love you, Bay. You're always on my mind."

He wasn't fooling anybody. "You want me to eat bacon when I'm in the bra."

"No, I want you to feed me bacon when you're in the bra."

I should've seen that coming. "Let's focus on the missing girl."

"I'm a great multitasker. You'll see."

TINA AND FELIX WERE INDEED DEVASTATED. Any amusement I'd felt regarding Landon's one-track mind fled the second I saw them.

"Any news?" Tina asked, her hand shaking as it approached her mouth. She looked so hopeful, and yet fearful. Her fingernails were ragged nubs.

"We're still looking," Chief Terry said in his softest voice. "That's why we're here. We need to look in Amelia's room. Just in case."

"In case of what?" Felix's forehead wrinkled. "You don't think this is her fault?"

"Absolutely not." Landon was firm as he shook his head. "This is definitely not her fault. However, it's possible somebody contacted her online. Maybe someone tried to lure her with the promise of ... something. We have to cover all the bases."

Felix dragged a hand through his disheveled hair. "Of course you do. Some pervert might've groomed her on the internet." His eyes were accusatory when he fixed them on his wife. "You said we shouldn't put a password on the wi-fi."

My heart sank at the hatred in his eyes. Landon was smooth as he stepped in to take control of the conversation.

"It's nobody's fault," he insisted, drawing two sets of bloodshot eyes to him. "It's certainly not the fault of those who live under this roof. Whoever took Amelia was meticulous and determined. He's to blame."

Felix didn't look convinced, but his cheeks colored with shame and he nodded stiffly. "Do what you have to do. I'll be in my office printing fliers."

"Thank you." A muscle worked in Landon's jaw as he watched the man stalk down the hallway. He almost looked as if he wanted to follow, perhaps to offer some sort of comfort, but he remained rooted to his spot and focused on Tina. "Can you show us Amelia's room?"

The tiny woman nodded. She looked beaten down, as if life had sucked all the energy from her, and yet she held it together as she motioned for us to follow. "You'll have to excuse my husband. He's not as hateful as he makes himself sound. He's just so ... angry."

"He has a right to be angry," Chief Terry intoned.

"He does, but he also feels guilty. He thinks he should've been able to do something to stop this from happening. He needs someone to blame, because if he allows himself to think too long he'll fall apart. At least right now he still thinks we'll get her back."

"And what do you believe?" I asked, the sound of my own voice shocking me. I hadn't meant to ask the question out loud.

"I know the statistics," Tina replied. "I know the longer she's gone the less likely she is to come back. I also know that there are miracles every single day. I'm really hoping for one of those miracles."

I nodded in understanding. "Then let's find a miracle."

TINA LEFT US ALONE IN AMELIA'S BEDROOM. She had hovered in the doorway a few minutes, her eyes cloudy, before wandering away. I figured it was too much for her. The room was a study of a girl caught between childhood and adulthood.

On the walls, posters of hot men stared lustily around the room. On the bed, three raggedy stuffed animals stood guard. They were obviously something Amelia had held onto since childhood.

"Let's look around," Chief Terry said, his eyes landing on me. "Bay, you know what to do. Winnie ... ." He trailed off as he regarded her. "Let Bay do her thing."

Mom shot him a withering look, one that promised payback. "I'm just as capable as Bay."

"Of course you are." Chief Terry refused to allow his broad shoulders to droop under Mom's warning look. "You're the most capable woman I know. Bay has worked with us before, though, and she's familiar with our rhythm."

"Yes, I'm totally familiar with their rhythm," I agreed, my eyes drifting to the closet. Something drew me in that direction. I sidestepped Mom and pulled open the door.

I don't know what I was expecting. Nobody jumped out. There was no monster lurking to grab me ... at least that I could see. There was no neon sign pointing and flashing to direct me toward a clue. Nothing but clothes ... and shoes ... and a stack of books on one of the shelves.

"What is it?" Landon asked from his spot at Amelia's desk. He was already accessing her computer.

"I don't know." I fingered a baby pink shirt and sucked in a breath. "I feel ... something."

"You feel something?" Mom shot Chief Terry a dubious look. "I don't want to be negative, but how is she in touch with your rhythm when she offers nothing solid?"

"Hey!" I was offended. Well, at least I thought I should be offended.

"I can offer more help than Bay," she promised. "You need to allow me to develop my own rhythm."

Chief Terry looked more tortured than someone with taste being forced to watch the Kardashians. "Winnie, you're going to be a great help. It's just ... what do you think you can offer that Bay can't?"

"For one thing, it doesn't appear that Bay has noticed there's a shadow monster crawling from that closet. If I wasn't here, who would point that out?"

It took a moment for the information to seep in, and when it did, I snapped my head up. There definitely was a shadow monster coming at me. It looked hungry ... and angry.

Before I could react, the creature's hands were on my shoulders. Landon jumped from his chair, but it was too late. The creature shoved me with enough force that my feet left the ground and I slammed through the window next to the bed and toward the ground below.

All I could think as I fell was that my mother's presence had turned out to be distracting after all, in more ways than one.

I was totally going to blame her for this ... if I didn't break my neck.

7
SEVEN

My instincts were to protect my face, so I threw up my hands. Despite the confusion coursing through me, my brain was working fast enough to realize that the drop coming my way was deep. Thankfully, it was a first-story room, but that didn't mean it wouldn't hurt.

I didn't have time to think, so I simply reacted, throwing out a blanket of magic to catch me. By the time I hit the ground, a net of sorts — like you might see under the high-wire at a circus — was waiting. The collision was mild. In fact, I almost bounced before rolling to a stop under a tree.

I sat there, my back against the trunk, dumbfounded.

"Bay!" Landon's face was awash with panic when he peered through the opening. His terrified eyes met mine over the distance. He looked surprised to see where I'd landed. "How ... ?" He didn't finish the question. Instead, he glanced over his shoulder and then hiked himself through the window.

"What are you doing?" Chief Terry snapped from behind him.

"Going to Bay." The determination lacing Landon's voice told me — and Chief Terry — that there was no sense arguing with him.

"Um ... who's going to explain what happened to the window?" Mom asked.

"That's your job." Landon hopped through the opening and landed on the ground, his expression grim as he raced toward me. "Are you okay?" He dropped to his knees, his hands roaming my shoulders and back. "Did you break anything?"

"I bounced."

"You bounced?" He arched an eyebrow, staring, and then moved his hands to the back of my head. "Tell me where it hurts."

Surprisingly, nothing hurt ... other than my forearms. Once I registered the pain, I looked down and saw a gash on one arm and a cluster of small cuts on the other. The gash wasn't deep, but there was enough blood to cause my stomach to tilt.

"I'm okay," I answered. "I'm ... bleeding."

"What?" He followed my gaze and growled. "You're definitely bleeding." Gently, he took my arm for a closer look. "Stitches?"

The single-word question jerked me wide awake. "It's not deep enough for stitches."

He didn't look convinced. "Baby ... ."

I shook my head, firm. "I'm fine. I just need a bandage."

"We'll see after we get it cleaned up." He leaned in and pressed a kiss to my forehead before letting out a pent-up breath. "You scared me."

"I'm sorry." That's when I remembered the shadow. "Where did it go?" I sat straighter and looked around the yard for the creature. I'd lost sight of it when I was crashing through the window.

"I don't know." He brushed my hair from my forehead and ran his finger over a tender spot. "You have a small cut here, too."

I forced a smile for his benefit. "I'm sure it will heal before the wedding. Don't worry about me being disfigured or anything."

"You're not funny." When he finally lifted his eyes to meet mine, I saw something odd there. "Did you really bounce?"

"I don't know if that's the right word," I hedged. "I didn't land like I should've." I stared at the broken window. "I don't know what that was."

"It looked like a shadow monster to me."

"Yes, but what kind of shadow monster?"

"I didn't even know shadow monsters were a thing until one tried to kill you."

I thought back to the way it had appeared. "I think it was hiding in the closet. What happened to me was secondary. It just wanted to escape."

"That doesn't make me feel any better."

"Yeah, well ... ." I shook my head and flashed a smile. "I can't wait to tell Aunt Tillie I can bounce. There's been a rumor about her for years that she can do the same. In fact, Stormy over in Shadow Hills mentioned it to me when we were having coffee the other day. I actually did it."

He looked as if he was struggling to remain stern, but he smiled. "You're turning into quite the witch."

"Does that upset you?"

"No. I always knew you were something special."

"Yeah, but ... now I can bounce. That kind of makes me a superhero. There's a superhero who can bounce, isn't there?"

He cupped my face. "You're my superhero. We're going to talk about this bouncing thing, but not here." He gave me a quick kiss and then looked back toward the window. "How do you think they'll explain that?"

I shrugged. "I'm sure Mom will come up with something."

AFTER STOPPING AT THE NEWSPAPER OFFICE long enough for Landon to bandage my arm — he still maintained that stitches might be necessary — we headed to the diner for lunch. The search at the Hart house had been fruitless.

"I'm starving," I announced as he held the door for me.

"Me too. It seems watching the love of my life get thrown through a window works up quite the appetite."

"Yeah." I tapped his chin. "Did I mention I can bounce?"

He smirked and shook his head. "Is it any wonder that I fell in love with you the moment I saw you?"

"I drove you crazy the day we met," I reminded him as he followed me inside. "You were undercover and I thought you were some dirty biker dude who might be selling meth."

"That's what I wanted you to think. There was a reason I was undercover with those guys."

"I know, but ... ." I broke off, considering. "You know, now that I think back on it, I was attracted to you from the start even though I thought you could be a criminal. What does that say about me?"

He laughed and put his hand to the small of my back. "That you're a good judge of character. Now, pick a table. I really am hungry."

I headed toward our usual table, pulling up short when I saw Chief Terry and Mom already sitting at it. They were engaged in intense conversation, and Chief Terry's expression told a nightmare of a story.

Landon, not paying attention, barreled into my back. "Ow, Bay." He rubbed his chin, which had smacked into my shoulder. "What are you doing?"

I inclined my head to the table.

"Oh." His expression didn't change, but I almost thought I saw a bit of light lurking in the depths of his eyes. "I guess Terry didn't shake your mother after all."

I was incredulous. "Shake her? Was that the plan?"

"There was no plan."

The way he averted his eyes told me there had been. "I saw you guys whispering outside the truck. You obviously had a plan."

"I don't. That's Terry's thing. I told him you were my responsibility and Winnie was his."

That sounded like a load of crap. "Can't I be my own responsibility?"

"In normal, day-to-day life? Absolutely. When it comes to official work? No."

There was something off about his response. "Should we sit with them or get our own table?"

"I prefer our own table, but your mother will take that personally."

"Right. A foursome for lunch." I shook my head. "This is going to be a really long day."

"You're okay," he replied, moving his hand up to the back of my neck and giving it a light squeeze. "There are worse things than having lunch with your mother and Terry."

Neither Chief Terry nor Mom looked up as we approached. Whatever conversation they were mired in looked to be serious, so much so that Mom had her "you're grounded for life" face on and Chief Terry looked as if he was trying to find a hole to crawl into.

"I don't see why you're acting like this, Terry," Mom complained. "It was a perfectly good explanation for what happened."

"What was a perfectly good explanation?" I asked as I took the seat next to Chief Terry, leaving Landon no choice but to sit next to Mom. The look he shot me when he realized what I'd done promised retribution.

"Your mother decided that the best story to tell the Harts regarding Amelia's broken window was that a swarm of bees attacked from the closet and in your haste to escape — you now have a debilitating bee sting allergy, by the way — you jumped out of the window to avoid being stung."

I sipped from the water glass in front of me. "How did the bees get in the closet?"

"Bees can get anywhere," Mom replied. "They're sneaky that way. Don't you remember when we used to have the hives on the property?"

"Ah, yes." I nodded. "The summer of 2008. You guys thought you were going to sell honey on the side."

"We did sell honey on the side."

"For, like, three weeks. Then Twila got stung on the lip and looked like a plastic surgery reject, and you guys abandoned the project."

"First, Marnie and I told Twila that she would be stung if she refused to wear the netting we provided her. That was on her. Second, we made good money from that honey. But it was more work than we thought."

It was a very practical argument. Unfortunately for her, I remembered things a little differently. "I thought you got in a fight with Aunt Tillie because she wanted to use the honey for spells and potions. She declared the honey was hers because the hives were on her land."

"I'm sure I don't know what you're talking about." Mom plucked the specials menu from the center of the table. "Oh, they have hot beef sandwiches. I love hot beef."

Across from me, Landon stared hard at his menu. I knew he was trying to refrain from reacting to the unintended double entendre.

"Landon loves hot beef too," I teased. "It's his favorite."

"I thought bacon was his favorite," Mom countered.

"It is," Chief Terry said. "They're doing something gross with the hot beef discussion. Ignore them."

"What's not to love about hot beef?" Mom asked blankly, causing me to choke.

Landon placed his feet on either side of mine and pressed inward, a silent acknowledgement that we were both feeling young and stupid today.

If I didn't change the subject, I would start laughing ... and perhaps never stop. "I'm pretty sure Aunt Tillie spelled the bees to chase you guys when you tried to gather honey." I rerouted to the previous topic. "She accused you of stealing her honey. You all got stung. Three bees flew into Twila's shirt."

"That didn't happen," Mom insisted.

"I remember it. She wasn't wearing a bra, so she wasn't hurt as badly as Marnie, who had four or five dead bees in her bra. How can you not remember that?"

"Because it didn't happen." Mom's eyes flashed with annoyance.

"It did. Marnie jokes about how Twila would finally have something to stuff in a bra if she'd been stung in the right place."

Mom leaned over the table — *far* over the table — and fixed me with her evilest glare. "Stop talking, Bay."

I knew better than to argue with that face. "Okay." I focused on Landon, who shot me a sympathetic look. "I should've just let her keep talking about hot beef."

Landon, sipping his water, choked so hard Mom slapped his back with enough force that it echoed throughout the diner. Embarrassed, I offered apologetic smiles to a few nearby tables. It was on the last table that I did a double take so pronounced I was glad I wasn't drinking water because I would've spit it all over my meal mates.

"That kind of hurt," Landon admitted morosely. "Did you box in another life?"

Mom snorted. "I raised your girlfriend and her mouthy cousins. That was training enough."

"Fiancée," Landon corrected.

"What?"

"Fiancée. Bay is my fiancée, not my girlfriend."

When I turned back, I found Mom eyeing Landon with disbelief. "We have a problem," I announced.

Mom didn't even look at me. "And why is that distinction important?" she challenged.

"Because I said so." Landon refused to back down. "A girlfriend can be temporary. Fiancée is forever."

"Wife is forever," Chief Terry corrected.

"Not if you're divorced," Mom countered. "I still don't understand why this is such a big deal."

"Because it is." Landon looked to me for support. "Tell her you're my fiancée. Girlfriend is too high school."

I felt as if I was caught in an unnecessary argument with Aunt Tillie about leggings. "Does nobody care that we have a problem?"

Landon sighed. "What's the problem, sweetie? Do you finally want me to take you to the hospital? I knew that fall through the window couldn't just be swept under the rug, no matter what you said."

I glared at him. "I told you I bounced. There's nothing wrong with me. That's not the problem."

Mom held up her hand to still me. "You bounced?"

I felt as if I was throwing words at a wall, desperately hoping some would stick. "I already told you this."

"You didn't tell me that part." Mom folded her arms over her chest and glared. "I don't think it's possible you bounced."

"Well, I did." There was no other way to describe what had happened. "I was there. I definitely bounced."

Mom didn't look convinced. "Is this like when Aunt Tillie bounced?"

"That didn't happen."

"The people in Shadow Hills think it did. That was one of the few stories Stormy related when she was here last week."

"Aunt Tillie started that rumor. It didn't really happen. With me, it did."

Landon scratched the side of his head. "I need more details. Why would Aunt Tillie start a rumor that she could bounce?"

"She was bored one day and decided to watch *Charlie and the Chocolate Factory*," I replied. "She likes the part when that girl blows up like a giant blueberry — we're talking the Johnny Depp one instead of the Gene Wilder version. She thought it would be fun to toss her around like a basketball. That started the discussion of people bouncing, and she claimed she could do it when she was a kid."

"Bounce?"

"Yes."

Chief Terry was already shaking his head when Landon looked to him. "Don't ask me. I can't explain anything these crazy witches do. I'm just along for the ride."

"I just don't understand why anyone would want to list 'bounce' on their résumé," Landon persisted. "It makes no sense."

"Oh, well, she didn't want to put it on her résumé. It's just one of those things that she likes to mention occasionally. Like the time she claimed Johnny Cash stopped in town and asked her to marry him. She didn't accept his proposal, of course, because she was already married to Uncle Calvin. That left Johnny broken-hearted, which is why he turned to drinking and song-writing."

Landon turned to me. "Were you saying something, Bay?"

I was about to explode. "Yes, I was saying we have a problem." I lobbed a dark glare toward Mom. "And I totally bounced, but not the same way Aunt Tillie bounced, because it was real when I did it." I looked back to Landon. "Don't look, but Aunt Willa and Mrs. Little are having lunch together in the corner."

Despite my admonishment, Landon's first instinct was to look, which caused me to kick him under the table.

"Ow!" Annoyance rolled over him as he reached under the table to rub his shin. "What is it with this family abusing me today?"

"I told you not to look," I reminded him.

"Well, excuse me for living."

"They really are sitting over there together," Mom said, pensive worry lining her forehead. "I wonder what they're doing. If I remember correctly, they weren't altogether unfriendly when they were younger."

She had to be kidding. "There's only one reason those women would join forces."

"We don't know they're joining forces," Mom argued. "They could just be having lunch."

"An evil lunch. I mean ... that's like saying Darth Vader and Sauron being at the same table could possibly be a coincidence."

"How did Darth Vader manage to find his way into Middle Earth?" Mom asked blankly.

"And why would they hang out?" Landon pressed. "I think Vader would be afraid of Mount Doom because he lost his limbs in a lava accident. Mount Doom should be the last place he'd want to visit."

I thought I might yank the hair out of my head. "Is that really important right now?"

"Just a point of clarification," Landon said.

"Focus on them." I gestured toward Aunt Willa and Mrs. Little, neither of whom had bothered to look in our direction. "They're flesh-and-blood evil instead of movie evil. I guarantee they're up to something."

"I maintain that we don't know they're up to anything," Mom countered. "It could be an innocent meal."

"Oh, you're so naive."

"And you get more like Aunt Tillie every day."

It was like a slap on a naked cheek. "That was the meanest thing you ever said to me." I turned my gaze to Landon. "Tell her she's mean."

"Yeah, I want to go back to talking about hot beef." Landon leaned back in his chair. "Anything is better than this conversation. I don't even know how we got here."

"I'll tell you how we got here," Chief Terry hissed. "You decided to play Take Your Future Mother-in-Law to Work Day, that's how."

Landon didn't blink. "How do you feel about hot beef?"

Chief Terry rolled his eyes. "I hate this family sometimes."

8
EIGHT

"We should leave now." Landon was serious as he stood with Chief Terry and me in front of the diner after lunch. "Right now."

Chief Terry gestured toward the door. "We are leaving. Winnie will be out in just a second and then we can go. I figured we would question Amelia's friends again."

"I'm all for questioning the girls, but we shouldn't wait for Winnie."

I stared at him. "What do you mean?"

"I love her — you know I do — but she's not an official member of this team." He moved his fingers between the three of us. "We work together well, have a certain rhythm. Winnie is a civilian."

"So am I," I reminded him.

"Yes, but you're special."

I couldn't withhold my grin. "How special?"

Before he could respond with a kiss, Chief Terry shoved his hand between our mouths and shook his head. "Don't even think about it." He was stern. "Our rhythm doesn't involve you two making out like morons."

"Actually, it does," Landon countered, nudging away his hand. "But I'm willing to forego that part of our rhythm if it means we can leave right now."

"You can't just abandon Mom in the middle of town," I argued. "She'll be mad ... and hurt ... and really mad. Do you know what she does when she's mad?"

"Yeah, she pouts."

"Oh, she's going to do a lot worse than that. She gets payback. That's what she does best."

"Aunt Tillie gets payback," Landon corrected.

"And she taught Mom. I don't know everything she'll do to us, but I promise it won't be pretty. I guarantee there will be no bacon for you anytime soon for starters. She'll probably start showing up at the guesthouse unannounced and invade the bedroom without knocking, too."

"She does that already."

"Not all that often. This will become a three-times-a-day thing."

His forehead creased as he considered. "We could change the locks."

"She's a witch. That won't stop her."

I turned to Chief Terry. "And you'll be cut off from the love machine. I don't particularly want to think about that, but you've been a bachelor for so long — and your last girlfriend turned out to be a homicidal maniac — so I'm guessing you don't want that to happen."

Chief Terry scowled. "I'm not comfortable having this discussion with you."

"Right back at you, but you'll be high and dry if we leave her."

"So you'll have nothing to entertain you but a hot beef sandwich," Landon supplied. "It might be worth it."

"Knock that off." Chief Terry gave Landon's shoulder a shove. "We're not leaving her. You, however, are going to talk her into going home."

It took me a moment to realize his eyes were on me. "What?"

"You're going to talk her into going home," he repeated, unruffled by how squeaky my voice had become. "You're her daughter. She'll listen to you."

He had to be joking. "Are you new in town? She's never listened to me a day in her life."

"That's not true. She thinks you're smart, that you have a good head on your shoulders. She told me."

Other than the "smart" part, that didn't sound like a compliment. "What else has she told you?"

"That she thinks you and Landon are a good fit, but she wants her grandchildren to be blond, so she'll be disappointed if they look like Landon."

"Hey!" Landon was affronted. "I'm a fine specimen of a man."

"If you say so."

Landon looked to me for confirmation. "Tell him."

"You're prime hot beef." I patted his arm but kept my focus on Chief Terry. "She'll listen to you more than she listens to me."

"She never listens to me. She'll listen to you."

"No, she won't."

"Yes, she will."

"No, she won't."

"What are we arguing about now?" Mom asked as she joined us on the sidewalk. She looked fresh-faced — as if she'd applied powder while in the bathroom — and her smile told me she knew more than she let on.

I decided to get ahead of potential trouble. "Chief Terry and Landon wanted to leave you behind, but I told them I wasn't having it. You're far too important to the team."

"Leave me behind?" Mom gripped her hands together and shot an accusatory look at Chief Terry. "Why would you want to do that?"

Chief Terry struggled to take a breath. He moved his mouth but no sound came out.

"Bay misunderstood," Landon countered calmly. "I didn't want to leave you. I just can't believe you're not bored. Isn't there something else you would rather be doing?"

"Other than spending time with my favorite daughter, the man she'll most likely marry as long as he doesn't irritate me, and the man I cook for three times a day? I can't think of a single thing."

Her message was clear, as was Landon's audible gulp.

"We should get going," Landon said. "You raise some compelling points, and I can't imagine not finishing the day without you by my side."

Mom flashed a bright smile and lightly clapped his cheek. "I thought you would see things my way. Come on, Terry. We have work to do. There's no sense standing around like lumps on the street."

Chief Terry was morose, but he rallied long enough to pin me with a look that promised retribution. "You'll be sorry you threw me under your mother's broom that way. Just wait."

He was all talk. "You won't hurt me. You love me too much."

"I do love you." He was matter-of-fact. "Vengeance is the Winchester way, though, and I have no problem giving you a taste of it ... Bradshaw style." He headed toward his vehicle. "Come on. If you two drag this day out one second longer I'll make you both cry."

Landon slid his eyes to me. "It's one thing to screw over Terry. I get it, it's every witch for herself. But I'm going to be your husband. You're supposed to protect me with your life."

"And if we were dealing with another witch, I would throw myself in front oncoming magic to make sure you were safe," I promised him. "We're talking about my mother. She won't kill you, just terrorize you."

"Well, if that's the way you feel, the same rules apply for me."

"What is that supposed to mean?" I was honestly curious. "Do you think she's going to take your side over mine?"

"I guess we'll just have to wait and see."

I didn't like the sound of that. "I'm her daughter. She'll always take my side." Even as I said it, I wasn't certain I believed it.

"We shall see."

"We definitely will."

ALL THREE GIRLS WERE AT PAISLEY GILMORE'S house. She lived in the ritzier part of Hemlock Cove — although that didn't necessarily mean much — and her parents, Richard and Anna, looked as if they were about to collapse when they allowed us in.

Chief Terry took charge this time and explained Mom's presence before a single question could be asked. "Marcus was hurt so Thistle made Winnie promise to help out. It makes Thistle feel better to have an inside person on the team."

Richard merely stared at him before ultimately nodding. "Whatever." He gestured toward the girls, who were spread out in the living room, staring mindlessly at the television. "They're very upset."

It didn't look that way. In fact, if I didn't know better, I would think Paisley and her clones were more interested in the Kardashians than their missing friend.

"She looks like Michael Jackson," Sophia said as we moved into the room, her gaze on the television. "She's had so much plastic surgery she's not even recognizable."

"She does look a little plastic," Paisley agreed, squinting at the screen. "But I like her hair better. And her body is sick."

"Totally sick," Emma intoned. "I can't believe she has that body so soon after having a baby."

"It's not that hard," Paisley said, her eyes moving to me. She seemed surprised to find new people invading her space. "You just can't let yourself turn into a fat cow when you're pregnant. Isn't that right?"

There was no doubt the question was directed at me. "I don't really have an opinion," I countered.

"You have to have an opinion." Paisley said it as if it were fact. "I mean ... you're going to have a baby one day." She looked at Landon. "If you get too fat and don't lose the weight fast, he's likely to leave you. Just look at that cousin of yours. She's gaining way too much weight. Her marriage will never last because there's no way she'll lose all that she's gained."

I was offended on Clove's behalf. "She'll be fine."

"She will," Landon agreed. He didn't look thrilled with the topic, but his expression never changed. "Something tells me Sam won't care about a few pounds here or there once she brings their child into the world."

Paisley snorted. "You can't possibly think that. I mean ... if this one gains fifty extra pounds and never loses the weight, how long do you think you'll last?" She pointed at me so there could be no confusion as to who she was talking about.

"I don't care." Landon was firm. "That doesn't matter to me in the least. I think most people fall in love with a person, not a body type."

Paisley shook her head and returned to the television. "If you say so."

"Did you find Amelia?" Emma asked, leaning forward. She obviously didn't care about the baby weight conversation as much as Paisley. "Is she back home?"

"Not yet," Chief Terry replied, glancing from face to face. "Can you turn that off? We need to go over your statements again."

"Why?" Paisley's attitude left a lot to be desired as she stretched on the couch. "Nothing has changed since last night. If you haven't found her yet, that's on you. There's nothing we can do for you."

"Actually, there is something you can do. You can turn off the television."

Paisley didn't reach for the remote control. "I don't want to talk about this. It makes me sad."

Richard, who had been loitering at the edge of the room, stirred. "This could be too much for them, Terry," he said. "Maybe you should come back another time."

"That won't be happening." Terry sat on the footstool in front of Emma, but his attention was directed at Paisley. They seemed to be engaging in a standoff. "Turn off the television."

"I'm in the middle of this episode," Paisley protested.

"Turn off the television." Chief Terry's voice was cold enough to cause my heart to sink. If he'd spoken that way to me when I was a kid, I would've curled into a ball and started crying.

"Fine." She hit the mute button rather than the power button and slowly tracked her eyes to Chief Terry. "What do you want me to say?"

"I want you to go through what happened to Amelia again," Chief Terry prodded. "We need to know everything that occurred behind that barn."

"It's already too late," Sophia said, her eyes wide. "If you don't find a missing person in twenty-four hours, then they're probably dead."

"We don't know that," Chief Terry argued. "All we know is that she's missing. We need leads. That's why we have more questions."

"Maybe the questions are too much for them," Richard interjected. "They were traumatized."

Paisley's smirk told me that she appreciated her father's insistence on inserting himself into the conversation. They shared an interesting dynamic. He was the father, but Paisley was clearly in control. His milquetoast personality made me think of plain oatmeal.

"Amelia is missing," Chief Terry pointed out. "How traumatized do you think she is right now?"

"I ... ." Richard wrung his hands but didn't finish his answer.

"If it was Paisley, what would you want us to do?" I challenged, my irritation with the girl overruling my common sense. I should've kept my mouth shut — Landon asked for just that before entering the house — but I couldn't stop myself.

Richard met my gaze for a full two seconds before he folded and stared at his shoes. "I would want you to find her by whatever means necessary."

"Well, this is necessary," Chief Terry insisted. "We need to know exactly what happened."

"Fine." Paisley threw her hands into the air. She realized she'd lost, that her father wasn't going to save her from invasive questions, and now that she'd come to this realization it was time to be as theatrical as possible for our benefit. "It was completely frightening." She focused on Landon for the duration of her tale, batting her eyelashes and twirling a strand of hair around her finger. The way she elongated herself, stretched in a flattering manner, told me she was testing him ... although why she thought that might benefit her was beyond me.

"That's all there is," she announced when she finished. She hadn't offered a single new tidbit. "She's gone and now we've lost our very best friend." Someone who didn't know her might think she was really on the verge of tears, but I recognized her glassy-eyed stare for what it was. She was mimicking emotions. Whether that meant she didn't actually feel anything or was simply hiding her true feelings was beyond me.

"What about earlier in the day?" Landon asked. If he noticed the girl was doing her best to flirt with him, he didn't show it. His expression remained impassive as he focused on her face.

"We did normal stuff earlier in the day," Paisley replied. "We hung around at the festival. We saw you guys there. You were eating a bunch of food and had your tongues jammed down each other's throats."

"Paisley," Richard scolded, shaking his head. "You shouldn't say things like that."

Paisley's eye roll was withering. "He said to tell him the things we noticed."

Richard was apologetic. "I'm so sorry. She's just acting out because she's a teenager."

"I remember being a teenager," I offered. "It wasn't that long ago. I would never have acted like this if my friend was missing."

"Well, you're not me." Paisley's eyes flashed with something dark and sinister. It was obvious she didn't like me, possibly because she had a crush on Landon. "I don't know what you want me to say. That's exactly what happened."

A muscle worked in Landon's jaw and I thought maybe he would push harder. Instead, he focused on Emma. "What about you? Did you see anything out of the ordinary during the day?"

"No." Emma solemnly shook her head. "It was a quiet afternoon. I mean ... there was that time we thought we saw someone watching us in the woods, but that turned out to be a trick of the light."

"Oh, yeah." Sophia sat up straighter in her chair. "I forgot about that. It was right before it happened." She giggled like the schoolgirl she was. "We were having our lattes and we saw something in the trees," she explained. "We thought someone was following us — Paisley always gets a lot of attention — but after we yelled at the shadow, like, ten times, we realized it was just a trick of the light."

I stiffened at mention of the word "shadow" and darted my eyes to Landon. He looked equally perplexed.

"You saw a shadow following you?" Landon kept his tone neutral. "Do you think it was a person?"

"It was nothing," Paisley countered. "We were so hopped up on caffeine we thought we were seeing things. It turns out we weren't."

Landon didn't look convinced. "And right after you saw the shadow, this man appeared to take Amelia?"

"Pretty much," Sophia confirmed.

"We didn't really see anything," Paisley insisted. "There was nothing there. We imagined it."

Landon glanced at Chief Terry and shrugged his shoulders. "Okay, change of plans. The state police have a very good sketch artist. We'd like permission to send him here and work on a sketch with the girls." He looked to Richard. "Is that okay with you?"

I didn't miss the fact that Richard appeared to look to Paisley for permission before nodding. "That should be fine."

"Great." Landon dug in his pocket for his phone, our gazes briefly connecting. "At least with a sketch we'll have something to work with."

"And then we can get Amelia back," Emma said. "I mean ... if she isn't already dead."

"We'll get her back." Landon flashed the girl a tight-lipped smile. "We're good at what we do. Whoever took her won't be able to hide from us."

I hoped that was true. A second mention of the shadow had me concerned things were about to spiral out of control.

"How about some tea?" Anna asked. It was the first time she'd spoken since the interrogation had begun. Her presence felt oddly forced.

"Tea would be great," I answered.

NINE

Getting three teenagers to agree on specifics regarding the facial features of a man over the age of thirty was harder than herding cats. Jensen Porter, the state police sketch artist, had the patience of a kindergarten teacher on pot, but even he looked at his limit an hour later.

"Tell me what it is that's wrong with the eyes," he demanded of Paisley, who to the surprise of absolutely nobody was the most difficult.

"They're not ... squinty enough," Paisley replied. "He was more like this." She made an exaggerated face.

"Uh-huh." Jensen flicked his eyes to Landon, as if to ask "Do you want to help me here" and then turned back to his tablet. "Let's see what I can come up with."

Landon put his hand to my elbow and nudged me out the front door. Mom and Chief Terry were already outside, sitting on a swing in the shade and talking.

"Anything?" Chief Terry asked as we approached.

"Paisley says the eyes aren't squinty enough," Landon replied. "She's being ... difficult."

"I'm pretty sure that kid idles at difficult. I thought Thistle was bad as a kid, but she was nothing compared to that one."

Thistle wasn't present to stand up for herself, so I felt the need to take up her cause. "Thistle wasn't that bad."

Amusement lit Chief Terry's features. "Oh, no? I seem to remember a time or two when I caught you guys down at Hollow Creek and she'd terrorized the other kids to the point they actually tattled on themselves for underage drinking just to get away from her."

"Those people usually picked on us before we picked on them."

"Toni Gibbons picked on you?" He arched a challenging eyebrow. "She must've weighed eighty-five pounds soaking wet. She was still wearing child-sized clothing when you guys were in high school."

"And she was vicious when provoked."

Chief Terry waited.

"She bit," I explained to Landon, who shook his head.

"Leave Thistle alone," he instructed Chief Terry. "Bay is feeling protective. She'll go after you if you're not careful. Just ... let it go."

"Fine. Thistle was an angel." Chief Terry shot me a sarcastic wink. "She never did anything wrong."

"You always did stand up for them, even when they were rotten," Mom said. "You can't suddenly turn on one of them after the fact. That won't go over well."

"Bay was never rotten." Chief Terry's voice was firm. "She really was an angel."

Landon rolled his eyes. "You've got him snowed."

I ignored him and graced Chief Terry with my prettiest smile.

"I'm not turning on them. I'm simply saying that I thought dealing with Thistle was going to be the worst the world had to offer me in regard to teenagers. Apparently I was wrong. That kid in there is so terrible her parents cower in her presence."

And that was what I'd been circling back to as well. "I don't sense any magic in her," I said.

"Did you expect to?" Chief Terry's expression was unreadable. "Did you think she was another witch?"

"I don't think so. It's possible, though." I thought back to Dani Harris, a local girl who had bamboozled me into believing she could be turned to white magic after embracing the dark side of the paranormal world. We spent weeks trying to prod her to what was right only to eventually bind her powers and send her away. She didn't want to be good, and even though it was one of the most difficult decisions I ever had to make, I had to let her go.

Chief Terry's expression softened. "If you're thinking of that girl ... ." He trailed off and held up his hands. He didn't fully understand our world. He tried, but some things were simply above his pay grade.

"It's fine," I reassured him. "I'm not dwelling or anything." Because I knew he worried about the same thing, I focused on Landon. "I mean it. I'm fine."

Landon slung his arm around my shoulder and tugged me close, pressing a kiss to my temple. "I know you're okay. It was difficult for you to let her go."

"It was, but I'm over it."

He didn't look convinced, but he nodded all the same. "I'm glad you're over it. We should probably focus on Paisley."

Something about the way he dismissed the topic told me he didn't think I was anywhere near over it, but this wasn't the time to battle over that topic. "I don't know if her parents are afraid of her or they just spoil her rotten. She's a difficult kid to get a read on."

"Agreed," Landon said. "She makes me nervous. It's as if she's undressing me with her eyes."

"That's because she is. She has a crush on you."

"Oh, come on. I'm an old man as far as she's concerned."

"A hot old man. Have you not noticed the way she looks at your butt when you turn around? It's a little distressing."

Mom straightened, suddenly interested in the conversation. "Was she looking at Terry's butt, too?"

I looked to Landon for help, but he was suddenly interested in staring at a random tree branch. "Do you think she was looking at Chief Terry's butt?" I asked him pointedly.

Landon acted surprised I'd aimed the question at him. "I haven't noticed her being inappropriate with either one of us. I'm oblivious to those things."

I was confused. "You don't have to worry about me thinking you return the interest," I reassured him. "You're probably the best one to answer the question about Chief Terry's butt."

"I didn't even notice her looking at me," he blatantly lied. "I certainly didn't notice her looking at anyone else."

He was acting too prim and proper. Normally he would puff out his chest and boast about how hot he was ... even if nobody cared to listen. Now, he was suddenly Mr. Unobservant.

"You're only doing this because of what happened outside the diner," I realized suddenly. "You're leaving me hanging because you think that's what I did to you."

He was the picture of innocence. "I can't believe you would think that of me." He rested his hand above his heart. "I'm shocked that you would accuse me of something so ... horrible. It's not my fault that I wasn't paying attention to a teenager, Bay. Most people would think that's a good thing."

AMANDA M. LEE

"He has a point," Mom noted. "The girl is hard to ignore. He was probably just focused on trying to get information. We are on a case, after all."

I wanted to knock some heads together, starting with Landon and Mom. "Well ... what were we talking about again?"

"How Paisley controls her parents." Chief Terry was obviously anxious to change the subject. "It's distressing the way she bosses them around."

"We were talking about whether or not you noticed Paisley checking out Terry's butt," Landon interjected. "You should answer your mother, Bay. It's a simple enough question."

I wanted to wrap my hands around his throat and start squeezing. "I ... ."

Mom had clearly moved on from the initial question because she was already making a tsking sound and shaking her head. "That girl is a menace. I can't believe she didn't think your butt was just as good as Landon's, Terry. It's criminal. That's your best feature."

Heat rushed to my cheeks, and I had to look away from Chief Terry's embarrassed face. I was mortified on his behalf. Thankfully, a fleeting hint of movement to the left caught my attention, and when I looked — desperately hoping the shadow creature hadn't returned to finish me off — I found Viola, the Whistler's resident ghost, watching me from the shadows of the trees. Even though I found her difficult to deal with on most days, I was thrilled to see her.

"Did something happen?" I blurted out. "You didn't see a shadow monster, did you?"

Viola shook her head. "That's not why I'm here."

"Who are you talking to?" Mom asked, glancing around.

"It's a ghost," Landon said. He was used to working cases with me and no longer questioned it when I started talking to no one in particular. "She's talking to a ghost."

"Oh." Mom folded her hands in her lap and sat up straighter. "We'll wait for you to do ... whatever it is you need to do. Then we'll finish our conversation."

"I can't wait," I muttered, doing my best to ignore Landon's twitching smile. "Do you need something, Viola?" I was filled with hope at the notion that she might be able to drag me away from the hell I was mired in.

"I've been looking for you." Viola's eyes were wild. "Something has happened."

"Did it involve a shadow monster?"

"What's with the shadow monster?" Viola made a face. "There is no shadow monster ... at least that I'm aware of. I'm here for a different reason."

"And that is?"

"I was sitting down in the lunchroom to watch my soaps — they say Dante is coming back to *General Hospital* and I'm on the lookout because he's the only dude with a tramp stamp that I find hot — when I heard it."

I was familiar enough with Viola's unnatural rhythm when it came to telling a story that I knew to hurry her along. "Cut to the chase."

"Someone was in your office."

"At the newspaper?" I still wasn't following. "Are you sure?"

"I'm sure. I realized that I was hearing real noises, and when I got up the courage to check it out, I found papers all over your office."

I had no idea what to make of the revelation. "Well ... ." I glanced at Landon, unsure.

"What did she say?" he asked impatiently.

I told him, cringing when his eyes caught fire. "She might not have heard what she thought she heard," I offered lamely.

"Well, we're going to find out." Landon grabbed my hand and dragged me toward Chief Terry's official vehicle. "Toss me the keys," he called over his shoulder.

Chief Terry shook his head. "No way. That's my truck."

"We have to get back to town. If someone has been in Bay's office, we need to check it out."

"You'll have to wait." Chief Terry planted his hands on his hips. "I can't leave until Jensen has finished his sketch."

"Call one of your other men to pick you up."

"You call one of my other men to pick you up."

"We need to leave right now." Landon was adamant. "That's her safe place. She should be allowed to work in her office without fear."

The statement was pointed enough — and emotionally manipulative enough — that Chief Terry sighed before reaching into his pocket. "Who am I supposed to call to pick us up?"

"Don't worry about that," Mom said. "Aunt Tillie is probably out in her truck about now. She likes to roam the neighborhoods and make lists of people she hates for the day. She can pick us up."

Chief Terry looked horrified at the thought. "I don't want to ride with her."

"It's perfectly safe," Mom insisted. "She has helmets for passengers. You have nothing to worry about."

Chief Terry looked as if he felt otherwise. "I'll make both of you pay for this," he threatened as Landon plucked the keys he'd tossed to him out of the air. "Just you wait."

. . .

LANDON FORCED ME TO STAY BEHIND HIM as we approached the newspaper office. I used my magic to scan the building to the best of my ability and came up empty, though I was far from infallible.

"Son of a ... !" He viciously swore when he caught sight of the groove marks next to the handle. "Somebody was definitely working on this door."

I pushed past him as he glared at the offending marks and grabbed the handle, prepared to walk inside. He caught me before I could.

"Together," he prodded in a soft voice. There was a plea in his eyes.

"If it's the shadow monster, I'll be fine," I assured him. "I can bounce now."

The statement had the desired effect, and he managed a crooked smile. "And what if it's a simple robber with a gun?"

The question caught me off guard. "It's never a simple robber with a gun."

"There's a first time for everything." He withdrew his service weapon from the holster at his hip. "Together."

That was a vast improvement over his "I'm going first and will serve as a human shield for you" mentality when we started dating. "Together." I nodded. Compromise was the name of the game in our relationship, and that meant we both had to give a little.

When we stepped inside I noticed the building felt different, almost chilly. Most days I was more than happy to spend hours working in my office. Something felt off today.

"I don't think whoever did this is still here."

"We're searching together." Landon was adamant. "We're start down there." He pointed in the direction of my old office, near the lunch and file rooms. I nodded and fell into step with him.

Landon was methodical as he picked his way through the building. The page designer now had my former office, though he was rarely present. That office was locked up tight, and it was easy to see through its windows that it was empty and intact.

Our next stop was the lunchroom. The television was still on — Viola hadn't been lying about leaving in a hurry — a soap opera playing out onscreen. "Which one has the tramp stamp?" I asked Viola as she materialized.

"Dante," Viola replied. I knew she'd returned after leaving us at the Hart house but had yet to see her during our search. Apparently she was still leery about being in the building alone. "He's not on right now. The actor left, but there are rumors he's coming back. I'm watching because I just know they're going to surprise us."

"And he has a tramp stamp?" That was hard to wrap my head around. "I thought that was a chick thing."

"Apparently some dudes like it too."

I shifted my gaze to Landon. "It takes all kinds, huh?"

He offered me a grin and a quick kiss before poking his head into the file room. It was old school — The Whistler didn't have the funds to hire someone to digitize everything — and empty. That left only the other side of the building.

"Let's go to your office next," he said.

I padded behind him, my heart pounding harder with each step. When we finally reached my office, I was convinced I would find everything I loved — the chair, desk, artwork — shredded. To my surprise, it looked largely the same ... except for about fifteen to twenty sheets of paper that had been strewn about the floor.

"What's this?" Landon asked as he knelt. Once he was certain the building was empty, he shoved the gun back into the holster and focused on the mess. "All these pages are blank."

My eyes went to the tempestuous printer on the table against the wall. "The printer spits out paper," I explained. "It does this weird thing of cycling through when starting up."

Landon held out his hands. "Someone still had to turn it on."

"This building is old. Sometimes the wind blows the power lines and they blink on and off. When that happens, the printer goes on and off."

"Did the wind put the grooves on the front door?"

Whoops. I hadn't gotten that far yet. "No."

"So, someone was definitely in here." He eyed the printer. "And whoever it was wanted to print something. Check your computer."

I did as instructed, booting it up. Nothing looked out of the ordinary. When I typed in my password and looked at my home screen, everything was the same. "I don't know that anyone was in here."

"Someone was definitely in here," Viola insisted. "I heard the front door close after I heard the other noises. I didn't imagine it."

She was sincere enough that I believed her. However, I couldn't wrap my head around someone breaking into the office to print something. "There's nothing worth stealing on the computer," I insisted. "I don't keep any financial data on this machine. I keep it on the computer at the guesthouse."

"Can you access the information on the other computer from this computer?"

"No. It's on a different computer."

"Yeah, but you have a cloud drive, baby. Most people do."

"I have one, but I never set it up."

He cracked a smile. "So, laziness might've saved us." A muscle worked in his jaw as he surveyed the paper configuration. "There's nothing here. If someone printed something, he or she took it."

"But what could it be?"

"I don't know." He folded his arms across his chest and pressed his lips together. I knew by his stance that he was already making plans.

"You're not going to stake this place out all night."

"Nope. But we are upgrading the security system."

My eyebrows winged up. "We did that not long after I bought the business."

"Yes, but I've had a few ideas since then. If this is where you'll spend most of your days, I want you safe."

"What did you have in mind?" His smile was so wide I instantly wished I hadn't asked the question. "Oh, you're going to go nuts, aren't you?"

"I prefer to think of it as keeping what I love most safe."

"So ... uber-nuts?"

"Pretty much."

I dragged a hand through my hair and looked around. "Well, if you're insistent, I'll agree to it."

"That easy?" He looked dubious.

"Compromise, right?"

"All the way, baby."

"Then let's do it. We might as well get a jump on it now. I know you won't rest until you feel I'm safe."

"You've got that right. Keep looking on your computer. I want to see if anything has been messed with on there. It could be something you don't ordinarily look at it. While you're doing that, I have to make a few calls for equipment. We might not be able to get all of it tonight."

"I'll look, but there's really nothing of note on here."

"Try for me, okay?"

"Whatever you think is best."

"Oh, don't tease me." He winked. "We'll play that game later."

10

TEN

Landon toiled over the new security system for hours. Chief Terry called him three times, demanding he return to work, but he refused. His focus was solely on my safety. At some point, Chief Terry showed up to help, saying he didn't have anything to do now that the sketch had been distributed to news outlets and law enforcement agencies. The two of them proceeded to bicker the entire afternoon.

"You're doing it wrong," Chief Terry insisted as he sat on the ground in front of the main door, watching Landon fuss with what looked like a small pen. "If you do that, then it has to be in a place where nobody sees it."

"I want people to see it," Landon shot back. "I want them to take one look at it, realize the building is under surveillance, and go on their merry way. If they know there's a camera, they won't break in."

"Yes, but if they don't break in, we can't catch them on camera and arrest them."

"I don't care about that. I want Bay safe."

"And I don't?"

"You want to use her as bait."

"I do not." Chief Terry rolled his eyes. "Don't be ridiculous. She won't be here."

"She might be the next morning." Landon refused to back down. "What happens if someone breaks in and she goes in through the side door?" He gestured toward the side of the building and an entrance I never used.

"I won't use that door," I promised.

"Shh, sweetie, we're talking." Landon shot me a wide-eyed look before focusing on Chief Terry. "Someone could break in and hurt her before she even registers someone is in the building. These cameras will ensure nobody bothers to break in, because they'll be afraid of getting caught."

Chief Terry hesitated and then nodded. "You're right. We should put twenty of these on the building to make sure she's safe."

"Four will do," Landon muttered. He was clearly chafing under Chief Terry's watchful eye. Even though Landon was an FBI agent, he often deferred to Chief Terry's wisdom. Construction was an entirely different matter.

"Is this, like, a dude thing?" I asked, sliding down the wall on the top step and unwrapping a candy bar as I watched them. "Do you guys need measuring tapes or something?"

Chief Terry grabbed the drill from Landon's hand. "We don't need measuring tapes, sweetheart. We have everything under control."

Landon's smirk told me he found Chief Terry amusing. "Yes, we have everything under control," he agreed.

"Well, awesome for you guys." I stretched out my legs and bit into the Twix. "Where did Mom go?"

"She wasn't interested in helping with the security system," Chief Terry replied. "She decided to head back home with Tillie after we left the Hart residence. I think she was tuckered out."

"I think it's weird you use the word 'tuckered,'" I said. "You know that dates you, right?"

He pinned me with a dark look. "Don't you have work to do?"

"Nope." I flashed a winning smile. "I'm done for the day." I took another bite and chewed with relish, drawing Landon's attention.

"Hey, where did that come from?"

I held up my free hand. "It magically appeared in my desk drawer."

He nodded in understanding. "You have a hidden candy stash."

"I'm the only one in the building regularly, so there's no reason to hide my candy. That said, Clove gets the munchies a lot and sometimes she visits because Thistle has hurt her feelings."

"Was that an elaborate way of admitting you have a candy stash?"

"Absolutely."

He chuckled. "How about you head back in there and get me a bar?" I shook my head, causing him to arch an eyebrow. "No?"

"Dinner's in thirty minutes. You shouldn't spoil your appetite."

"You're spoiling your appetite."

"Yes, but I'm bored." I leaned into him and rested my head on his side as he watched Chief Terry insert the pen-looking thing into the wall. "What is that?"

"A camera. We're putting one on each side of the building. They'll do infrared at night. This way, nobody will be stupid enough to try to break into the building. The cameras will frighten them away."

"It looks like a pen."

"It's a camera."

"I thought it was a pen."

Landon pinned me with his most exasperated look. "You know I love you, right?"

I nodded. "That's the word on the street."

"Well, it's true. I love you so much." His smile told me he was about to say something I didn't want to hear. "You're the love of my life, Bay Winchester."

"Thank you."

"You're also a righteous pain. We know what we're doing with the cameras. Leave us to it."

I watched him for a moment, an odd surge of love threatening to overtake me.

"Why are you still staring at me?" Landon groused. "We have to finish this."

I loved him, even when he drove me crazy. That was never more evident than now. "Are you going to be like this for our entire marriage?"

He blinked several times and then nodded. "I'll always want to keep you safe. Sorry if that bothers you."

"It doesn't bother me. I think it's kind of sweet."

"Oh, geez." Chief Terry stared so hard at the camera mounting that I thought he might pop a blood vessel. "Are you guys trying to make me barf?"

Landon chuckled. "We're working on compromise." He brushed my hair from my face. "I probably should've asked if you were okay with the cameras. Instead I ran off to the hardware store and spent a bunch of money without talking it through with you."

"You did," I agreed.

"Are you okay with it?"

I cocked my head, considering, and then nodded. "I like the idea of scaring people off. We don't know if it was a human being or something else that broke in. It could've been the shadow monster for all we know."

"You think the shadow monster has pressing printing needs?"

"No, but I wouldn't think a random human being would either."

"That's fair." He pursed his lips and watched Chief Terry put the finishing touches on the camera. "I don't know the answer, Bay. These cameras will make me feel better. They also might point us in the right direction if someone comes back, notices the cameras, and takes off. They're an extra layer of protection."

"And an extra layer of protection is always good." I handed him the other half of the Twix bar and grinned.

He took the candy bar and gave me a kiss. "Did we compromise twice in one day?" he whispered as he pulled back. "It might be a Hemlock Cove miracle."

"Or we're just growing up."

"That would be nice," Chief Terry grumbled, shaking his head. "One camera down. Let's get the other three."

Landon held my gaze a moment longer and then stood. "It shouldn't take long, Bay. We'll make it to the inn in plenty of time for dinner."

"We're eating at the Dragonfly tonight," I reminded him. "We have to leave in five minutes if we want to get there in time."

He stilled, surprised. "Right. Dinner with your father."

I sensed where he intended to take the conversation and immediately shook my head. "We promised. We haven't caught up with him since the engagement. I know it seems weird that he's so interested, but I think it's kind of sweet. And it's a way to include him without stepping on my mother's toes."

I realized what I said too late to yank it back and shot a questioning look at Chief Terry. "I didn't mean that in a negative way, in case you decide to repeat it to my mother."

He chuckled. "Don't worry," he reassured me. "I don't tell your mother everything. We're not gossip buddies."

Landon shot him a dubious look.

"We're not," Chief Terry insisted. "We talk, but I don't feel the need to tell her everything. As for this ... ." He looked momentarily lost and then held out his hands. "I know this is hard for you. Your relationship with your father is a work in progress. Your mother wouldn't want to stand in the way of that."

"I know it's not easy for you," I admitted, my heart rolling at the brief flash of discomfort that glinted in the depths of his kind eyes.

"He's your father." Chief Terry refused to meet my gaze. "I want you to be happy. You're getting married. Even if it's to this chucklehead. Go and have dinner. I'll finish up the cameras. It won't take more than an hour."

I balked. "That's not fair. This is Landon's job."

"It is my job," Landon agreed. "One camera is up. I can install the rest tomorrow."

"We should put all of them up."

"I've got it." Landon laid his hand on Chief Terry's forearm. "This is the main door and the camera is done. It won't take me long to finish up tomorrow. Bay is right. It's my job. If you do it, I'll just come here and tear it all down tomorrow so I can make sure it's done right."

Chief Terry scowled. "I am doing it right."

"I know, but she's going to be my wife." Landon's tone was soft. "I want to do it. You should go to the inn. Let Winnie wow you with whatever she cooked. And make sure you ooh and aah over her stories about what happened today. She enjoyed being part of the team."

"You're giving me relationship advice now?" Chief Terry looked horrified at the thought. "I don't think I like that."

"We're going to be a family ... forever. We all need to get used to different things. Believe it or not, I'm smarter than I look."

"You would have to be." Even though he was talking gruff, Chief Terry clapped him on the shoulder. "You can finish the cameras tomorrow. I'm going to the inn."

"Take my advice."

"And you put the cameras up correctly tomorrow or I'll be around to tear them out and install them correctly."

DAD MET US AT THE DOOR OF THE DRAGONFLY, immediately pulling me in for a hug before checking out the large engagement ring on my finger.

"I saw it when he proposed, but it's even more impressive under good lighting," Dad noted as he ushered us inside. "You did a good job."

Landon grinned at the compliment — his relationship with my father wasn't always easy — and extended his hand for Dad to shake. "I wish I could take all the credit for it, but Winnie helped."

"She did?" I jerked up my head, surprised. "You didn't tell me."

"I bought the ring myself. However, about a week before the big day, I got nervous and showed the ring to Winnie. She started crying and said you would love it. I couldn't decide if she was being schmaltzy or truthful, so I considered taking the ring back twice before I realized that you would love it no matter what."

"No way." I vehemently shook my head. "You got me the perfect ring. All other rings would pale in comparison. A different ring would've made me cry, and not for happiness."

He smiled. "It's been an interesting couple of weeks."

Dad laughed as he led us to the dining room table, which was decked out with candles and the nice china. "I made prime rib," he said. "I know it seems decadent for five people, but I wanted something nice. It is a monumental occasion, after all."

"I love prime rib," I reassured him.

"And I'll eat anything," Landon added.

"And he'll eat anything," I agreed.

"It's still about fifteen minutes from being done," Dad said. "I thought we could have a drink and catch up while waiting."

He filled wine glasses, smiling when Teddy and Warren joined us. He'd opened the inn with Thistle's and Clove's fathers — making it a family affair of a different sort. We were still wading through the tangled relationships that had taken over our lives. It was getting markedly easier.

"So, when is the big day?" Teddy asked as he got comfortable.

"We don't have an official date yet," I replied. "We're thinking August."

"That quick?" Dad couldn't mask his surprise. "I thought you might take some time to enjoy the engagement."

Landon stiffened next to me and a burst of worry wormed through my chest. I had to keep things on an even keel if I wanted this to work out ... for everyone.

"We've been living together for some time now," I pointed out. "Even before then, we essentially lived together half the week. When he wasn't in Traverse City, he was with me at the guesthouse."

"I think you misunderstand," Dad said. "There's nothing wrong with August. I remember being engaged to your mother. She enjoyed all the ritual that went along with the planning, like picking out the dress and selecting a cake. I thought you might enjoy that."

"Oh, well ... ." I didn't know how to tell him that I was more excited for the marriage than the wedding. Heck, I didn't know how to tell Landon.

"We want to get married outdoors," Landon explained, his hand moving to my back to rub my shoulders. "That means it has to be summer, early fall at the latest. Weather in Michigan is unpredictable."

"We have Aunt Tillie, so we don't have to worry about that," I reminded him.

"That's true." He smirked for my benefit and then sobered when looking at my father. "We don't want to wait. I've loved her since I met her. The only reason I waited to propose was that Sam proposed to Clove. When we found out Clove was pregnant, everything took a backseat until their wedding."

"Yes, that was quite the surprise," Warren agreed. Clove was his daughter. He didn't seem bothered at the prospect of soon becoming a grandfather.

"I know it seems soon to you, Jack, but it's what we want," Landon continued. "We want you to be part of it, the planning and the execution. We definitely want to get married before summer is over."

Dad held Landon's gaze for what felt like a really long time and then nodded. "Then we'll make it happen."

That was it. Dad and Landon agreed the wedding was happening this summer and then moved on to other matters. Because it seemed wrong not to tell them, we related what happened at the festival the previous day, including the appearance of Willa and Rosemary. When we got to the part about Amelia being kidnapped, they were horrified ... and intrigued.

"Did you see the sketch?" Dad asked. "Is it anybody you know?"

I was sipping my wine, so I had to swallow and wipe my mouth before I could shake my head. "No. It's a pretty generic sketch. We're hopeful that someone will use their imagination to enhance the drawing."

Teddy looked sick to his stomach. "That's awful. I'm not a big fan of teenagers — we've had our fair share of them haunting the woods out back for the past few weeks — but nobody would wish this on anybody."

Landon stretched out in his chair, kicking out his legs in front of him. He looked intrigued. "You've had problems with teenagers?"

Dad nodded. "Ever since you guys shut down the last party spot they started showing up here. It sucks because they scatter when we go out to confront them. We hear them all hours of the night."

"How long has this been going on?"

Dad held out his hands and shrugged. "A couple of weeks. Does it matter?"

"Probably not." Landon slid his eyes to me. "It's interesting, though."

"More like loud and annoying," Warren corrected. "They're rude and crude."

"Just like Thistle," I said, earning a laugh from those assembled. Landon was lost in thought. "Do you want to party with some kids tonight?" I asked.

He lobbed a grenade of a smile at me, one that exploded with charm, love ... and even a bit of lust. "Do you want to party with me if I go?"

"Absolutely."

"We'll check it out. It will likely turn out to be nothing."

ELEVEN

"How do I look?"

Dad had let me borrow a dark shirt to cover my lavender one. He seemed amused when we said we were going out to engage with the kids. Now that I was dressed in his oversized shirt, I felt ready for action.

"You look like you're carrying about twenty extra pounds," Dad said.

Landon shot him a warning look. "She does not. She looks adorable."

Dad's forehead wrinkled. "That shirt is way too big on her."

"She still looks adorable," Landon insisted. "Seriously, haven't you learned anything from being divorced? The woman in your life never looks anything less than perfect. Get with the program."

I gave my reflection a cursory look in the mirror. "I do look a little hefty," I hedged. "I don't think the kids out there will believe I'm one of them."

"Sweetie, you don't have to be one of them," Landon reminded me. "You're mature ... and with an FBI agent."

Honestly, that wasn't what I wanted to hear. "I could still pass for a teenager." As if to prove it, I stared hard at myself in the mirror, making a duck face for good measure. "I mean ... I look the same as I did when I was seventeen."

Landon nodded as Dad snorted, earning a narrow-eyed glare from me.

"I look the same," I insisted.

"You do not." Dad moved away from Landon, probably to make sure my intended didn't lash out and give him a hard slap. "I love you dearly, Bay, but you can't pass for a teenager. You look thirty."

"I am thirty."

"Well, then you look your age."

"I could be a teenager if I wanted," I muttered, leaning closer to the mirror and studying my face. "I don't have any wrinkles."

"Try smiling," Dad suggested. "Laugh lines are the first to appear."

"I think I'm good." I focused on Landon. "Ready?"

"Absolutely." He held out his hand to me and then met Dad's steady gaze over my shoulder. "Really, take a class or something before you start dating again. You need to learn how to deal with a woman properly."

Dad glared at him. "I've been on this planet twice as long as you. I think I know what I'm doing."

Landon pressed his hand to the small of my back. "You have one failed marriage under your belt. As far as I can tell, you haven't had a successful relationship since. I, on the other hand, gave your daughter the perfect proposal. A proposal for the ages. Women will weep for centuries over that proposal."

"It was a pretty good proposal," I agreed when Dad's eyes narrowed. "What? I'll never forget that moment as long as I live. He went above and beyond."

Landon bestowed Dad with an "I told you so" smirk. "If you want to have a woman gush over your proposal anytime in the future, I suggest you get it together. Women don't want to be told that they look old. Of course, in this case, Bay really does look like a teenager. It's uncanny."

I beamed at him. "You say the sweetest things."

"It's easy when they're true." He brushed a kiss against my cheek and then fixed my father with a challenging look. "Get it together."

"Unbelievable," Dad muttered as we moved out of his bedroom. "Bay, you're not really falling for this, are you?"

Of course I wasn't. I knew I looked older. The fact that Landon was willing to play the game correctly was all that mattered. "We're going to be forever young together," I explained as I slipped into the hallway. "I'm really looking forward to the 'forever' part."

This time the smile Landon shot me was genuine. "You and me both."

"Good grief." Dad growled. "I can't tell you how annoying the two of you are."

"You'll get used to us." I slipped my hand in Landon's as we descended the stairs. "We plan to be this way for the rest of our lives."

"Yes, we're really looking forward to being the sort of parents who make out at school functions and embarrass their children," Landon volunteered. "We're thinking of having matching shirts made up."

"Un-freaking-believable," Dad grumbled. "I just ... you get more and more like Tillie with every year, Bay."

"Stop saying things like that. It bugs me."

"Well, it's the truth." Dad refused to back down. "Can you see yourself married to Tillie in fifty years, Landon? That's the life you're setting up for yourself if you insist on spreading utter nonsense."

Landon didn't flinch. "As long as I'm with Bay, I'll be happy forever."

Instead of pushing things further, Dad merely sighed. "God, you guys are too cute to be annoying."

I beamed at him. "That's how we roll."

I WAS MORE FAMILIAR WITH THE AREA surrounding the Dragonfly, so I led the way through the woods.

"Your dad says it's about a quarter mile out," Landon noted. He insisted we maintain a slow pace so we didn't trip over tree roots. "What can you tell me about this property?"

"Not much." A hint of movement to my left caused me to snap my eyes in that direction. I hadn't yet given up on seeing the shadow monster again. Thankfully, the only creature running wild in the woods tonight appeared to be a raccoon. The glare it shot me before scampering into the underbrush told me he didn't much like our intrusion on his evening. I forced my heartbeat to return to normal and returned to the question at hand.

"When I first came back to town and started working for William, I thought the best thing I could do was familiarize myself with the land deeds around town," I explained. "Believe it or not, for a very brief time, Clove, Thistle, and I talked about opening our own inn. The Dragonfly was on our short list."

Landon's pace slowed. "Are you kidding me?"

"No."

"I've never pictured you as the sort of person who would enjoy running an inn."

"I wouldn't. But at the time, I was feeling restless. I wanted a business of my own. I never thought I would be able to run The Whistler by myself." I was sheepish as I flicked my eyes to him. "You made that happen for me. We were going to try to buy the Dragonfly property on a land contract, but we thought better of it before things went too far."

"You made the deal for The Whistler happen by being a hard worker and knowing what you're doing," Landon countered. "I provided a bit of money, that's all."

"I couldn't have done it without your money."

He hesitated and shook his head. "Our money. We're getting married."

"It wasn't our money at the time and, technically, it's still not our money."

"I don't like this yours and mine stuff. Everything is ours from here on out. I still can't see you running an inn. I've seen the way your mother and aunts work, and while you're far from lazy, those aren't the sort of days you want to put in."

"I don't disagree." I went back to picking my way through the darkness. "At the time, I felt like a failure for having to return home. I wanted something to call my own. I mean ... desperately. I thought working on the Dragonfly would give me a sense of purpose. I thought that writing for a weekly would be a letdown after the hustle of covering stories in Detroit."

"And?"

I shrugged, noncommittal. "I realized that I was being a complete and total idiot. My heart has always led me to writing. Things have worked out better than I ever dreamed they could, and for the record, that includes you."

He squeezed my hand tighter. "I appreciate that. I want you to have everything you've ever desired. If that means owning your own inn, we'll make it happen."

I chuckled. "I don't want to own an inn. The idea wasn't about actually owning an inn, it was about being my own boss. I am my own boss now, so I'm perfectly happy with how things turned out."

"Okay." He didn't sound convinced. "You mentioned the land deeds. What did you find?"

"Oh, well, the only thing I knew about this area is that we would occasionally party out here when we were kids. The woods are thick. A lot of this property is government land, but since it would take a lot of money to clear it and build — more than any business or housing development could ever earn — it's going to stay wilderness ... except for one thing."

"I'm a captive audience. I'm not sure I could find my way back to the Dragonfly. You might as well tell me."

"Bootleggers ran an operation out here. It was the perfect setup because the Dragonfly had a basement for storage and access to a road. A story claims that five men used the property and paid the former owner of the Dragonfly to allow them access to the parking lot and storage buildings.

"This was back in Prohibition times, of course, so keep that in mind," I continued. "Something happened back then that resulted in four of the five bootleggers disappearing. I don't have their names, but I found references in old notes from the time."

"The Whistler has been around since then?" Landon let loose a low whistle. "That's pretty impressive."

"The Whistler is old, and I'm happy to be a part of history even if it means most of the stories I do are of the fluffy variety. Hemlock Cove is my home, and it's where my heart is. It's full of stories, and this property was home to a few of them."

"Do you think the bootleggers died out here?"

"I think it's likely they were killed, and probably because someone else wanted to move in on their territory."

"Or one of the other bootleggers wanted all the profit."

"Possibly," I acknowledged. "Whether they were all killed out here I couldn't say. It's one of the stories I'm considering digging into for my special editions."

He slowed again. "What special editions?"

I glanced over my shoulder, sheepish. "Yeah, well, I've been meaning to bring it up to you. I guess I was afraid you'd think it was a silly idea. The more I think about it, though, the more I believe it's a good idea."

"I'm waiting."

"I can see ghosts."

His forehead furrowed. "I'm aware."

"We live in a town of humans pretending to be witches and cater to tourists who desperately want to believe in the paranormal."

"I'm aware of that, too."

"I thought there might be a way I could marry the two." My stomach constricted.

Landon stopped and held my hand tightly. "Just tell me your plan. You're the prettiest and smartest woman I know and yet occasionally you're riddled with self-doubt. I don't understand it."

"It's not self-doubt," I offered hurriedly. "I honestly do think it's a great idea, and I think I'll do it well. It's just ... it might open us up to talk."

His expression never changed. "Your great-aunt rides around town on a kick-scooter wearing a cape and occasionally causes fire hydrants to explode."

I blew out a sigh to steady myself and went for it. "I've been thinking of tracking down ghosts — like the bootleggers out here, if they're still around — and interviewing them for historical issues. Then I'll print the stories, including interviews with the ghosts, and sell them as official ghost stories to the tourists while securing advertising for the issues at the same time."

He was quiet for so long I thought for sure he was trying to keep from laughing. He ultimately cracked a smile that signified amazement rather than disbelief. "You would quote ghost bootleggers and write stories about the historical places in Hemlock Cove. They would be true, but everybody would think they're made up because nobody would be able to prove you were talking to ghosts."

"Nobody would be able to prove I wasn't talking to ghosts," I pointed out. "It's an idea I've been toying with for a few weeks now. I ... um ... what do you think?"

He broke into a huge grin. "It's genius. Do you have access to photos from back in the day?"

I nodded, some of the tension I'd been carrying around easing. "Yeah. We have a full morgue of old photos. I might need Thistle's help scanning the negatives, but ... I have plenty of art."

"I think it's inspired, Bay." Landon wrapped his arms around my waist. "It's a real moneymaker of an idea. Why didn't you tell me?"

I wasn't certain how to respond. "Well ... ."

"It's the ghost thing," he surmised, not waiting for me to get up my courage to answer. "You were worried I thought you were being reckless and exposing yourself to ridicule."

"Maybe a little," I conceded. "The town is always watching us. We're used to it. I have to discuss the idea with Mom and the aunts, too, in case they object. But I think they'll be fine with it.

"You're another story," I continued. "Your job requires that people take you seriously. Do you really think that will continue if your wife is conducting interviews with ghosts?"

"Yes."

I couldn't contain my surprise. "You do?"

"Bay, my co-workers will think it's an ingenious way for you to expand your business. They'll assume you're making it up. Even if they are suspicious, I won't care. This is what's best for you. I love the idea."

I wanted to throw myself on him and kiss him senseless right there, but I managed to refrain. "Thanks for always being in my corner. It's important to me."

"Well, you're important to me." He lightly brushed my hair from my eyes.

"I knew when I met you that you were special. That's one of the reasons I fell in love with you. I don't ever want you to change."

I knew he meant it. "Well, I'm glad, because I think I'm starting to grow into my own skin. For a time, it wasn't always a comfortable fit. But it is now, and you have a lot to do with that."

"Aww." He pulled me tight against his chest and lowered his mouth to mine for a sweet kiss. "You're my favorite person in the world," he whispered when he pulled his head back.

Before I could respond, a teenage boy pushed through the foliage to our right. He was tall, on the lanky side, and seemed as surprised to see us as we were to see him. "Um ... ."

"Hello." Landon released me and squared his shoulders. "We ... um ... ."

The boy didn't appear interested in what he had to say. Instead, he looked over his shoulder and yelled back to his friends, who we could hear carousing in the woods. "Hannah, your parents are here!" His eyes were full of annoyance when he turned back to us. "No offense, but nobody is supposed to have their parents pick them up here. It's embarrassing."

"We're not parents," Landon replied.

"We're definitely not old enough to be your parents," I added, disgusted. "We're still young and fun."

"Right." The boy rolled his eyes. "If you're not parents, who are you? Wait ... did those old dudes from the inn send you? Are you doing their dirty work?"

"We're here for a different reason," Landon reassured him, pulling his badge from his pocket. "We have a few questions."

The boy's eyes went wide and I sensed trouble before he started barking out warnings.

"Cops!"

The excitement we'd heard through the trees only moments before diminished, and then other kids picked up the call.

"Cops! It's the cops!"

"They're going to arrest us!"

"Run!"

And just like that, not only were we officially old, but something to fear on top of everything else.

TWELVE

I stood there for what felt like a really long time, frustration threatening to make me yank out some hair. The teens had all scattered, so there was nobody to attack but Landon, but he hadn't spiked my irritation.

"We don't look like parents," I announced as Landon began picking through the discarded items abandoned by the fleeing kids. "I mean ... we're young and hip."

"Sweetie, I don't think that people who are actually young use the word 'hip.'"

I glared at him. He didn't seem bothered in the least by the fact that the kids had mistaken us for parents. "You know what I mean."

He knelt and looked inside a cooler. "They have some pretty good stuff here."

He almost looked impressed, which only served to bolster my agitation. "It's beer," I argued. "What's impressive about beer?"

"It's Oberon. When I was a teen all we had was Bud Light and Busch. Well, and Milwaukee's Best, which is best left forgotten. Who do you think is buying for them?"

He had to be kidding. "How should I know? You heard those kids. I'm not up on who is doing what in the teenager realm. I've been relegated to the parent realm."

He smirked. "This is hardly the first time you've been mistaken for an old person by teenagers. It happened out at Hollow Creek."

I'd worked overtime to forget about that. The fact that he felt the need to remind me was simply another blow I wasn't keen to absorb. "Do you love me?"

He glanced up, his face unreadable. "Is that a trick question?"

"I really want to know."

"I love you more than anything. I thought we already established that during my proposal that will go down in history as the best ever."

It took everything I had not to smile. He was ridiculously proud of that proposal, as he should be. Still, he needed to understand certain things about my psyche and now was a good time to explain one of them. "I don't want to be old."

"I'm well aware, but you're not old, so I don't see the problem."

"Those kids think I'm old."

"Those kids think anyone over the age of twenty is old. It's always that way with teenagers. I don't see why you're getting so worked up over it."

"Because I'm not old. We don't even have children yet. I don't want to be mistaken for a parent until I'm actually a parent."

He grabbed the Styrofoam container and stood. "Are you ready?"

I narrowed my eyes. "Are you taking that?"

"Absolutely."

"Why?"

"Those kids left hoodies and shoes here. They'll be back for them. As a duly sworn officer of the law, it would be a mistake to leave this beer for them to reclaim. I refuse to make that mistake."

It sounded reasonable on the surface and still ... . "Are you going to take that beer home and drink it?"

His smirk was pronounced. "That's a horrible thing to ask."

"You could just dump it out and leave the mess for them to pick up."

"That seems like a waste." It was only when he moved closer that I could see the glint in his eyes. "Besides, what's more young and hip than stealing a group of teenagers' beer and taking it home to have a private party?"

I wanted to argue but he had a point. "What else do they have in there?" I leaned closer and peered inside. "Ooh, White Claw. I guess we can steal it."

"And we'll be young and hip in the process."

I pinned him with a dubious look. "I thought you said young people today would never use the word 'hip.'"

"I did say that and I meant it. But live a little. It might be fun."

"Are you going to include beer theft in your report to your bosses?"

"Oh, I'm not writing a report on this. We didn't find anything and I don't want the guys in my office thinking my future wife looks old enough to be the mother of a teenager. They'll give me endless grief about it."

I glared at him. "I don't look that old."

"Of course you don't, Bay. You look like a spring flower on a sunny day."

I glared at him.

"Took it too far, didn't I?" he lamented, frowning when I nodded. "I always take it too far."

"Live and learn."

"Yeah." He pressed a quick kiss to the corner of my mouth. "Do you want to be young and foolish with me tonight?"

I surveyed the contents of the cooler again and sighed. "Okay, but I expect you to try to get to third base if we drink all this. You have to be bad at it, too, because all teenage boys are bad at it."

He shook his head. "Not me. I was always good at it. A total champ. The other kids wanted me to teach classes."

"You're making that up."

"I'm not."

I shook my head but gave in to the bubbling laughter. "Let's go home and act like teenagers."

He offered me a saucy wink. "You read my mind."

I EXPECTED TO WAKE WITH A HANGOVER, but once I popped some aspirin and had a cup of coffee I was fine. Landon seemed almost cheerful as he held my hand, swinging it like kids in the heat of young love, as we trekked to The Overlook in relative silence. Once we reached the family living quarters, however, he began chirping.

"There's my girl." He dropped to his knees when Peg ran up to him. Today she wore a Motley Crue T-shirt, her hindquarters wriggling with excitement. "How are you today?"

Snort. Snort.

"Did you miss me last night?" Landon continued, as if he'd understood whatever message Peg was trying to convey. "I know I missed you. We had to go to the Dragonfly for dinner. It sucked being away from you, but it won't happen again anytime soon. I promise."

Snort. Snort.

I shook my head as I stepped around them. "I'm starting to think you prefer Peg to me."

"Don't be ridiculous. You're a much snappier dresser." He winked at me and stood. "I don't see why you have so much attitude where she's concerned. She's just a little pig."

Snort. Snort.

Landon beamed at her. "What was I thinking? She's the world's best pig."

"Whatever." I moved into the kitchen, Landon and Peg following. It was five minutes to eight, so I expected my mother and aunts to be putting the finishing touches on breakfast. Instead, I found the kitchen empty. The lingering smell of pancakes told me they'd been here not long ago.

"Where's my bacon?" Landon focused on the scattered dishes, Peg seemingly forgotten. "Has the Wiccan Rapture really happened? Am I not getting breakfast? Man, this day already sucks."

I nudged him with my hip to jostle him out of the way and pushed through the swinging doors to the dining room. To my relief — and annoyance — I found everyone settled around the table already eating.

"What the Hecate is going on?" I demanded, moving toward the table. "Breakfast isn't for another five minutes."

Mom, a forkful of pancake halfway to her mouth, fixed me with a dubious look. "So what?"

"So ... breakfast isn't for another five minutes." I turned my attention to the end of the table, where Thistle and Marcus sat, and caught Thistle's steady gaze. "How could you let this happen?"

Thistle looked as if she hadn't slept in days. I realized it had been more than twenty-four hours since I'd seen her and was fairly certain she hadn't slept in all that time.

"What are you going on about?" Thistle rasped.

"Breakfast," I said. "Breakfast is never served early. It's still five minutes early. Right?" I looked to Landon for support, but he was already moving toward his usual seat.

"As long as there's bacon, I don't care." He pulled out my chair but didn't wait for me to take it before plopping into his seat. "Are those blueberry pancakes?"

"Blueberry, regular, and chocolate chip," Twila volunteered. "And sausage links."

"I'm good with the bacon." Landon smiled at her. "What's with the pancake selections, though? You guys usually have eggs the mornings before guests arrive."

"We can shake things up," Mom argued, irritation evident. "You act as if we're slaves to a routine."

"You are," I insisted. "Breakfast is never early. Never."

"Sit down, you big whiner," Aunt Tillie ordered from her regular seat. Her expression was as dark as mine. "You're way too loud so early in the morning."

"Maybe I won't be as loud in five minutes," I suggested. "By the way, that's when breakfast is supposed to start."

"Bay, are you trying to say something specific?" Mom asked, cocking her head. The glint in her eyes told me I should be wary.

I hesitated. "Well ... yes. Breakfast is never early."

"Well, it is today," Mom said. "The food is still hot, so you're fine."

"Awesome," Landon enthused as he put his bacon on top of his pancakes and doused both with syrup. "I love blueberry pancakes and bacon."

"There are sausage links, too," Twila offered.

"I'm good with bacon." Landon smiled at her. "Marcus prefers the sausage links. He can have all of those."

"There are fifty of them," Marcus noted, speaking for the first time. He looked pretty good for a guy who had been knocked unconscious only thirty-six hours earlier. "I can't eat all of them."

"Take the extras home," Mom suggested. "Thistle can heat them up as snacks."

"Yes," I drawled. "Here are your fifty sausage links for snacks. That won't create a gastrointestinal explosion or anything."

"Leave him alone," Thistle snapped, her gaze flashing dark as it locked with mine. "If he wants fifty sausages, he can have fifty sausages."

I was taken aback. "It was just a joke."

"Maybe you should mind your own business instead of telling jokes this morning," Thistle suggested.

Landon forgot about his breakfast long enough to give Thistle a measured look and then he held his hand out to me. "Bay, sit down with me. You need to get some food in you. I know you said you're not hungover, but pancakes will make you feel better."

I still wasn't over being mistaken for a teenager's mother — and the change in the morning routine had thrown me. "We were supposed to have eggs. We usually have eggs."

"We're having pancakes today," Mom hissed. "If you don't want pancakes, cook your own breakfast. Now sit down and shut up."

"What is going on?" I demanded. "I don't understand any of this."

"Bay?" Landon shook his extended hand, insisting I take it. "Come sit next to me. Have some pancakes. You'll be fine."

I was still grousing as I sat next to him, but I kept my complaints to myself rather than risk another blow-up.

Marcus broke the uncomfortable silence that had descended around the table. "This is all for my benefit," he explained, sheepish. "Thistle wanted me to have all my favorites today, but we don't have any food at home. She called your mothers last night to see if they could cook a special breakfast. I'm sorry if it's thrown everybody off."

I felt ridiculously guilty ... and obnoxious. "It's my fault," I reassured him. "We were up late. And I'm used to a certain routine here. I want you to have your favorite breakfast." Marcus was the only member of our family who never issued a word of complaint. He was also the first to pitch in with a helping hand. He was practically a saint, for crying out loud, and here I was whining. "I'm sorry."

"Why were you up late?" Chief Terry asked. He looked perfectly happy with his pancakes and sausage. "Wait ... do I even want to know? If you guys were doing something gross, don't tell me."

"We broke up a party at the Dragonfly after dinner," Landon said. "We confiscated their beer and hard seltzer."

"You broke up a party?" Chief Terry made a face. "Why would you do that?"

"Jack and the others mentioned ongoing parties out there and we thought it might be a good chance to question teenagers about Amelia."

Chief Terry nodded in understanding. "Makes sense," he said around a mouthful of pancake. "What'd they tell you?"

"Nothing. We ran into one kid who thought we were there to pick up somebody named Hannah. He lectured us about how picking up our kid at a beer party was embarrassing. When I explained who I was, they started screaming 'cops' and took off."

Chief Terry snickered. "Well, what did you expect?"

"I'm not old," I glowered, grabbing several slices of bacon and adding them to my plate. "I know I'm older than them, but that doesn't mean I'm old. I could totally pass for a teenager if I wanted."

Everybody at the table snorted — Aunt Tillie and Thistle extra hard — which caused my irritation to double. "I could totally pass for a teenager," I hissed, glaring.

"Right." Thistle rolled her eyes and added more syrup to Marcus's pancakes without him asking. I didn't miss the sidelong look he shot her — it was one that made me think he was having a rough morning — but he didn't say anything. Knowing him, he was probably biting his tongue until they could talk privately.

"I could pass for a teenager," I insisted. "I still have great skin and bone structure."

"I'm confused," Aunt Tillie interjected. "Are we supposed to laugh or feel sorry for her because she feels this way?"

I sulked as I focused on my plate. "I know you guys like messing with me, but it's true."

"You're a beautiful creature, Bay," Landon offered. "You light up every room and yes, you could pass for a teenager."

"Thank you."

"You're welcome."

"Yeah, let's book a return trip from La-La Land," Aunt Tillie suggested. "I want to know the plans for the day. Are we heading out to look for Amelia Hart?"

"How do you figure you're involved in this?" Chief Terry challenged.

"I wasn't talking to you." Aunt Tillie made a face and focused on me. "What are your plans?"

The question caught me off guard. "Oh, well ... ."

Landon swallowed some bacon and reached for his juice. "She's going to the party spot in the woods in an attempt to talk to some of the kids if they come back to reclaim the stuff they left behind."

My mouth dropped open. "How did you know?"

"I know you." He grinned. "You figure the kids will have no choice but to talk to you because they won't want you tattling about their party habits to their parents. It's a good idea."

It wasn't like him to agree so easily. "I thought maybe you would be worried about me going out there."

"I'm not particularly worried," he hedged. "It's not far from the Dragonfly and it's the middle of the day."

I grinned. "Compromise?"

"Yes." He bobbed his head. "And you're going to compromise too."

My heart sank. "I am?"

"You're taking someone with you."

"Okay, um ... ." I looked to Thistle, but she was already shaking her head.

"Don't even think about it." Her tone was cold. "The doctor says that Marcus has to stay quiet the next few days. I'll be with him ... making sure he stays quiet."

"Oh, right." Aunt Tillie shook her head. "Because you're the expert at being quiet. This should go well."

"Don't make me come down there, old lady," Thistle growled. Her demeanor was completely devoid of any playfulness, unlike the other times she'd decided to take on Aunt Tillie. Marcus' injury had obviously thrown her, and she wasn't reacting all that well.

"I think it's sweet that Thistle wants to take care of Marcus," Twila said, worry lurking in her eyes. She clearly wasn't thrilled at Thistle's attitude either. Nobody wanted to push Thistle, because it could end in an ugly scene.

"I'll go with you," Mom offered. "We had a lot of fun yesterday. We can be partners again today."

I could deal with a lot, but that possibility was completely off the table. I had no idea how to turn down the offer without infuriating my mother — until my eyes landed on Aunt Tillie. I fixed Mom with an apologetic smile. "Aunt Tillie wants to be involved, so I planned to take her along."

Mom didn't look convinced. "That seems ... strange. I can't remember you ever willingly spending time with your great-aunt."

"Hogwash," Aunt Tillie countered. "She loves spending time with me ... and who wouldn't? I'm tons of fun." She beamed at Mom before letting her eyes drift to me. "I would love to spend the day with you in the woods questioning teenagers."

The fact that she was so excited about the prospect had me reconsidering, but it was too late. "Then right after breakfast," I gritted out. "We'll head out then."

"I'm looking forward to it."

That made one of us.

13
THIRTEEN

Landon met me outside while I was waiting for Aunt Tillie to gear up.

"Be good, huh?" He leaned in and gave me a kiss.

Suspicious, I waited for him to say something else. When he didn't, I folded my arms over my chest. "That's it?"

His smile was automatic. "What were you expecting?"

"You usually threaten to lock me up if I break the law."

"I haven't threatened that in a long time."

"Old habits die hard."

"Do you want me to threaten you with jail for old time's sake?"

"Not particularly."

"How about with a spanking?"

He said it in such a flirty manner I had trouble holding back a smile. Somehow I managed, though it took effort. "I'm surprised you're not giving me a list of things to be careful about," I admitted. "I'm not complaining, but it seems strange for you."

He brushed his finger against my cheek and made a face. "I'm trying to grow."

"Okay."

"I mean it. I don't want us constantly bickering about things like this." He hesitated and then barreled forward. "I'm an FBI agent. It's my job to uphold the law."

"I never would've guessed," I teased, poking his side. He seemed unusually serious, and it was the last thing I wanted to deal with. "I'm sorry I brought it up. Don't worry about it."

"No, I want to talk about it." He pursed his lips and then smiled. "When we first started dating, I was always worried ... but not for the reasons you might think. It wasn't that I didn't think you could take care of yourself as much as I feared someone else might catch you breaking the law and I would be put in a bad position at work."

Understanding dawned. "You thought I would mess up and cost you your job."

He fervently shook his head. "I feared that if someone else other than Terry took you in that I wouldn't be able to protect you. That nearly happened, as you recall, and it almost broke me."

My heart went out to him. "I'm always safe when I go out investigating."

"Yeah, don't run that bull on me. You're strong and capable, but you're not always safe. I've come to the realization that's who you are, though, and I don't want to change who you are. So, instead of warning you about getting caught, I'll just ask you to be careful."

"That seems like a mature decision."

"I'm always mature."

"Says the guy who stole Oberon and White Claw from a bunch of teenagers last night."

He laughed as he wrapped his arms around me and tugged me tight against his chest, absolute adoration shining back at me from the depths of his fathomless eyes. "I thought you enjoyed that. You seemed to when I finally got to third base."

"You were definitely more adept than all the others."

He narrowed his eyes. "What others? I thought you were a chaste white witch when we met."

"Oh, you wish."

He buried his face in my hair and made chomping noises as he kissed my neck, making me laugh. It was only Aunt Tillie's arrival that caused him to stop.

"Oh, could you guys be any grosser?" she complained, her nose wrinkling. "Fornicating in public is against the law."

Landon gave me another hug before releasing me, his eyes trained on my great-aunt. "So is making wine and whiskey without a license."

"Ah, that's where you're wrong." Aunt Tillie wagged her finger. "It's only illegal if I'm selling it."

"You are."

"You can't prove that."

"If I tried I could prove it."

"Please." Aunt Tillie's eye roll was pronounced. "We all know you have no interest in proving it because then you would put Bay in a sticky situation and you hate it when she's sad. Don't bother denying it."

"I have no interest in denying it." He stroked his hand down my hair. "I don't want any of you in jail. I simply want all of you to live happily ever after — with me — and not get in so much trouble that I can't get you out of it. I don't think that's too much to ask."

"It's not," I reassured him. "We all want to live happily ever after."

"I don't," Aunt Tillie countered. "People who are happy all the time are likely insane. Besides, what's the fun of not being able to rant? I happen to think a good rant is always welcome."

I pulled away from Landon to give her a good once-over. She'd dressed in baggy camouflage pants, pairing them with a bright orange shirt. She was without her combat helmet today, for which I was thankful, but her boots were military. All I could tell with any certainty was that she was locked and ready for bear.

"Speaking of good rants, what's up with Thistle?" I asked.

"What do you mean?"

"You know what I mean. She seemed ... out of sorts."

"Oh, *that*." Aunt Tillie shook her head. "She's upset about Marcus."

I stilled. "Is there something wrong with him? I thought his prognosis was good."

"It is. That doesn't mean she's good. Marcus getting hurt has made Thistle realize she loves him."

I didn't know what to make of the statement. "I believe they've been saying 'I love you' to one another for more than a year. I'm pretty sure they said it before Landon and me."

Landon scowled. "I said it better."

I patted his arm. "You do everything better than everybody else. That's a given."

Aunt Tillie made an exaggerated face. "You two are so annoying. I thought you were bad before the engagement, but you're ten times worse now. How long is this lovey-dovey phase going to last?"

"Forever," Landon replied, moving his hand over my back. "Or until it no longer bothers you and Terry. We haven't really decided yet."

"Yeah, yeah, yeah." Aunt Tillie appeared to have limited patience this morning. "I'm not telling you how to live your lives, but if you put everything on display like you do, the second you have a fight everybody in town will know about it. Then they'll start spreading rumors and you will have to dispel ridiculous assumptions. Is that what you want?"

"I don't know," Landon replied blankly. "What sort of assumptions are we talking about? Do I look good in these rumors?"

"You look like a ninny. Everybody in town will take Bay's side because she was born here. You're still an outsider."

"I won't be when we get married."

"Don't kid yourself." Aunt Tillie was winding herself up, which was the last thing I wanted to deal with. "It's like certain southern communities. It doesn't matter how long you live there, or who you marry. Unless you're born there, it doesn't count."

"Are you saying that the people of Hemlock Cove will gladly stone me if they get the chance?"

"They like you fine. They'll just always take Bay's side because she's one of them."

"Not all of them," I countered. "Mrs. Little will never take my side."

"You let me worry about Margaret." Aunt Tillie's gaze eyes darkened. "She's been hanging around Willa. They're up to something. I'm going to handle it, though, so there's nothing to worry about."

"Did Mom tell you about them having lunch together at the diner yesterday?"

"No." Aunt Tillie straightened. Age had given her bad posture, but when she was spoiling for a fight she looked almost a foot taller than she really was. "Was Rosemary with them?"

"No." Suddenly, I was the suspicious one. "Do you know what they're up to?"

"Not exactly. I only know that Rosemary is supposedly engaged and they're hanging around town and trying to fly under the radar."

"Maybe they really did feel a yearning for home," Landon suggested.

Aunt Tillie pinned him with a withering look. "Don't be an idiot. Willa never had any love for Walkerville. None. When she heard about the rebranding, she said it was the stupidest thing she'd ever heard and actually said she was glad she had no ties to the town."

"To be fair, I don't know anyone who would think the rebranding you guys did would turn out the way it has," Landon said. "When I heard I was going undercover in a town where grown-ups pretended to be witches, I thought all of you should be locked up for the foreseeable future. I didn't see how great it was until I'd been here for a few weeks."

THE WITCH IS BACK

"You didn't see how great it was until you stumbled across this one," Aunt Tillie countered, jerking her thumb in my direction. "The only reason you think Hemlock Cove is so great is because you look at it through Bay-colored glasses. That's annoying and gross, by the way, but it's a conversation for another time."

"I'm just saying that holding her doubts about the rebrand against her seems like a waste of time."

"She's a waste of time," Aunt Tillie said. "But don't worry about it. I'll handle Willa. Whatever she has planned, I'll stop it before it becomes a thing."

"I'm sure you will." Landon leaned in and gave me a kiss. "I assume you two will wander everywhere today. Do me a favor and watch your backs. There's a shadow monster running around out there, and even though Bay thinks she can bounce, I still want both of you to be careful."

Intrigue lit Aunt Tillie's well-lined features. "You can bounce?"

"It's a long story."

"You can tell me on the way to town. We should start behind the stable and then work our way out to the woods. We need to cast a locator spell if we're really going to find the answers we need."

I'd been thinking the same thing. "I still to want to head out to the Dragonfly."

"I know."

"That means you'll have to get along with Dad."

"I can get along with your father. He's the one who doesn't want to play nice with me."

It was mutual, but I had no time for arguments. "We'll figure it out as we go along." I swiveled to face Landon. "As for you, I'll text you with updates so you don't worry. How does that sound?"

He broke out into a huge grin. "More compromise?"

"If you can do it, I can do it."

He grabbed me for another hug. "I think we're turning into adults. How fun is this?"

I glared. "Not the sort of adults who have a teenaged child."

"Of course not. We're decades from that."

"Just checking."

"It's always good to check."

AUNT TILLIE HAD HER EYES PEELED AS WE parked in front of the stable and made our way to the rear of the property. I heard activity through the barn door and was curious enough to poke my head inside. I found Marcus, working alone. He looked lost in thought.

"Um ... we don't want to bother you or anything," I started.

He jerked up his head, surprised to see me. "I didn't realize you were here." He flashed a genuine smile, although it wasn't of the megawatt variety, which told me that circumstances were starting to lay heavy on him. "Do you need something?"

I glanced around to make sure we were alone and then shook my head. "Aunt Tillie and I are using some magic to try to find Amelia. We're going to cast a locator spell and go from there. I wanted to do it the night she was taken, but Chief Terry and Landon didn't think it was a good idea. It feels late to be doing it now, but it's worth a try."

"Do whatever you need to do." He was earnest. "I wish I could be of some help. I just don't remember what happened."

"Don't push yourself. You'll remember eventually. It'll pop into your mind when you least expect it."

"Except the information would be helpful now."

"Yeah, well ... we have to work with what we're given." I offered him a smile, which he didn't return. "How is Thistle?"

He growled. "She's hovering and it's driving me crazy."

"You were hurt. She can't help herself."

"Yeah, well ... I'm not hurt any longer. I'm fine."

I hesitated, briefly wondering if I should keep my nose out of their business, and then barreling forward anyway. "It's hard when the person you love most is hurt. The doctor was hopeful you would wake up, but there was no guarantee. She had a lot of time to think about her life, what she wants. I'm pretty sure the only thing she really wants is you."

His expression softened. "And that makes me love her all the more. It's just ... I'm used to doing what I want when I want. We're not codependent like you and Landon. We can go without seeing each other for a few hours."

I frowned. "I don't think that makes us codependent. We just work together a lot."

He laughed. "Oh, please. You guys are all over each other because you can't help yourselves. I'm not saying there's anything wrong with the two of you being codependent or anything. Thistle and I usually spend our days apart and then regroup for dinner. She's been on me for more than twenty-four hours now. Everywhere I go she has questions and then demands that I rest. I need a little break here and there."

"She doesn't mean to smother you," I explained. "She's fearful right now. That will fade. Give her a bit of time."

"I'm trying. I almost suggested she go out adventuring with you and Aunt Tillie this morning, but I knew that would be an ugly business."

"Probably," I agreed. "You have to let her work through things at her own pace. In fact ... ." I broke off when Aunt Tillie poked her head into the barn.

"If you two are done gabbing, I cast the locator spell and it's buzzing for us to go ... back out of town."

"You cast the locator spell without me?" I looked outside and found the orb of light zipping around, excitedly making a chattering noise and then racing to the east to get us to follow. "Why didn't you wait?"

"I don't need your help casting a spell," Aunt Tillie replied, annoyed. "I've been doing this since long before you were even a speck in your mother's eye. Heck, I've been doing this since before your mother was a speck in Ginger's eye."

"I'm aware." I shot Marcus a rueful smile. "Sorry. Apparently we'll be going now."

"It's fine." He offered up a wave and a genuine grin. "I like the idea that the two of you are out there looking for Amelia. I haven't been able to stop thinking about her since I heard what happened. She's the reason I wish I could remember. I just ... what if something horrible is happening to her?"

"That's why we're going to find her," I promised. I meant it. "Don't worry. We've got this."

"We definitely do," Aunt Tillie agreed. "Now, if you'll excuse us, we're on a mission from the Goddess."

He offered up a half-salute. "Good luck."

"We don't need it. I'm here." Aunt Tillie paused before exiting the barn. "If Thistle is bothering you, give her a good crack on the head. Maybe then she won't be so annoying."

Marcus's smile disappeared. "I think I'll refrain from hitting her."

"I'm just saying that she's one of those people who has to learn the hard way."

"I'll keep that in mind."

AUNT TILLIE GROUSED THE ENTIRE WAY OUT of Hemlock Cove. I drove while she kept an eye on the locator sphere. It zipped forward at a fantastic rate and then fell back until we caught up before zipping forward again.

"We'd better hope nobody sees it or we'll have to answer a lot of questions," I muttered, removing my foot from the gas pedal and frowning when the orb darted to the right. "Wait ... ."

"I know how to cast a locator spell without anybody noticing," Aunt Tillie groused. "Don't worry about it. Have I ever let you down?"

That felt like a trick question, but I ignored it in favor of following the orb. "It's taking us to Hollow Creek," I noted, my stomach clenching. Hollow Creek had been a regular hotbed of paranormal activity the past two years. In recent months, though, thanks to a little help from some magical circus friends, it had been much quieter. We'd performed a ritual to ease some of the magic clinging to the area. We hadn't been back in weeks to see how our hard work was paying off.

"I wonder why." Aunt Tillie was suddenly alert and ready. "Park in that clearing and we'll walk in. It's safer that way."

It was impossible to park anywhere but the clearing, so I didn't comment. I navigated the narrow road until I reached our destination. Aunt Tillie was out of the car before I even killed the ignition.

"Look at that," she said once I pocketed the keys and joined her in front of the vehicle.

She needn't have pointed. I could see the glowing energy ball zipping about without anyone drawing my attention to it. The multiple magical fragments that had been hanging over the area months before had dwindled, though several remained ... and they appeared to be growing in size.

"What's happening?" I squinted for a better look. "Are things exploding out here or something?"

Aunt Tillie shook her head. "I think it's more that the small fragments are joining together in an attempt to survive. We're going to have to come out here and break them up again."

I was afraid she was going to say that. "Okay." I rolled my neck until it cracked and blew out a sigh. "Let's start looking around."

I moved to the left, Aunt Tillie the right. We'd barely taken three steps before Aunt Tillie made a gagging sound. When I turned, the hair on the back of my neck already standing on end, the shadow monster had Aunt Tillie by the throat.

She lashed out with a burst of magic before I could react, knocking the creature back a good two feet. Aunt Tillie landed on her feet, but she looked shaky as her eyes locked with mine.

"I found something," she said.

14
FOURTEEN

I sent a burst of magic directly toward the shadow monster, impulse telling me that protecting Aunt Tillie was most important. I raced forward far enough to grab her arm and gave it a vicious yank. I was trying to pull her behind me so I could take on the monster.

She had other ideas.

"Foul hell beast," she bellowed as she unleashed her own barrage of magic into the creature, red flames exploding from her fingertips.

I recognized her fire magic but couldn't figure out why she was trying to set the creature aflame. It made no sense because the shadow's form was ethereal. That didn't stop Aunt Tillie from giving it her all.

I had other plans. I raised my hands, calling on my necromancer powers, and drew two spirits from the woods to do my bidding. I unleashed them on the shadow monster before it could fully recover from Aunt Tillie's assault, whipping my hands in the creature's direction and sending a small tornado directly for its head. Right before the magic collided with the monster, a pair of yellow eyes flashed hot and hard.

"*Witch*," it hissed.

"I'm the queen of witches," Aunt Tillie barked, preparing to unleash yet another wall of fire magic.

I grabbed her arm before she could. "You're wasting magic," I complained. "Fire magic won't stop that thing."

"Oh, and air magic will?" Aunt Tillie sneered. "Have I taught you nothing?"

"The air magic is a distraction."

"So you can do what?"

"That." I pointed toward the ghosts swooping in from different angles. The monster didn't immediately see them — why would he think to look behind him, after all? They were on him in seconds.

At first, I thought it sounded as if the air was slowly being let out of a mattress, but then I realized the creature was screaming, mouth open and emitting a high-pitched noise that I never wanted to hear again.

"Oh, well, that's just cheating," Aunt Tillie complained, hands landing on her hips. "I can't call ghosts to my rescue."

I kept my eyes on the monster, watching as the ghosts seemed to rip it to pieces. Within seconds, the monster was gone. The ghosts remained hovering.

I leaned over, resting my hands on my knees, and sucked in a calming breath.

"Who are you guys?" Aunt Tillie asked as she eyed the ghosts. I'd inherited the ability to see and talk to spirits from her. Nobody else in our family could claim that particular brand of magic. She opted to stay away from the ghosts most days, but I didn't have that choice.

"I recognize this place," the female said. She looked to be about nineteen, but her clothes were dated, bell bottoms and a peasant blouse, both of which looked authentic rather than rediscovered. Her parted hairstyle was popular in the seventies.

"Hollow Creek," I said, giving her a long once-over. "What's your name?"

"I ... um ... ." Suddenly shy, the ghost lowered her voice. "I'm not sure what I'm doing here. I was in another place when you called, a sad place. It was quiet."

I hesitated, unsure how to proceed. I had a feeling the place she'd been was her own mind. Ghosts who didn't interact with people were often known to go mad. This woman, however, seemed relatively put together ... for the most part. That probably meant she'd been zoning in and out of this world. Eventually, she would just fade into memory.

"I CAN HELP YOU," I offered in a soft voice, doing my best not to frighten her. "If you tell me your name, I can help you move on."

"Just send her on her way now," Aunt Tillie instructed. She seemed more interested in the male ghost, suspicion lining her eyes as she stared at him. "There's no reason to keep her here."

That was true. The shadow monster was gone. And still, a niggling cascade of fear worked its way up and down my back. "She's young. She died sometime in the seventies. Why was she out here?"

Aunt Tillie's forehead wrinkled as she peered at the ghost. "Oh, man. You're Carol Umber."

My shoulders jerked. "You know her?"

Aunt Tillie nodded. "She lived in the area. She was older than your mothers by a bit. She babysat them a few times, as I recall. Your grandmother was still alive."

The math made sense. "What happened to her?"

For her part, Carol had completely lost interest in me, and now focused on Aunt Tillie.

"People said she ran away," Aunt Tillie replied. "She had a yen for the beach, as I recall. She told people she was going to become a famous actress in Hollywood. When she disappeared, everyone just assumed that's where she went.

"You have to remember, it was a different time," she continued, barely taking a breath. She looked lost, as if she couldn't quite believe what she was seeing. "It wasn't unheard of for kids to take off as soon as they hit nineteen then."

"Or they didn't and you guys simply didn't realize something had happened to her," I argued, tugging on my bottom lip. I wasn't certain what I should do, and yet Carol's disappearance — and now reappearance — fit in to my new plan for The Whistler, so I was reluctant to send her on her way just yet. "Do you know what happened to you?"

Carol looked positively apoplectic. "No. I ... don't like it here." Her eyes momentarily flashed on Aunt Tillie and then she floated backward. "You seem familiar, like I've met you before. But that can't be right. You're ... too old."

"Hey!" Aunt Tillie's eyes caught fire. "I'm middle-aged. I'm not old."

"She probably remembers you from forty-five years ago," I pointed out. "She can't quite put it together."

"I don't want to be here," Carol repeated, looking around. "I'm going to leave now."

I thought about stopping her, but given her emotional reaction, that seemed cruel. "I'll be back to talk to you when you're feeling better," I said.

"I ... you don't have to." She shook her head. "I'm going back to sleep. I don't know why I woke up in the first place."

I did, but now wasn't the time to explain. "I'll be back," I promised, turning my attention to the man. His clothing reminded me of fishing gear I'd seen in a movie. "Were you out here fishing or something?"

He nodded. "Yeah. I was minding my own business until you somehow called me into your mess. That's rude, young lady. I hope you know that."

I held my hands up in a placating manner. "I'm sorry. Kind of."

Aunt Tillie extended a finger, as if she was going to touch the ghost, and then she yanked it back. "That's Carter Culpepper. He disappeared about seven years ago. He was an avid fisherman. It was assumed he was down on the Au Sable River. That's where they looked for him when he went missing."

"He was here, so they never found him," I mused.

"Yeah, and I like it just fine," Carter snapped. "I want to fish and be left alone. Can't you understand that?"

I worked my jaw.

"You could set him free," Aunt Tillie suggested. "I'm sure there's fishing on the other side."

I was certain of that too. "I'll be back to help you as well," I said to Carter finally. "Try to remember where your body is. I'll have it moved to town for a proper burial. Then I'll send you on your way."

"I don't care about any of that. I just want to fish."

"Find your body and you can visit the best fishing places ever, and whenever you want."

"I ... is that true?" He directed the question to Aunt Tillie. "Is she pulling my leg?"

"It's true," Aunt Tillie promised. "She can do what she says."

"Well, then I'll try to find my body." He looked pleased. "Maybe this day won't be just like the rest after all."

"It's not happening today," I warned. "I will be back at some point, though. I promise."

THE LOCATOR SPELL HAD LED US TO HOLLOW Creek, but once the shadow monster was removed from the equation we found nothing of note. We spent hours searching without success, at which point Aunt Tillie lost interest in being my sidekick and insisted we return to town.

I left her on Main Street, something I was loath to do because I knew she would find trouble, but she insisted it was fine and she would find her own way home. I watched her for a few minutes, convinced she would head straight to the Unicorn Emporium to mess with Mrs. Little, but she ultimately headed in another direction. What she was up to, I couldn't say.

I headed to The Whistler office next. I was surprised to find Landon there, sprawled on the couch and reading a magazine. He didn't look up when I entered.

"I think that's a fine idea," he said. "You should totally do that."

He must be on the phone, I thought, but I found his phone on the floor next to him ... and there was no voice coming from it.

"Did you say something?" he asked after a beat, his eyes narrowing. "If you did, I can't hear it. I'm sorry."

"Who are you talking to?" I asked, confused. There was nobody in sight.

"Viola," Landon replied, offering me a smile. "You look a little windblown but otherwise okay. How did your mission go?"

"The shadow monster is dead ... but let's talk about you. How are you talking to Viola?"

"What do you mean the shadow monster is dead? Did it attack?" He rolled to a sitting position, his eyes fierce. "Come over here. Are you hurt?"

I did as he demanded, but only because I was curious. "I wasn't hurt. It didn't come near me. It did grab Aunt Tillie by the throat and try to kill her. She tried to burn it and it was a whole big thing, but I killed it because I'm awesome."

He arched an eyebrow and looked caught between amusement, relief, and annoyance. After a few moments, he sighed and shook his head. "Well, you did what I knew you would do. I can't get worked up." The last part he almost uttered to himself, as if trying to eradicate his fears. "At least that thing is dead. How did you kill it?"

I told him about the ghosts. When I was finished, he held out his arms and tugged me to him, settling us both on the couch before speaking. "You really are turning into a badass."

I glanced over my shoulder for a better look at his profile. "Does that upset you?"

"No. It makes me feel a lot better. I just ... don't know what to make of it. What are you going to do about the ghosts?"

"I'm going to help them find their bodies and put them to rest ... after I interview them for the newspaper."

His lips curved against my cheek. "That's my girl, working the angles. That's a pretty good idea."

"Yeah, well, it makes me feel a little guilty."

"They've been out there for years, Bay. A few more days won't hurt."

"That's what Aunt Tillie said."

He stirred and craned his neck to look at the door. "Where is Aunt Tillie? I thought she was supposed to stick with you."

"She got bored hanging around Hollow Creek and ordered me to bring her here. If you want to know the truth, I think she's plotting something against Mrs. Little ... or maybe Aunt Willa ... or maybe both of them."

He chuckled and tightened his arms around me. "She's a great multitasker. What did she think of you sending the ghosts to kill the shadow monster?"

"She said it was cheating. But she was trying to burn a being that didn't have physical form, so I'm taking it with a grain of salt. I mean ... I love her, but she's a real pain when she wants to be."

"I'm right there with you."

We lapsed into silence, happy to be with one another in a relaxed environment, and then I remembered what he'd been doing when I entered the office. "How are you talking with Viola?"

"Oh, well ... ." His cheeks were slightly tinged with pink when I turned to face him. Ever since I'd put a couch in my office, he'd stopped by for regular naps when his shifts allowed. We'd grown accustomed to navigating the small area without risking a fall.

"You don't have to tell me if you don't want to," I hedged. "I mean ... I would like it if you told me, but you don't have to if you're embarrassed or something."

"I'm not embarrassed," he reassured me, tucking a strand of hair behind my ear. "Not at all. I just ... seeing Erika again at the proposal made me remember a few things. Maybe remember isn't the right word. It got me to thinking."

"You could see them that night," I mused. "The ghosts."

"I think I saw all of them."

"At least most of them," I agreed.

"They disappeared after that. I didn't see them again. It was as if I could see them for a moment — one of those wondrous moments you never forget — but then they were gone."

I was having a hard time keeping up. "And you want to call them back?" I considered the conundrum. "I don't know that I feel comfortable doing that."

"I don't want to call them back," he reassured me quickly. "I don't want to disrupt them. I just ... they're a part of your life. When you first told me you could see and talk to ghosts, I thought maybe you were a crackpot. But I got used to it and now I'm comfortable with your gift."

"That's great, but I still don't understand."

"I want to be a part of your life as much as possible. Erika came to me that night and told me you were in trouble. At the time, I didn't know what to make of it, but I had this ball of fear inside of me that couldn't be quelled. I couldn't think beyond what you needed ... so I went after you."

"You arrived in the nick of time."

"Yes, and that bolstered my ego for a bit. But now I know you would've figured a way out of that situation on your own. That's who you are ... and I'm really proud of how powerful you've become."

A lump formed in my throat. I hadn't expected him to take this tack. "Thank you."

"Oh, so cute." He swooped in and kissed my cheek, a grin taking over his handsome features. "You're not the best at accepting compliments. You need to get over that."

"I'll work on it."

"Good." He moved his hand up to cup the back of my head and stared directly in my eyes. "I want to be able to participate in your life as much as possible."

I protested. "You are my life."

"I'm the love of your life," he corrected. "And, no, that's not just my ego talking. I believe it, just like you're the love of my life. I'm not your entire life, though, and I shouldn't be. You have things that don't revolve around me and I'm fine with that. This ghost thing is different.

"I've seen Erika," he continued. "I've seen your grandmother. I saw the ghosts at the proposal. I want to be able to see and hear them regularly in case ... well, in case they ever need to warn me that you're in trouble again."

It was a really sweet sentiment.

"I also want to be able to hear them when they give you tips. I don't like being left out."

That made me laugh. "So, you've been working on it on your own?" I asked when I'd recovered.

"I have."

"And how is it going?"

"Sometimes I can hear Viola. It's very faint. I haven't been able to see her yet. I guess you could say it's a work in progress."

I looked around, confused. "I haven't seen Viola since I've been here. Are you sure she was talking to you?"

"Yeah. She says she doesn't like to interrupt us in the office too much because she'll be jealous if she sees us doing the bump and grind. That's how she phrased it, by the way."

"That sounds like her."

"She's an interesting ghost. I kind of like her."

"I'm glad." I rested my head on his shoulder. "You know, you don't have to do this for me. I mean ... I don't want you to be who you don't want to be."

"I know who I am," he reassured me. "I don't want to do everything you can do, but I figure this little bit can help."

"I bet it can."

We lapsed into silence, comfortable just to hold one another. I was close to drifting off for a nap — which I was certain was his goal — when the office door flew open.

"I figured I'd find you here," Chief Terry growled. "I thought you were just putting up the cameras and then coming back to the station."

I'd forgotten about the cameras. "I distracted him," I offered hurriedly. "I'm sorry."

"She didn't distract me," Landon said. "We were just ... talking. I thought you'd call if something popped up."

"Well, something has popped up." Chief Terry was grim. "The Harts received a ransom demand."

Landon sat up. "What?"

"They've gotten a ransom demand. They have to get a million together, in cash, by tomorrow at midnight. Then they'll get further instructions later in the day tomorrow."

"That's it?" Landon was clearly flummoxed.

"That's it."

"Well, that's not normal." Landon shifted his eyes to me. "We need to figure this out."

"The family doesn't have that sort of money. We have to come up with a plan ... and we have to be quick about it. I don't think we're going to get a second chance, so we need to make the first one count."

15

FIFTEEN

"What do you think a ransom means?" I waited until Chief Terry had left to ask Landon the most obvious question.

"I don't know." He sat on the couch, his expression clouded. He was thinking things through. "Maybe this was always a money grab."

He didn't look convinced. "You don't believe that."

"Hmm." He slid his eyes to me and offered up a half-smile, his thumb going to my cheek so he could absently brush at it.

"You don't believe that," I repeated. "You think something else is going on."

"I think that it's a weird way to make a ransom demand," he admitted. "I also think we don't have a choice but to treat it as a real demand."

Deep down, I knew he was right. "What do you want me to do?"

He cracked a grin, one that filled his eyes with warmth. "I don't suppose you would consider going home and cooking bacon all day?"

I made a face. "No."

"I didn't think so." He leaned forward and rested his forehead against mine, falling into silence. I was about to prod him when he opened his mouth. "Do what comes naturally, Bay. You're good at figuring things out. You have amazing instincts, and they rarely lead you astray. Just ... be careful."

"The shadow monster is dead," I reminded him. "There's nothing for you to worry about."

"That would be nice to believe but ... I don't. How do you know the monster is really dead? If it didn't have form, there was no body for you to check."

I almost tripped over my tongue I was so surprised by the statement. "I didn't consider that."

"I just want you to be careful. I know you're capable of doing anything you set your mind to. I don't want you hurt in the process."

"I'll be good."

His lips curved. "Not too good. I like my girl when she's a little bad." He swooped in and gave me a kiss before standing. "I have to go work on this."

"Go." I made small shooing motions. "I'm going to check in with Clove and Thistle. If I come up with any ideas, I'll let you know."

"I would appreciate that. If I get any new information, I'll let you know."

I couldn't hide my smirk. "Is this us compromising?"

"Apparently so."

"It's kind of nice."

"It is."

"It won't last. We'll fight again eventually."

He tapped the end of my nose. "Don't go begging for trouble. Let's enjoy it for now, huh?"

"Absolutely."

CLOVE AND THISTLE WERE BUSY WORKING on a new window display when I entered Hypnotic. Unlike previous redecorating, it wasn't joy they were sharing in a new artistic endeavor as much as annoyance.

"You're putting it in the wrong spot," Clove complained, hands on hips as she watched Thistle hang stained-glass moons and stars from the rafters above the display. "They should be more spread out."

From her perch on the ladder, Thistle scorched Clove with the darkest look in her repertoire. "If you don't like how I'm doing it, maybe you should come up here and do it yourself."

Clove rolled her eyes. "I can't get on a ladder and you know it. I'm growing human life here." She gestured toward her expanding midriff. "If I get on a ladder and fall I could kill the baby."

"At least then we wouldn't have to hear you constantly whine," Thistle muttered.

I shot her a quelling look — even for Thistle that was taking it a step too far — and held up my hand to help her down from the ladder. "I'll put up the moon and stars," I offered.

Thistle's eyebrows drew together. "Why are you offering? It's not your responsibility."

"You have enough to deal with." I shook my hand to get her to take it, but being Thistle, she slapped it away and climbed down on her own.

"You're up to something," Thistle announced, folding her arms over her chest as she regarded me with overt suspicion. "I just can't figure out what it is."

I tried to meet her gaze for as long as possible, but she had a masterful ability to beat people down without saying a word. She'd inherited it from Aunt Tillie. "I'm not up to anything."

"Leave her alone," Clove admonished as she lowered herself into one of the chairs in the middle of the room, letting loose an unearthly grunt as she did. "Just because you're mad at the world, Thistle, that doesn't mean you get to take it out on Bay."

I let my gaze drift to Clove, dumbfounded that the noise I'd just heard could've really come from her. "Did you just give birth to an alien or something?" I asked.

Clove's ski-slope nose wrinkled. "Why would you ask something like that?"

"Because that noise you made was unbelievable. I mean ... un-freaking-believable. You're like a human Whoopee Cushion or something."

The wounded expression she'd used to great effect when we were kids to get whatever she wanted took over Clove's face. "I'm sorry if my discomfort offends you. I'm creating human life." She ran her hand over her stomach as evidence. "Sometimes my back hurts and I make noise. Goddess forgive me, but I'm not up and perky all the time."

"Oh, well ... ." I pressed my lips together and looked toward Thistle, only to find her glaring daggers into the back of Clove's head. They were clearly in the middle of a thing, and for some reason I felt left out.

"You guys can't fight without me," I said, moving toward the couch. "It's not allowed."

"Hey, I thought you were putting up the moon and stars," Thistle called to my back.

"I will ... later."

"Whatever." Thistle stomped — yes, actually stomped — as she went to the counter to pour cups of tea for everybody. She delivered Clove's first, which I found interesting because they were obviously caught in a fight. She practically threw the cup at my head when she delivered mine.

"Seriously," I pressed as I lifted the cup to my lips. "You cannot fight without me. I have to be aware of any fights because I get joy from picking sides. You know the rules." I sipped the fragrant tea and immediately had to fight the urge to gag. "What horror is this?"

Thistle smirked as she sipped her own tea. "It's herbal. No caffeine."

"Ugh." I set the cup aside. "What's the point if there's no caffeine?"

"Clove can't have caffeine." Thistle took another sip, her expression never changing. "That means all the tea we have in the store has to be herbal because she might accidentally slip and have the real stuff and the world will end." Another sip. "Everything in my life now revolves around Clove."

The bitter way she said it told me something very bad was going on. Before I could ask about her mental state, Clove decided to push things ... and in the exact wrong manner.

"Nobody is forcing you to drink the tea," Clove snapped. "If you hate it so much, drink water or something."

"Oh, no." Thistle emphatically shook her head. "I live to serve you."

I worked my jaw as I glanced between them. This was so much worse than I'd anticipated. "So ... um ... how's it going?"

Thistle's scowl was pronounced. "How does it look like it's going?" She sipped the tea again. "I'm drinking herbal nonsense and catering to a crazy person."

"Hey!" Clove's dark eyes flashed with hurt. "I'm not crazy. I'm carrying human life. What do you want from me?"

I could almost see the tiny devil sitting on Thistle's shoulder shouting instructions. Before she could respond, I took control of the conversation. "Thistle, if you don't like the tea, you probably shouldn't drink it."

"I pretend it's the tears of my enemies," Thistle replied. "That makes it tolerable."

"That was a really freaky thing to say," I complained. "I mean ... that was horror movie creepy."

"I stand by it."

"She doesn't care," Clove interjected, her voice higher than normal. "She doesn't care that I'm carrying human life. What I'm going to do in a few months is miraculous. Like ... actually miraculous. I'm going to provide the world with a miracle. She makes everything about herself, though, so she doesn't care about my miracle."

Thistle emitted a low growl and I thought she might launch herself out of her chair and grab Clove by the throat.

"Okay, how about a timeout?" I held up my hands and made a T. "You guys are going at each other and now isn't the time."

Clove sniffed. "Tell her. She's being horrible to me."

I knew Clove well enough to recognize her tactic. She was a master at manipulating people when she bothered to put forth the effort. Her diminutive size and puppy-dog eyes had people practically tripping over themselves to wait on her. Now that she was pregnant, she had another method of getting what she wanted.

"You need to stop that." I jabbed a finger in her direction, earning a narrow-eyed glare. "You're acting like a baby. Thistle is going through something right now. You should take pity on her."

Clove's face was blank. "And what exactly is Thistle going through?"

"Last time I checked, her boyfriend was knocked unconscious and left for dead. She sat vigil with him all night. That deserves a few days of quiet."

Clove's mouth dropped open. "Oh, well, I see you're taking her side."

"In this particular instance, I am."

"Even though I'm creating human life," she muttered darkly. "I'm providing the miracle but Thistle gets all the attention."

I felt as if I was talking to a brick wall ... and it had Clove's face. "Stop being a pain." I focused my full attention on Thistle, who almost looked amused. I had no doubt she was deriving enjoyment out of Clove's misery. "You need to stop sticking her with tiny needles, too," I admonished, drawing Thistle's eyes to me. "I get that you're upset."

Thistle straightened in her chair. "I'm not upset. Why would you think I'm upset?"

Was that a trick question? "Anybody would be upset. What happened to Marcus was terrifying."

"I was never afraid. I knew he would be okay."

Now that was an outright lie. I'd sat next to her for an entire night, her emotions seeping into my soul, and there was no denying the terror running through her. "Thistle, you're taking things a step too far."

"That's what she always does," Clove groused. "She can never just be calm and collected like the rest of us."

I tried to hide my snort ... and failed.

"It's true," Clove insisted, reading the merriment in my eyes. "She always makes a big deal out of things, which makes the rest of us look like idiots."

"Okay, Miss 'I'm creating a human life,'" I drawled.

"It's a miracle!" Clove's eyes flashed and the lights overhead momentarily flickered.

I looked up. "What was that?"

"The baby," Thistle replied. "When Clove gets upset, the baby gets upset and weird stuff happens."

This was the first I'd heard about that. "Have you guys mentioned it to anyone?"

"Who would we mention it to?"

"Um ... our mothers." I stared at the light fixture a minute longer and then focused on her. "How can we be sure that's normal?"

"Why wouldn't it be normal?" Clove sat straighter in her chair. "You said it was normal. Were you lying to me? Oh, Goddess, help me. What if I give birth to an evil child? Worse, what if I give birth to Thistle's clone?"

My mouth dropped open and I cringed when Thistle's laser scalpel eyes cut holes into me.

"Are you happy?" Thistle hissed. "This is on you. I hope you know that."

I had no idea what to make of the situation. Luckily — or perhaps unluckily — the chimes over the front door sounded to alert us of an incoming customer. I turned toward the door to find Rosemary entering.

It was strange to realize that I'd practically forgotten she was in town. Over the course of a normal week, that would've been impossible. Somehow she'd managed to slide under the radar — mostly. I was instantly alert.

"Good afternoon." Rosemary offered up a smile that had the hair on the back of my neck standing on end. "It's good to see you all."

Thistle and Clove immediately forgot their fight and focused on the common enemy.

"I heard you were back," Thistle noted, shifting her attention to the girl we were raised to think of as a cousin ... at least superficially.

"I'm back." Rosemary's smile was serene. "I ran into Bay the other day. I would've thought she'd already filled you in on my return."

"She told us." Clove grunted as she tried to situate herself to see Rosemary better.

"None of us were all that impressed," Thistle offered.

"I see you're still as delightful as ever." Rosemary had always hated Thistle more than the rest of us, although the distinction wasn't all that wide. It wasn't as if she found anything to like about any of us.

"I am a delight," Thistle agreed. "People will write songs about how delightful I am."

"Totally," I agreed, smirking. "I'm betting the Jonas Brothers will sing them."

"Don't go there," Thistle warned. "You know how I feel about boy bands."

"Boy bands are fantastic," Rosemary offered. "They know how to find the beat."

"Well ... that's awesome." I rubbed my hands over my knees, suddenly uncomfortable. "Um ... what are you doing here, Rosemary? I thought we agreed that it would be best for everybody if we didn't interact."

"We did agree on that." She bobbed her head. "I just ... well, I realized I wanted to see all of you together. We're family. Maybe it's time to let go of old grudges."

"And why would we want to do that?" Thistle challenged. "I like an old grudge. Heck, I like new grudges. Either way, I'm comfortable with the grudges I'm holding against you."

Even though I would've preferred she not be so overt with her disdain, I couldn't help agreeing with Thistle. "You said you didn't want trouble," I reminded Rosemary. "I agreed with you that it would be best if there was no trouble for any of us ... and yet here you are."

Rosemary had to drag her dour glare from Thistle to focus on me. "I don't want trouble. Why do you naturally assume I do?"

"Because you seem to bring trouble wherever you go."

"That's funny. My grandmother says the same about you."

"Your grandmother is trouble too," I shot back. "Don't think we haven't noticed her out and about with Mrs. Little. If she really wants to steer clear of trouble, she's going about it the wrong way."

Thistle straightened. "Wait ... Aunt Willa and Mrs. Little have been hanging out? Why didn't anybody tell me about this?"

"You've been dealing with other issues," I reminded her. "Marcus is your primary concern right now, and that's okay."

"I still want the family gossip." Thistle was incensed. "I'm going to totally make you eat dirt over this. You can't keep gossip like that to yourself."

"I agree with Thistle." Clove rubbed her belly and glared. "Just because we're not living together any longer doesn't mean we can't share in the family gossip. I think my eyes are going to leak over this one."

"Oh, geez." I rubbed my forehead and stared at the ceiling, gratified to find the lights weren't flickering.

"I don't think it matters who Grandma has been hanging around with," Rosemary countered. "She's an adult, and she's been keeping far away from all of you."

"Not exactly, but close enough," I said. "We don't have time to deal with her. We have other things going on. If you could keep her out of our way, explain that she's not wanted on our turf, that would be great."

"I don't know that I would phrase it like that, especially to her," Rosemary hedged. "It's a free country. She's allowed to go wherever she wants and interact with whomever she wants."

She wasn't fooling anybody. She could make as many grand pronouncements as she wanted but she was here with an agenda. But what was it? What could she possibly want? Their claim to the family land had been denied. There was nothing here for them.

"If Aunt Willa wants to hang around with Mrs. Little, that's her right," I agreed, changing course. "Just remember that Aunt Tillie will consider it an act of war."

"And not a fun war either," Thistle warned. "She's not afraid to get her hands dirty ... or bloody, for that matter."

As Rosemary's gaze bounced between us, I could tell she was struggling, perhaps arguing with herself over what to say. Finally, she held out her hands and shrugged.

"Grandmother isn't afraid of Tillie," she offered. "We've talked about it, at length, and we both agree that Tillie only has power because people give it to her. We have no intention of giving it to her."

"You'll realize what a mistake you've made in the end," I said. "But it doesn't matter. You're not part of our lives. If Aunt Willa and Mrs. Little want to take on Aunt Tillie, they'll lose."

"And I'll be looking forward to the payback heading in their direction," Thistle added. "It's going to be entertaining."

Rosemary narrowed her eyes. "You really think that old bat you've sworn loyalty to will come through in the end every time, don't you?"

"Pretty much." I leaned back in my seat. "If that's all, Rosemary, we're having a family discussion."

"That's all." She reached for the door and paused. "You guys think you're so special. You were raised thinking you were better than me."

"That's where you're wrong," Thistle countered. "We weren't raised to think anything of you because you were a non-factor in our lives. We didn't think of you at all."

"Well, you're going to have to think of me now." Rosemary's sickly-sweet smile was back. "You won't be able to ignore me. You're no longer special."

What was that supposed to mean? "We never thought we were, but I'm curious why you believe things have changed."

"I know what's to come." Rosemary sucked in a calming breath and then pushed open the door. "I look forward to you figuring it out too. I think we're entering a whole new ... world, the four of us here in this room, and I can't wait to see how it comes together."

With those words, she was gone, leaving Clove, Thistle, and me to come to grips with what had just happened.

"She's up to something," Clove intoned.

"Oh, you think?" Thistle's eyes flashed before landing on me. "What are we going to do?"

That was a good question. Now I had two problems to contend with. One was definitely more important than the other. That didn't mean I wasn't open to answers on both.

16
SIXTEEN

My agitation level was high when I left Hypnotic. Even though I knew I shouldn't be worried about Rosemary's presence in town — what was going on with her and Aunt Willa was hardly life-threatening — I couldn't help but wonder. Now was not the time for the two of them to start digging for trouble.

I grabbed a coffee from the bakery to wash the taste of the nasty tea from my mouth and plopped down on a bench in front of the police station. That's where Chief Terry found me as he went to pick up his own coffee.

"What's up, Buttercup?"

I laughed at the old term of endearment. He'd dropped it on me a few times when I was younger, along with a few others like Sunshine and Sweetie Pie. "I haven't heard that one in a long time."

"Once you hit eighteen it didn't seem appropriate." He sat next to me. "What's wrong?" He looked genuinely concerned.

"Nothing. Why do you think something is wrong?"

"Because I've known you your whole life ... or at least for the better portion of it." He leaned back and stretched his long legs out in front of him. "Do you want to tell me what's wrong or should I call Landon out here so he can drag it out of you?"

I shot him a warning look. "I don't need Landon to fix things for me."

"I never said you did. He seems to be able to read your moods better than anybody else, though, and since I don't like when you're upset, he might be the only one who can fix things."

I blew out a sigh. "I'm not upset ... completely."

He arched an eyebrow. "Bay."

His tone told me he meant business, and because Landon was busy working, I decided to unload my troubles on Chief Terry. He once told me that's what he was here for, and I opted to put that to the test.

"Clove and Thistle are fighting," I volunteered. "Clove won't stop saying she's creating human life out of nothing and that it's a miracle. Thistle is being mean to her, but that's only because Thistle went through a trauma and that's how she reacts when she can't control her emotions."

Chief Terry pursed his lips. "Sounds like normal stuff," he said. "Clove and Thistle are always fighting."

"Yeah, but this is different. Our lives are about to be different. Clove is married, for crying out loud. She's going to have a baby in two months. I'm engaged." I looked at the ring for proof. "In two months I'll be married. I guarantee Marcus proposes soon. He's worked up about Thistle hovering because it's not something she normally does."

Chief Terry waited patiently for me to finish and then chuckled when I didn't continue. "Is that all?"

"Isn't that enough?"

"I think you're overreacting to all of it."

"I'm not overreacting. They really have been fighting."

"Of course they have. Clove is a walking hormone. She was theatrical long before she got pregnant. That's simply who she is. She likes attention and she's more than happy to have all eyes on her. She's the most dramatic of the Winchesters." He said it with equal parts amusement and love.

"If she's the dramatic one, what does that make me?"

"You're the thinker. You chew on a problem until there's nothing left but masticated bone and gristle."

I frowned. "That sounds ... lovely."

"It's not so bad. I've always been a fan of how pragmatic you are."

"I'm pretty sure that makes me the boring one."

"You're not boring. You think hard and puzzle things out. You're a good girl in general but you occasionally let your baser urges take over. That's something you get from all those wacky women in your family.

"Still, when it comes to it, you're the one who will point out the gas tank is on empty before it becomes an issue," he continued. "That makes you a hero."

I chewed my lower lip, annoyed. "Yeah, now I'm certain that you're saying I'm the boring one. Landon called me a prude the other day. He believes the same thing."

"And here we go." Chief Terry pinned me with a quelling look. "This is that dramatic thing you can't quite make a break from even though Clove has claimed ownership of the family theatrics. You're not boring, and I don't want to talk about the prude stuff because I'm certain Landon only said that because he wanted you to be filthy in public with him."

That was true, so I decided to change topics. "Rosemary stopped in at Hypnotic."

Very slowly, very deliberately, Chief Terry turned so his entire body faced mine. "What did she want?"

"She said she didn't want anything, but I don't believe her. They're clearly up to something."

"I agree. They're definitely up to something."

"What, though?" I honestly hoped he would have some sort of answer for me. Even if his response promised Armageddon, I needed something to lead me in the right direction.

"I don't know. Willa has always been wily, like Tillie. She doesn't have a sense of ethics."

"And you think Aunt Tillie does?" I couldn't hide my surprise. "I love her, but she's fine hurting people to get what she wants."

"Not entirely." Chief Terry's shoulders sank with weariness as he shook his head. "While it's true that she's willing to do whatever it takes to get what she wants, there are limitations to her efforts. She won't hurt the innocent. In fact, she'll sacrifice of herself if she believes someone is being treated wrongly. She's gotten in a bit of trouble with that over the years."

I thought about Mrs. Gunderson, the baker who had a husband who beat her. Aunt Tillie had covered up the man's death for years because she assumed Mrs. Gunderson had killed him and needed help putting the death behind her. In the end, it turned out there was another culprit, but Aunt Tillie never faltered in her support.

"She's also gone above and beyond for you guys," Chief Terry volunteered. "She likes to torture you, but if somebody else tries to torture you, then she's all up in arms about it. She'd die for all of you. Heck, she'd die for a virtual stranger if she thought it was the right thing to do."

"I guess." I rubbed the back of my neck, weariness threatening to overtake me. "Rosemary said some weird stuff about how we weren't special any longer and how she was just as good as us. Do you think we treated her poorly when we were kids?"

Chief Terry hesitated and then shrugged. "You weren't great to her."

I balked. "We weren't horrible."

"You were exclusionary. You girls had your own little club and nobody else was allowed to join. For someone like Rosemary, a person who status meant a great deal to, it would've been difficult to accept that she was being shut out. On the flip side, she didn't like you girls. She didn't want to be excluded from the gang. It would've been better for her if she could've told you where to stick your club."

That made sense, at least on the surface. "So, we're all at fault."

"I don't know that I would phrase it that way ... but yes." He grinned when I frowned. "Bay, what's this about? It's not like you to be worried about Rosemary or what she thinks. There's no reason to get worked up. Just ignore her."

"Except she's here with Aunt Willa, who is in cahoots with Mrs. Little, and they're all planning something. I know it here." I tapped the spot above my heart. "I can feel it, and I don't like worrying about what it is they have planned."

"Does it matter?"

"I don't know. It feels like it should matter ... but we don't have time to be distracted. We have other things going on. Amelia has to be the priority."

"I agree with you there, which is why I'm going to have to leave you now. I thought I had time to pick up coffee and head back, but it's time for our next interview."

My forehead creased as I turned my attention to the sidewalk, where JD was hurrying toward the building. "You don't suspect him of taking Amelia?" I blurted out. "I'm pretty sure we saw him right before she was taken. He didn't have time to kidnap her. Besides that, he looks nothing like the man the other girls described."

"He's not here for that." Chief Terry's tone was grave. "Even though we're not convinced the ransom drop is going to go down, we still have to be ready ... just in case."

My heart did a long, slow roll. "I didn't think about that. Is he going to help you?"

"We're still ironing out specifics." Chief Terry stepped to the center of the sidewalk and extended his hand. "JD, thanks for coming."

"Don't mention it." The banker flashed a smile that didn't make it all the way to his eyes. "I'm sorry I'm late. I was working on a project and couldn't ignore the final details." Suddenly, his smile turned genuine. "We closed on the old Lakin house and I can't tell you how relieved I am."

I stilled, the words flowing through me, and then raised my chin. "The house across from the campground Landon bought."

"I believe he wants to build a house for both of you out there," JD said. "That means it's your property too. You shouldn't shy away from that. Being a property owner is important, and as soon as you're married, it's half yours."

"I know. I just ... ." I took a moment to regroup. "Who bought the Lakin house?" I couldn't believe he'd managed to turn around the property so fast. In recent weeks, several people had died at the expensive house. Even the state newspapers out of Detroit had published articles. The line of inheritance had been somewhat vague.

"We got things worked out, and the new buyers moved fast," JD replied. "It was almost like magic, the way things fell together so fast."

I hated it when people who didn't understand what that word meant threw it around. A house sale was not magic. "Oh, well ... that's great." I tried to smile but it felt more like a grimace. That property had caused nothing but heartache the past few weeks. "Who bought it? Was it anybody local?" Immediately my mind went to Mrs. Little. She'd been trying to get her hands on the property for years — supposedly because she believed there was pirate treasure buried out there. I wouldn't put it past her to find a way to claim ownership. Landon and I were planning to build a house directly across the lake, so we needed to know our neighbors.

"I can't say just yet," JD replied with a chuckle. "The buyer has chosen to remain anonymous."

Suspicion wormed through my chest. "Once the sale goes through, those documents become public record."

"They haven't gone through yet." He held up his hands in resignation. "I'm sorry. I can't tell you just yet, although you'll want to write a story on it at some point."

"Eventually," I agreed, pushing myself up from the bench. JD wasn't going to tell me what I needed to know, but I was convinced that Mrs. Little had somehow procured the property. That meant she was back on my radar as a threat. "Well, I should probably let you guys get to it. I know you have a lot to deal with."

"We do," Chief Terry agreed, his hand shooting out to land on my shoulder. "Before you go, sweetheart, you need to remember that not everything is your responsibility. You're letting all this family stuff wear you down.

"Clove and Thistle are adults and can work out their own problems," he continued. "The same goes for the rest of them. All you need to worry about is you. Focus on your wedding. Have fun with it. That's the most important thing."

He was so earnest all I could do was smile. "I'll do my best."

I WANTED TO TALK TO LANDON ABOUT my suspicions regarding Mrs. Little and the Lakin property, but I could hardly interrupt him when he was making plans regarding a ransom drop for a missing teenager. I had to focus my attention elsewhere ... which had me across the road from the Unicorn Emporium.

I sat on a bench there, exposed to Mrs. Little's dark glare from inside the shop, watching the hubbub in the store. Compared to Hypnotic, the porcelain unicorn store did paltry business. That was only on a sliding scale, though, and I happened to know that Mrs. Little did quite well. She had the means to buy the house. Probably not in cash, but if she wanted to secure a line of credit on all her properties she could likely manage it.

I watched Mrs. Little schmooze two customers who appeared to be sweet old ladies from another part of the state. They were enthusiastic and chatty as they picked out their souvenirs, and Mrs. Little was much more animated than I'd ever seen her when working with me or another member of my family.

I stared for a long time, lost in thought. It was only the high-pitched sound of young women arguing that turned my attention to the sidewalk. There, less than half a block away, Paisley, Sophia, and Emma bickered as they trotted down the sidewalk.

"You can't wear pink," Paisley insisted. "We're talking about our final homecoming dance. Only a moron would wear pink."

Emma made a face. "I look good in pink. It's my favorite color."

"It's a stupid color," Paisley countered. "And you look stupid in it. Nobody wears pink, not on a beach or anywhere else. Why can't you see that?"

Rather than fight back, Emma stared at the ground. "If you say so."

"I do say so."

They were snotty girls and yet they were fascinating. Their emotions seemed all over the place. I would've pegged Amelia as the one most likely to succeed. Had that somehow worked against her? Was someone in the school jealous of her potential? Did the shadow monster have anything to do with her disappearance? I had a million questions where these girls were concerned but no idea where to start looking for answers.

The girls stopped outside the coffee shop and read the menu in the window. I thought the argument was over, but then Paisley snapped her gum.

"Don't sit there and pout," she insisted. "Pink is the dumbest color out there. You'd look much better in a blue ... or a green."

"I was thinking gold," Sophia offered helpfully.

Paisley shot her a withering look. "Gold? Who wears a gold dress?"

"It was popular in the seventies," Sophia shot back. "I've seen photos. They say that everything old is coming back. Maybe gold is coming back."

"Nothing old is coming back," Paisley snapped. "Once it's gone, it's gone forever."

"Kind of like Amelia," Emma said in a low voice, speaking for the first time since Paisley had vetoed her pink dress. "She's gone and never coming back."

My stomach constricted at the matter-of-fact way she delivered the line, dislike for the girls rolling through me. Emma burst into tears and dropped to the pavement, resting her face in her hands as she cried. "I can't believe she's gone. I thought for sure she would be the one to get out of this town and do something. Do you think she's coming back?" Her eyes were plaintive when they locked with Paisley's vacant orbs. "You don't think she's gone forever, do you?"

"Of course not." Rather than make fun of the sad girl, Paisley joined her on the pavement and wrapped her arms around Emma. "She's going to come back. Just wait and see. Think about the stories she'll have to tell when we see her again."

"She'll be the center of attention," Sophia noted as she sat with the other two girls. If any of them were bothered that others might point and stare, they didn't show it. "She'll have everybody talking about her. She'll be on all the news channels. She'll have celebrities wanting to talk to her and stuff."

"She probably will," Paisley agreed, her voice clogged with tears. "We can't give in to bad thoughts just yet. There's still a chance she'll come back."

"And if she doesn't?" Sophia asked darkly. "What if it's just the three of us forever?"

"That is not going to happen." Paisley sounded sure of herself. "Amelia will come back. You just need faith."

Watching the scene, I was struck by an odd thought. Either the girls really did care about each other, which was something I'd yet to see, or they were excellent actresses. The latter possibility sent chills down my spine. If they were acting, whose benefit was it for? The thought that it could've been mine made me distinctly uncomfortable.

What were they up to? And, if nothing, why did they pluck every suspicious nerve in my body? There was something very dark happening here. And what did the shadow monster have to do with it? It was far more than coincidence that a strange monster appeared the same time a girl was taken. There had to be something tying it all together. It was my job to figure out what.

17

SEVENTEEN

I stopped at the guesthouse long enough to drop off my car and change clothes before dinner. I still wasn't sure what I'd heard. The girls' emotions were all over the place. I was certain at least part of it was an act, but which part?

I was about to head to the inn when Landon pulled up. He hopped out of his Explorer and grabbed me around the waist, giving me a twirl and planting a kiss on my lips potent enough to rock me back on my feet.

"What was that for?" I asked when we separated.

"Maybe I missed you."

"Why really?"

"Because I missed you." He gave me another kiss, this one quick and chaste, and then moved toward the guesthouse. "I'm going to toss my keys on the table and then we can get going. I'm starving. I hope they have something good."

I waited for him in front of the guesthouse. It didn't take long for him to rejoin me, and he immediately linked his hand with mine as we started down the pathway to the inn. He seemed to be in a good mood, which had me curious.

"Did you find Amelia?"

He slid me a sidelong look. "Do you really think I would keep that from you?"

That was a fair point. "You're just so ... happy."

"I have you. Why wouldn't I be happy?"

It wasn't that he was a morose guy, or generally unhappy. In fact, he was the exact opposite. He was only sad when circumstances warranted. He was unusually happy today, though. "You didn't see Aunt Tillie, did you?"

"Not since this morning. Why?"

"I just thought that maybe she cast a spell on you or something."

"What sort of spell?"

I shrugged. "A happy spell. I don't know. It could be a thing."

He chuckled. "I'm happy because my shift is over and we're about to eat amazing food. After that, I have several uninterrupted hours with my favorite woman in the world. Nothing makes me happier."

I watched him for a long moment and then shook my head. "Okay. You're happy. Who am I to get in the way of that happiness?"

"Only a selfish person would get in the way of my happiness," he agreed.

We walked in silence for a bit, both of us taking in the nature that surrounded us and letting go of the dregs of the day. We were halfway to the inn when I decided to tell him about my day. "So, do you want to hear what I did today?"

"Is it going to ruin my happy day?"

"I don't think so."

"Then go for it."

I told him about Rosemary's stop at Hypnotic and then wound around to the girls. When I finished, his expression hadn't changed.

"What do you think about that?" I prodded.

"We knew Rosemary and Willa were up to something. As for the girls ... I don't know what to say. I find teenaged girls freaky ... and not in a fun carnival way."

I made a face. "Could they be involved?"

"I don't see how. They were all there when Amelia was taken. Someone would've seen something if they had a hand in it."

"Except nobody saw the guy who took her."

"That's a point." Landon used his free hand to stroke his chin, all earlier merriment missing from his handsome features. "I still don't see how they can be involved. I mean ... how would that work?"

"Maybe the reason the ransom is so messed up is because kids are making the demand. Maybe Amelia is in on it and isn't really missing. Maybe they're all trying to get money because they have some cockamamie idea to go to Los Angeles to become soap actresses."

"That's a really specific hunch, sweetie." He released my hand and slipped his arm around my shoulders, tugging me closer so he could press a kiss to my forehead. "I need to think about it. Can we return to this topic after dinner?"

I nodded. "Yeah. I don't really want to mention it to anyone else anyway. They'll laugh at me."

"What makes you think I won't laugh at you?"

"You love me."

"So do they."

"Yeah, but it's different with them. They get off on making fun of me. You only do it when you're really bored."

He pulled open the door that led to the family living quarters and ushered me inside. I'd barely made it a step when a screeching I recognized as belonging to Aunt Tillie assailed my ears. We exchanged cursory looks — it sounded as if someone was dying, but Aunt Tillie was more likely the culprit than the victim — and then bolted into the kitchen. Landon was the first through the door, and even though he'd left his service weapon back at the guesthouse, he looked ready to throw down.

There was no obvious enemy when we entered the kitchen. All we saw was Mom, Twila, and Marnie as they faced off with Aunt Tillie. They were all red-faced and furious.

"Not under my roof," Aunt Tillie barked. Even though she was clearly in the middle of a meltdown, I couldn't stop from looking at her leggings. "Are those ... legs?" I found I was focused on her backside.

Aunt Tillie glanced at me over her shoulder. "It's good you're here. You'll never guess what your mother did. It's good you're here too, Fed. I need you to shoot Winnie. You don't have to kill her, but a good flesh wound would be appreciated."

"I'll pass," Landon said dryly. I noticed he was looking anywhere but at what looked to be the fluffy legs on Aunt Tillie's butt. "Why are you screaming?"

"And what's on your leggings?" I pointed for emphasis. "Is that supposed to be a bunny butt?"

"Corgie," Aunt Tillie replied. "I got them on sale. They fit my personality." She wiggled her rear end for emphasis and then snapped her fingers in my face. "Focus. Your mother has set into motion a chain of events that will result in the deaths of us all."

Oh, well, I should've seen this coming. "This doesn't have anything to do with the Wiccan Rapture, does it? I'm really not in the mood."

"It does, but tonight is just the opening volley," Aunt Tillie replied.

"Okay, well ... I'm sure you have everything under control." I patted her arm and moved closer to the stove. "What's for dinner?"

"Stuffed peppers," Mom answered.

I made a face. "I hate stuffed peppers."

Landon draped himself over my back and looked in the pan Mom was removing from the oven. "That doesn't look very good."

"The peppers are stuffed with sausage," Mom offered.

"It still doesn't look like dinner." Landon's hand was warm when it landed on the back of my neck. "What are our other options?"

"Cooking for yourself," Mom said coolly.

He rested his chin on my shoulder. "Maybe we should order pizza or something, Bay. I can't eat peppers and sausage and call it a meal."

"There's rice and side dishes, too," Marnie offered. "Marcus likes stuffed peppers. We made it for him."

"Are they here again?" I didn't mean for it to sound as petulant as it did. "That's two meals in the same day."

"You and Landon eat at least two meals here a day," Mom pointed out. "Sometimes you eat three. And Landon has been known to find his way down here for a midnight snack."

I flicked my eyes to the man in question. "Is that true? Were you cheating on our snacks?"

"If that happened I must've been sleepwalking." He mimed crossing his heart. "I swear it wasn't on purpose."

I didn't believe him but it hardly mattered. "I didn't mean that I'm not happy to see them," I explained to my mother. "It's just ... they usually only show up once or twice a week. Why are they here twice in one day?"

"Thistle wanted Marcus to have stuffed peppers," Mom replied. "Given what happened to him, I think it's only fair that he gets to eat his favorite meals."

"So if I were to get hit over the head, you'd make my favorite meals?" Landon asked.

Mom rolled her eyes. "Maybe, but you get your favorite stuff at least once a month. Marcus never makes requests."

"He's low-maintenance, so I guess that means he's the new favorite. I see how it is." Landon folded his arms over his chest and focused on me. "I've been supplanted, Bay, and I don't like it."

I elbowed his stomach to quiet him. "Are stuffed peppers really all there is?"

"There are mixed vegetables, roasted potatoes, rice, and macaroni salad."

I made a face. "Who eats stuffed peppers and macaroni salad?"

"Apparently Marcus loves the combination," Twila explained. "It's one night. I'm sure you'll survive."

Survival wasn't my worry. "Fine." I threw up my hands. "At least tell me there's good dessert."

"Chocolate lava cake, ice cream and hot fudge," Marnie said, a twinkle in her eye.

I perked up. "Well, that's worth hanging around for."

"I guess." Landon squeezed my hip. "I still think you should hit me over the head with a frying pan so I can make meal requests for a bit."

"Don't tempt us," Aunt Tillie warned. "Forget about the food. We have other things to worry about."

"A bad dinner is something to worry about," Landon complained.

Aunt Tillie raised her hand and shoved it in his face to silence him while focusing on me. "Did you not hear me about the first step of Armageddon being upon us?"

"Yes," I drawled. "It's the end times. We need to run for our lives."

"It is the end times," she agreed, agitation on full display. "It's the end times in the form of the devil and her favorite minion."

I looked to Mom for an explanation. "What's she talking about?"

"I invited Aunt Willa and Rosemary for dinner," Mom replied primly. "She's upset."

All the oxygen whooshed out of my lungs and I thought I might fall over. "You did what?"

Mom was used to dealing with high-strung women — Aunt Tillie was only the oldest and loudest — so she immediately went on the offensive to cut off conversation. "I don't want to continue an unnecessary war. There's no reason we can't have a meal together and discuss our issues.

"Who knows?" she continued. "We might be able to come to a meeting of the minds and strike a truce. Don't you want that?"

Was she kidding? "No, I don't want that. They're up to something."

"Dirty shenanigans," Aunt Tillie hissed. "They're planning our downfall. We're all that stands between them and world domination."

That was a bit extreme, but I didn't want to look a gift ally in the mouth. "All of that but without me sounding like a nut," I agreed. "They're not here because they want to make nice. They're here to mess with us."

"Destroy us," Aunt Tillie corrected. "They'll mount our heads on pikes on the bluff and dance around the remnants of our bodies to collect power from the evil one."

"Okay, don't put those images in my head before dinner," Landon warned. "I don't want to think of Bay without a head."

"Oh, thank you," I deadpanned. "It's nice to be loved."

He smiled. "And I love you best."

"Knock that off." Aunt Tillie rocked to her tiptoes and smacked Landon across the back of his head. "Focus. Your mother has invited the enemy into our inner sanctum, Bay. We must prepare for war."

"There won't be any war," Mom insisted as she transferred the stuffed peppers to a serving platter. "You're going to sit in your chair and be nice." She paused a beat and studied Aunt Tillie's face. "Or you're going to sit in your chair and make passive-aggressive faces and be quiet. I don't care which you choose."

"I would go for the faces," Landon offered.

Aunt Tillie smacked the back of his head again, never moving her eyes from Mom's face. "I don't want them in my house."

"It's one meal," Marnie countered. "How bad can it be?"

As if on cue, a ringing filled the air. The buzzer for the lobby desk, signifying guests had arrived and needed assistance at the front desk.

"I bet that's them now." Mom removed her apron and wiped her hands on a counter towel. "I'll greet them. You all should finish up in here."

She was gone before anyone could respond.

"Satan's minions are here to lead us astray," Aunt Tillie warned. "The devil takes the face that most appeals to it. Willa has always looked like a bucket full of worms. We must cast them out."

Landon had apparently had enough. "Okay, you need to calm down." He grabbed Aunt Tillie's wrist before she could slap the back of his head again. "Come on. Let's get you settled in your chair. It will be easier for you to make faces if you're already in the power seat before they get to the dining room."

Aunt Tillie put up a minor struggle. Landon led her to her normal spot, pulled out the chair, and made sure she was secure before flicking his eyes to me.

"Maybe you should sit down too," he suggested.

"What's going on?" Thistle asked from her seat at the end of the table.

"Apparently it's the end times," I replied.

"Wiccan Rapture?" Thistle looked less than impressed. "She's been talking about it nonstop all afternoon. By the way, when you abandoned her in town I had to bring her back home, so you owe me."

"I didn't abandon her. She took off."

"I had things to do," Aunt Tillie said. "I had ... big things to do."

"Yes, well ... ." I darted my eyes to the door. I couldn't hear Mom talking to our dinner guests. In fact, outside the room, it was eerily quiet. They should've found their way to the dining room by now.

"Where are you going?" Landon's arm snaked out and grabbed me around the waist.

"I'm just checking on my mother. I believe that's allowed."

He stared into my eyes for what felt like a long time and then released me. "If you commit a murder, you drag those bodies outside right away so I don't see them. In this case, what I don't know can't hurt me."

"I'll keep that in mind." I flashed a worried look to Thistle, who didn't rise to follow, and then disappeared down the hallway. I was almost to the lobby before I finally heard voices.

"It was very nice of you to invite us for dinner." Aunt Willa's tone was stiff, which was nothing new. "I wasn't certain we should come, but Rosemary suggested it was probably best if we want to move past what happened."

"I think we would all like that," Mom agreed.

"Tillie?" Aunt Willa sounded dubious. "Do you think she wants that?"

"She'll learn to deal," Mom replied. "I ... um ... is there are reason we're waiting in the lobby? You can head to the dining room now."

"Oh, we have one more," Rosemary said. I couldn't see her, but I recognized her saccharine voice. "My fiancé is joining us. I hope that's okay. He wasn't due to arrive in town until tomorrow, but he finished his work early. I didn't want to miss a meal with him so I asked him to join the entire family."

"That's fine," Mom reassured her. "I can't wait to meet him. Why is he meeting you here? I was under the impression that you guys were only in Hemlock Cove for a short visit."

"Oh, no."

I looked over Mom's shoulder to see Rosemary's mischievous grin as she shook her head. One look at Mom told me she sensed trouble too. I had a feeling she was regretting her decision to invite the devil's rejects to dinner, but it was far too late to rescind the offer.

"You're staying longer?" Mom was the picture of politeness even as beads of sweat gathered on her upper lip.

"We're moving here," Willa replied. "We bought a house. We just closed on it today. It's by a lake."

Realization hit me hard and fast. This was the secret JD had been keeping. He'd sold the house to Rosemary and her fiancé, and they'd asked him to keep quiet about it.

"You bought a house?" Mom looked positively stunned. "I guess congratulations are in order." She didn't look convinced, but she said the words all the same. "Is your fiancé okay with moving to Hemlock Cove? There isn't much for people to do here unless they own a business."

"Oh, he's familiar with the town," Rosemary said. "He's the one who suggested we move back." She cocked her head at the sound of footsteps on the other side of the door. "Here he is now." She skirted around Aunt Willa and opened the door, a huge smile crawling over her features. "You're just in time."

The man who walked through the door had a friendly enough smile, but it was more smarm than charm. I recognized him of course. He'd been my boss at one time. We'd run him out of town when he tried to take my job from me.

Brian Kelly's eyes glinted with amusement as they met mine. "Hello, Bay. I can't tell you how good it is to see you."

18
EIGHTEEN

"What are you doing here?"

It made no sense ... and yet here he was, standing in front of me, grinning that stupid grin that made my stomach churn.

"What do you mean?" Brian was the picture of innocence as he looked between Mom and me. "I'm having dinner with my soon-to-be wife." He sent Rosemary an adoring look that was clearly for show. "It's nice that you guys are trying to repair your relationship. Since we're moving back to the area, that will make things more comfortable for all parties concerned."

I had no idea what to say. "You're engaged?" It was all that would eke out of my mouth.

"We're in love," Rosemary countered, batting her eyelashes at Brian. "We're going to live happily ever after."

"That's right," he enthused. "I've finally discovered what matters most in life. Isn't that what Landon suggested when I left?"

Landon. Oh, geez. I hadn't even thought about how he would react. He hated Brian with a fiery passion. If the stuffed peppers didn't completely ruin his mood, this would.

"You have to go." Decisively, I moved forward to shove him out of the inn. "You can't be here."

Brian caught my hands before I could make contact with his chest and snorted. "That's not very welcoming."

"You have to go," I insisted, refusing to back down. I sent an imploring look to my mother. "He can't be here for dinner. I ... Landon ... ."

Mom fixed Rosemary with a hard look. "I can't help but feel this was a set-up from the start. It's probably best that you go."

Aunt Willa's eyebrows hopped perilously close to her hairline. "You invited us. It would be rude to rescind that offer now. Who taught you manners? Oh, wait, I already know the answer to that."

I tried to give Brian another shove but he refused to release my wrists. I was debating using magic — having a ghost drag him out might be entertaining, especially if he crapped himself, which was a definite possibility — but the sound of footsteps on the floor behind me told me I was too late.

Landon was to me in a shot and he grabbed Brian's shirt before I could issue a warning. "Take your hands off her," he growled, his eyes flashing with menace.

Despite his smug demeanor upon seeing me, Brian paled once Landon was in the mix. "I ... what are you doing?" His eyes were so wide I thought they might pop out of his head.

"Don't touch her," Landon ordered.

Brian immediately released my wrists. Landon's dislike of Brian was well-known and I was worried punches might be thrown.

"Landon." I tentatively reached out and wrapped my fingers around his wrist. His eyes blazed when they met mine. "He's not worth it." I kept my voice low. "Just ... he's not worth it."

Perhaps reading my fear, Landon slowly released Brian and took a step back, making sure to draw me with him. "Why are you here?" he gritted out.

"Rosemary and Brian are engaged," I volunteered before Brian could respond. "They're getting married and moving to Hemlock Cove."

"Like hell." Landon's temper flared again. "Why would you want to come back here?"

"I like Hemlock Cove." Brian made a big show of smoothing his shirt. "It's my home. I was forced out against my will."

"Forced out?" Landon shook his head, his eyes on a spot above Brian's shoulder. "You created that entire situation. You weren't forced out. You tried to ruin Bay and got what was coming to you."

"That's not how I see it. Bay was a suspect in a murder. I had every right to remove her from her position."

"The town didn't see it that way," Mom argued. "The town recognized that Bay did all the work. They wanted her to be in charge."

"Oh, that's cute," Brian said. "The business owners only came together because Terry Davenport threatened to cut off police protection if they didn't."

I was appalled. "Chief Terry would never do that," I argued. "He's not that type of person."

"I happen to know that's not the case." Brian was firm. "I've talked to one of the business owners. She told me exactly what happened."

There was no need to ask which business owner he was referring to. "Mrs. Little."

Landon cast me a sidelong look, a muscle working in his jaw. If he flew off the handle, Brian would be able to use his actions and words against him. It was the last thing I wanted.

"You should go," Landon said. "There's no reason for you to be here."

"We were invited to dinner," Aunt Willa countered. "It would be rude to change your minds now."

The fury that kindled in the depths of Landon's eyes made me cringe. "We can go to town for dinner," I suggested hurriedly. "Let them stay. We'll go. You don't want the stuffed peppers anyway."

He looked conflicted, but ultimately nodded. "Fine. We'll go to town."

"Maybe you should take Aunt Tillie with you," Mom said hurriedly.

"Maybe we will." Landon flashed a smile for my benefit. There was no warmth to it, though. "Let's get out of here."

I nodded in relief and started moving with him. "We'll get you something with bacon ... and maybe some mashed potatoes. You know, comfort food."

This time the smile was genuine. "I'm fine." He managed another glare for Brian. "We won't let them get to us."

"Believe it or not, this has nothing to do with you," Brian said. "This is about us, about our new home. We're thrilled to be moving here. I hear, eventually, we'll be near you and Bay."

"You'll never be close to us," Landon snapped. "You can try, but it's simply not going to happen."

My heart did a long, slow roll. He didn't yet know about the Lakin house. I leaned in close and whispered the tidbit. The fury he'd been feeling only moments before doubled.

"Son of a ... !" He started toward Brian again, but I wrapped my arms around his waist to stop him. I was desperate to keep them from coming to blows. It wasn't that Brian could hurt Landon — he was a sniveling wimp of the highest order — but he would report Landon to his superiors, possibly costing him his job.

THE WITCH IS BACK

"Don't." I was adamant as I dug my heels in. "He's not worth it, and this is what he wants."

Landon ceased struggling and stared into my eyes. The disgust reflected back at me, the horror, had my heart hurting for him. "Fine." He held up his hands in defeat. "He's definitely not worth it."

Aunt Tillie picked that moment to join the fray. If I thought Landon was furious at Brian's arrival, she was apoplectic. "I told you it was the end times! Satan has drawn another hell beast to his cause ... and this one has been marked with the pox as our evilest foe."

I stared at her, confused, and then remembered one of the curses she'd unleashed on Brian before he left town. She'd turned his — um, private area — into a poxed unholy mess. Obviously Brian remembered, too, because he cringed upon seeing her.

"Stay away from me," he warned, extending a finger. "I'll have you arrested if you come anywhere near me."

Aunt Tillie sneered. "I'd like to see you try." She lifted her hand and leveled a finger directly in his face. Then, slowly, she lowered it until it was aimed at his groin. "I have a few ideas now that an old friend has come for dinner. I've been stocking up on ... ideas. Now I have someone to use them on."

Brian swallowed hard. "I'm not afraid of you."

"Then you're dumber than you look."

Before Aunt Tillie could take things further, Landon snagged her around the back of the neck and directed her toward the hallway. "Come on," he prodded. "You're coming to town for dinner with us."

Aunt Tillie didn't look thrilled at the prospect. "I can't torture him if I'm not here."

"No, but we can come up with some fun ideas for you to torture him with in the future." Landon cast Brian a pointed look. "That will be more fun. Besides, nobody wants stuffed peppers."

"Isn't that the truth." Aunt Tillie wrinkled her nose. "Fine, but I'm going all out. We're talking multiple courses ... and you're paying."

"I have no problem with that." Landon cast me a look to make sure I was following but kept his hand on Aunt Tillie's back. She was wily and he likely feared she would pull a disappearing act. "We'll see you soon, Kelly."

"I'm looking forward to it," he called out boldly. "I'm happy to be back in town, and I'm thrilled we're going to be neighbors ... when you actually have a house, that is. I'm guessing that won't be anytime soon."

"Never say never," I snapped, my eyes moving to Rosemary. She looked altogether smug. "You really shouldn't have inserted yourself into this situation. You're going to end up hurt."

"Is that a threat?" Rosemary challenged. "I don't react well to threats."

"It's reality." I held her gaze a moment longer and then chased after Landon and Aunt Tillie, not catching up until they were at the rear of the inn and Aunt Tillie was slipping on her shoes. "Grab your combat helmet," I instructed when I'd had a moment to collect myself. "We have a mission after dinner."

"Do I even want to know?" Landon groaned. "I thought we were going to have a private mission between the two of us after dinner."

"We will," I promised. "Eventually. We need to focus on Amelia. The sooner we find her — and hopefully alive — the sooner we can focus on Brian and Rosemary. I don't think we'll be able to ignore them as easily as I initially thought."

Landon hesitated and then nodded. "What's your plan for after dinner?"

"I'll tell you once we're out of here." I cast a final look back toward the interior of the inn, where I was certain Thistle was getting her first gander at the dinner guests. "You're probably not going to like it, but I think it's our best shot."

"Then lead the way." Before I could open the door, he leaned in and planted a kiss on my pursed lips. "I won't let him hurt you." He was fierce. "Not again. Don't be afraid of him."

Fury, not fear, was threatening to overtake me. I had a target now. Still, Amelia was the priority. Brian Kelly would get what was coming to him ... just as soon as Amelia had been found and returned to her family. Rosemary and Brian would eventually get their due. I wouldn't be able to live with myself if I didn't take them on myself.

"I DON'T UNDERSTAND."

Landon stood in the Dragonfly parking lot two hours later and watched as Aunt Tillie's hands started to glow.

"It's pretty simple," I replied. I'd pondered the plan for the entire ride to town and throughout half of dinner. The more I thought about it, the more convinced I became that it was the right idea. "The teenagers are the key. They won't tell what they know to adults because it's their unwritten code."

"A code, huh?" Amusement had the corners of Landon's mouth curling. "What sort of code are we talking about?"

"The sort where they don't squeal on one another. Even if they overhear something bad, something that can only lead to ruin, they still close themselves off from adults. They can't help themselves."

"And you think they're going to somehow tell you this information because you look like teenagers?" He folded his arms over his chest and watched as Aunt Tillie positioned the mirror on the passenger side of the Explorer so she could see her reflection.

"It's a glamour," I said. "We'll still be the same people. We'll just look younger."

"I get that part of it. What I don't get is why you think that these kids will talk to virtual strangers."

We'd returned to the Dragonfly because I was convinced the kids would be out partying again. The noise emanating from the woods told me I was right. It was only then that I filled Landon in on my plan. He was taking it better than I'd envisioned.

"It'll work," I insisted.

"I don't know." He rolled his neck and stared at the moon. "I don't understand why you think the kids are involved."

He was buying time to come up with a better argument, but I opted to play the game because I wanted him to be comfortable. "I don't know that they are involved," I admitted. "I do, however, believe they're likely to have more information than they're letting on."

"How do you know Paisley and the others will be here?"

I shrugged. "It's just a hunch. They strike me as the sort of girls who like to be in the thick of things."

"And you're just going to start questioning them?" Landon was incredulous. "They might be young, but that doesn't mean they're dumb."

"I don't need to question them. I just need someone else to question them when I'm nearby."

"And you think that will magically happen?"

"Amelia's disappearance is the talk of the town. The teenagers aren't immune from that no matter how much the adults might want to protect them. She's one of their own. They'll want to talk to those who saw what happened. I don't have to be on top of them when that happens, just close enough to overhear what they say."

He dragged a hand through his shoulder-length hair, debating, and then nodded. "Okay. I can't say that I think it's a good idea, but because we have nothing else going on I don't see what it could possibly hurt. But I'm going with you."

I paused and then shook my head. "If you show up, they'll just flee again.

Besides, you heard the kid the other night; nobody is going to trust the newbies who bring their father."

Landon's mouth dropped open at the same moment Aunt Tillie turned to me. "I'm done. What do you think?"

I jolted at her appearance. "You can't make yourself look like Britney Spears." I was horrified. "And why would you pick the outfit from that video where she's wearing the plaid skirt? That's just ... so wrong."

"These kids don't even know who Britney Spears is," Aunt Tillie argued. "She's an old woman as far as they're concerned."

I vehemently shook my head. "Some of them will know who she is because she's still in the news because of her mental problems. You can't pick a celebrity."

Aunt Tillie turned back to the mirror. "That sucks."

"You want to know what sucks? The fact that my fiancée just referred to me as her father. That's what sucks." Landon had turned petulant. "I don't look old enough to be your father, Bay."

"Not now," I agreed. "In a few minutes ... ."

"No." He wagged his finger. "I'm young and hot, and I have no intention of going to the party with you. I'm just going to get close and spy from the bushes."

I made a face. "I don't think you phrased that correctly. Perverts do that."

"I'll be spying on you and Aunt Tillie."

Aunt Tillie turned around again. "What about this?"

Her new hairstyle was dated and I had trouble placing the face. "Wait ... are you supposed to be Gidget?"

"Of course not. Gidget was a stupid character. I'm Sally Field as Gidget."

"Oh, well, that's so much better ... and no." I was adamant as I fixed her with a serious look. "You need to be reasonable with this. Why can't you just look like you did as a teenager and modern-up the hair or something?"

"That's no fun."

I turned back to Landon. "You need to be careful you're not caught," I warned. "If you go to jail, I'm not going to have nearly enough pull to get you out."

"Don't worry about me. I can take care of myself. I'm worried about you. What are you going to do if those kids question who you are?"

"We'll say we're guests at the Dragonfly, heard the party, and decided to check it out." I'd already covered that scenario when dreaming up the idea. "The worst they can do is shun us, but I doubt they'll do that."

"Definitely not," Aunt Tillie agreed, turning a final time. "What do you think?"

My breath caught in my throat. She'd made herself look like Clove, back when we were kids, and the resemblance was uncanny. "I ... why did you pick Clove?"

She shrugged. "I kind of want to know what it's like to be a kvetch. I figure this is my chance to test it out."

I nodded and turned back to Landon. "This will be okay. Trust me."

"I trust you." He watched as I took Aunt Tillie's spot in front of the mirror and moved my hands over my face. "Please don't make yourself look too different," he pleaded. "It will freak me out."

"Don't worry about that." When I turned back to him, his mouth dropped open. I was wearing a familiar face, but only because he'd traveled through time with me at a certain point and been introduced to teenaged Bay. "What do you think?"

He merely blinked.

"Is it good?" I looked to Aunt Tillie for confirmation.

"You look like you did when you were seventeen, though your nose is a little different."

"Yeah, I stole Thistle's nose so it wouldn't be exact." I was imploring when I looked at Landon again. "Do I look okay?"

He let loose a sigh and a nod. "Yeah. You look like Bay, but not the Bay they'll recognize."

"See. I told you it would work." I rolled up to the balls of my feet to give him a kiss but he pulled away, his lip curving into a sneer. I tried not to allow the hurt to show on my face. "What's wrong?"

"I can't kiss you when you look like that."

I fought a smile. "Does it make you feel dirty?"

"Yes, and that's not good. I can't kiss you again until you look like yourself."

"Well, hopefully that won't be long." I gave his hand a squeeze. "It'll be okay. This is just another adventure, and it's going to be quick."

"If you say so. I want you looking like my Bay again ... and fast. This entire thing is going to give me nightmares."

"You're such a baby," Aunt Tillie groused. "Man up." She smoothed her hair. "If I start crying and complaining about Bigfoot, don't pay any attention. I'm a method actor, and that's how I plan to get into character to play Clove."

I blew out a resigned sigh. "Knock yourself out." I glanced toward the woods and squared my shoulders. "Let's do this."

19

NINETEEN

"Let me do the talking," Aunt Tillie warned as we cut through the woods toward the sound of revelers. Her gaze was intent on the path in front of her, and even though she looked like a young Clove, a fall could incapacitate her.

"Why should I let you do the talking?" I asked, grasping her arm to lend support when she started climbing over a fallen tree.

She pinned me with a dark look. "Don't ever do that. I can take care of myself."

I released her, although I refused to look away from her glare. "Asking for help isn't a crime. I believe you told me that."

"I did not." She struggled with the log a moment longer and then found her footing. "See. I'm perfectly fine."

"You're amazing," I agreed. "It's still okay to ask for help."

"It's okay for *you* to ask for help. You should ask for help. There's no shame in it."

"But there's shame for you?"

She rolled her eyes. "I don't need help. I've got this."

Rather than argue, I nodded. It was an old argument we could revisit later. "Let's see what we can find."

The clearing hummed with activity, the only light coming from the bonfire in the center of the circle. I counted thirty people, give or take. It was hard to keep track of them as they bopped from one group to the next.

"Do you recognize any of them?" Aunt Tillie asked.

My gaze fell on a small group east of the fire. Paisley, Sophia, and Emma were there, along with a few others. They clutched drinks and seemed to be having a grand time.

"Those are the ones I want." I inclined my head.

Aunt Tillie pursed Clove's lips — the resemblance was uncanny — and then nodded. "Okay. I've got this."

"Wait." I tried to grab her arm but she was already gone, her expression determined as she closed in on the girls. "How's it hanging?" she called out.

Paisley turned her eyes to Aunt Tillie and frowned. "Who are you?"

"Gidget."

I wanted to groan. "Gidget?" Paisley's eyebrows drew together. "What kind of name is Gidget?"

"My parents are potheads," Aunt Tillie replied. "Apparently there was some show or something a long time ago."

"That sucks." Paisley shook her head. "Weird names are the worst. Thankfully my parents didn't make that mistake."

It took everything I had not to burst out laughing. Only someone with supreme self-esteem could believe that.

"Yeah, I'm thinking of killing them," Aunt Tillie said as she plopped down on a log next to Sophia. "So, do you guys come out here often?"

Paisley looked confused. "I'm sorry, but ... where did you come from?"

I inserted myself into the conversation before Aunt Tillie could offer a ridiculous answer. "We're staying at the inn over there." I gestured vaguely in the direction of the Dragonfly. "Our parents made us come here for some stupid reason. I mean ... this town is lame. We were bored, hanging outside, and heard you guys out here so we thought we'd check it out."

Sophia appeared to be the most suspicious member of the group because the looks she kept shooting Aunt Tillie reminded me of a scene from a bad horror movie. "Why would your parents bother to come to this town?"

"They're interested in the paranormal," I answered. "They think real witches live here."

"Real witches do live here," Paisley said. "It's not the entire town or anything — I don't know who they think they're fooling with that — but there are a couple of people here who really are witches."

"Like who?" I had to ask, if only to know what they would say about us behind our backs.

"There's a whole family of them who live out on the bluff," Emma volunteered. "There are, like, seven of them. They're all mean and nasty."

"They're not all nasty," Sophia countered. "The one who came to question us about Amelia was nice enough ... and her boyfriend is smoking hot. I want to know why she gets to go on assignments with him. Is that, like, a normal thing?"

"Of course not," Paisley replied. "That's not normal at all. She only gets to go because she's put a spell on him. Everybody knows it. He's way too hot for her."

I frowned. "Maybe he loves her," I said.

"Her family is too nuts for him to love her. I mean ... he's hot and she's kind of cute and all, but she's nowhere near as hot as the other women he could get."

I had to restrain myself from reaching across the fire and dragging her into it. "Well, that's weird."

"Totally weird," Aunt Tillie agreed. "Hey, have you guys ever seen Bigfoot out here? I totally want to see him ... and then cry like a baby."

It was an absurd statement, and obviously I wasn't the only one to think so, because Paisley was suddenly looking at Aunt Tillie with fresh eyes.

"Bigfoot?"

Aunt Tillie nodded. "I want to see him and then cry. That's my life goal."

"What are you doing?" I hissed. "You'll make them think we're nuts."

"I'm getting into character," Aunt Tillie replied, her eyes never moving from Paisley's face. "I just figure, if this town is full of witches, maybe there are a few other creatures hanging around."

"I wouldn't get your hopes up," Emma shot back. "There are only a few witches here. And I guarantee there's no Bigfoot."

"Ignore her," I offered lamely. "She just likes to mess with people. She smokes a lot of pot."

Rather than be impressed, Paisley wrinkled her nose. "Potheads are gross. I've seen them on television. You should really talk her out of that."

"I'll get right on it." I struggled for a way to redirect the conversation. "Why are you guys out here? This place seems pretty isolated."

"That's why we like it," Sophia said pointedly, her gaze never leaving Aunt Tillie's face. "We don't want to be bothered. This way the tourists don't find us ... most of the time."

Only a moron could miss what she was saying, but I pretended all the same. "It's a nice area, don't get me wrong, but it's kind of ... dark."

"We used to have a better place," Paisley supplied. "It was by this creek and really cool, but the cops found out about it so we had to give it up. We keep hoping they'll forget about it so we can go back."

"That's a total bummer."

"Total," Aunt Tillie agreed. "I bet Bigfoot would like to hang around the creek."

Sophia's dislike of Aunt Tillie was on full display as she rolled her eyes. "There is no Bigfoot, you moron. Why can't you get that?"

"Don't be mean," Aunt Tillie replied. "You'll make me cry. I'm a whiner and I do it on command."

I wanted to find a hole and crawl into it. "It was some pretty wicked pot," I volunteered to Paisley's unanswered question. "She says stupid stuff when she's high. Ignore her."

"Um ... okay." Paisley made a wide-eyed expression that was supposed to be mocking, but I ignored it.

"What were you guys talking about?" I asked, hoping I wouldn't come across as too eager. "We're going to be stuck in the area for a few days and we want to know what's fun to do."

"There's nothing fun to do," Paisley answered. "I mean ... nothing."

"There's the festival," Emma countered. "They might like that."

"Nobody likes the festivals. They're for loser tourists. Nobody who lives around here ever goes to the festivals."

"I see locals at the festivals all the time," Sophia argued. "I mean ... they're not cool locals, but they go."

"Only the business owners participate," Paisley insisted. "They have to because they have no choice. Everybody else thinks it's stupid."

"Maybe you're stupid," Sophia muttered.

As much as dissension in the ranks intrigued me, I needed to keep the conversation focused. "If you weren't talking about things to do when we walked up, what were you talking about?"

"All the perverts in town," Paisley replied, her lip curling. "We have this friend — Amelia — she was kidnapped." The statement was delivered without inflection.

"We think it was probably a pervert," Emma added.

"It's the only thing that makes sense," Sophia agreed, darting a glare toward Aunt Tillie. "You probably don't have to worry about that."

"It's okay," Aunt Tillie reassured her. "I happen to like a good pervert."

"Of course you do." Sophie rolled her eyes. "Why am I not surprised?"

Despite the sarcasm, I was intrigued. "You have perverts here?"

Paisley nodded. "It's really gross. They dress up and pretend to be participants in all the town stuff, too." She leaned closer, as if imparting some great wisdom. "Like the guy who runs the kissing booth. He totally tries to get us to go inside with him so he can take photos of us."

"Is that true?" I couldn't believe it. I knew Todd Lipscomb. He was older than me, had graduated from high school when I was still in junior high, but I'd never heard whispers about him being untoward when it came to teenage girls.

"It's totally true," Paisley intoned. "Then there's the guy who runs the food truck at the festivals. He doesn't want anyone to know, but he doesn't wear pants when he's serving up the hot dogs."

I just had to know if that was a euphemism for something. "What kind of hot dogs is he trying to serve?"

"Oh, don't be gross." Paisley wagged her finger. "He doesn't let us see — not that we would want to — but he totally puts his hands on it when he sees us."

"He also says nasty things about putting hot dogs in buns," Sophia added. "You know what that means."

I honestly didn't. After all, it was possible he really was talking about hot dogs and buns. Of course, it was also possible he'd slipped under the radar and the girls were right. "Anybody else?" I was almost afraid to ask.

"This town is full of perverts," Paisley replied. "I mean ... *full* of them. It must have something to do with dressing up and pretending to be something you're not."

"That's a pretty advanced take on life," I said.

"I'm going to be a therapist." Paisley preened as she ran her hands over her knees. "I don't want to be one who sits in an office and listens to people's problems. I want to be on, like, *Oprah* ... and *Dr. Phil* ... and that guy with the bad hair and eyebrows who desperately needs a makeover but is on a lot of shows anyway."

"Dr. Oz," Aunt Tillie supplied. "I think he might've been a troll in another life."

Paisley snorted. "Good one."

I pushed forward. "Anyone else?"

"Are you sure you want to know?"

I was resigned. "I need to know who to avoid, right?"

"Good point." She launched into a list of supposed perverts, and with each name my stomach clenched a little tighter. If even a fraction of her stories were true, Hemlock Cove had quite a problem on its hands ... and Aunt Tillie was going to be doling out karma curses until she got carpal tunnel syndrome.

. . .

AFTER AN HOUR, I DECIDED IT WAS TIME to leave. I sent Aunt Tillie off first while I made a final lap around the party circle. We'd left Paisley and her buddies twenty minutes before, and if the way they carried on and put on a show for anybody within hearing distance was to be believed, they didn't miss us.

Once I was convinced there was nobody left to talk to, I headed for the path back to the Dragonfly. I was almost back to the inn — convinced Landon had led Aunt Tillie back to his Explorer — when a figure appeared on the path in front of me.

We were heading in opposite directions. I was certain it was a man because the shoulders were too broad for a woman. I almost gasped when the individual flicked on a flashlight and slowed his pace.

"Leaving so soon?"

Brian. He was here. In the woods. With a bunch of a teenagers. How did that even happen? More importantly, why? Was he one of the perverts the girls had been talking about?

"I have to get back to the inn," I replied, lifting my hand. "We're staying there."

"That's convenient." Brian said. "Why leave so early?" He checked his phone screen. "It's barely after ten. Come back to the party and have a good time."

That was the last thing I wanted. "If I don't go back now, my parents will notice," I replied hollowly.

"Or maybe they won't."

"They will." I was thinking of Landon. He would definitely notice if I didn't return. "My sister already headed back. My parents will come looking if I don't join them."

"Out here?" Brian looked surprised. "Would they even know to look out here?"

"They would if my sister told them where we were."

"Oh, right." He moved to the side, leaving room for me to traverse the path without having to touch him. "Then you should definitely get back. You don't want to ruin it for anybody else."

I swallowed hard as I stepped around him, keeping my eyes on his hands as I headed in the direction of the parking lot. I waited until I was a good thirty feet away to slow my pace, and when I glanced over my shoulder Brian was gone. What was he doing in the woods with a bunch of kids? There was no answer I could come up with that wasn't bad. Still, I forced myself to go to the parking lot rather than follow him. If I went back now, I would draw suspicion.

Landon was indeed trying to wrestle Aunt Tillie into the Explorer when I caught up with them. He seemed agitated, and it appeared Aunt Tillie was pressing every single one of his buttons.

"My eyes will leak if I don't sit in the front," Aunt Tillie argued. "And not because I'm crying or sad, but because I'll throw up. Do you want me to throw up all over your vehicle?"

"Don't be a pain," Landon complained. "Turn yourself back to normal and get in the truck."

"I need to be up front." Aunt Tillie was adamant. "If I'm not, I'll totally puke. I'm not kidding."

"Just let her sit up front," I instructed as I appeared out of the darkness.

The relief on Landon's face was palpable. "Where have you been? Why didn't you come back together? I was about to head in and look for you."

I waved off the question. "I wanted to make sure I saw everybody. Amelia wasn't there, as far as I could tell, but I needed to be sure."

"I know. I was watching. Did you really expect her to be there?" He raised his hand, as if to brush the hair from my face, and then dropped it before touching me. "Turn yourself back to normal."

"Just a second." I shifted from one foot to the other, contemplating the best way to tell him about who I'd met on my way back. I finally decided the only way to share the news was as bluntly as possible. "Brian Kelly is on his way out there. I saw him on the trail."

Landon snapped up his head. "What?"

I nodded. "I couldn't believe it was him. He tried to get me to stay until I told him I had to go back to the inn or my fictional parents would start looking for me. He didn't seem to want that, so he sent me on my way."

"And you're certain he didn't recognize you?"

"There's no way. He would've said something if he suspected, maybe tried to test me or something."

Landon again reached out to put his hand on my shoulder and then snatched it back. "Seriously, you need to make yourself look like you. I need to touch you."

"At least we don't have to worry about this one being a dirty pervert with teenagers," Aunt Tillie noted, jerking her thumb in Landon's direction. She'd dropped her glamour. "He can barely look at you."

"It's kind of cute." I flashed a smile and then acquiesced, running my hands over my face and hair to put my features back in place. Landon looked so relieved when he realized I was back to my old self that I thought he might cry. "Better?"

"Yes." He pulled me to him for a hug, inhaling deeply. "But you smell like bonfire."

"Is that bad?"

"It reminds me of when you were a teenager." He released me and conjured a rueful smile. "You're going to have to take a bath when we get home."

He was taking this to a ridiculous level. "I'm me. It's not like you're doing anything dirty."

"You'll still have to take a bath. I can't ... with all of this." He put his hands on his hips and gazed at the woods. "We can't just leave Brian out here with the kids. We have to break up the party."

"How do you suggest we do that?".

He tilted his head toward Aunt Tillie. "You can make it rain?"

Her eyes lit with glee. "I can."

"That's actually a good idea," I offered. "That way Brian won't be suspicious of us."

"I couldn't care less if he knows it's us. The kids are another story. We might need to talk to them again. For now, we'll go with the storm idea. They'll scatter like rats and we'll be free to think and regroup."

"Okay." I focused on Aunt Tillie. "Make it rain."

"Can I send down lightning to give Brian a scare? I won't let it hit him, but it might be funny if he wets his pants."

I expected Landon to shut her down. Instead, he grinned. "Do your worst."

Always the negotiator, Aunt Tillie wasn't finished quite yet. "Can I sit in the front seat for the ride back?"

"If you make him crap his pants on top of everything else, you've got yourself a deal."

"Consider it done."

20

TWENTY

Breakfast the next morning was a dour affair. Mom felt the need to apologize before anyone was allowed to eat.

"I'm sorry I tried to make things right with them," she started. "I thought maybe there was a chance we could all get along. I was wrong."

"Oh, you think?" I muttered, flicking my eyes to the empty end of the table. "No Thistle and Marcus this morning? I guess that means there's something good for breakfast."

Mom pinned me with a dark look. "I think Thistle was feeling better last night. She perked right up as soon as everyone started sniping at one another. As for breakfast, have you ever had a bad meal here?"

That was a trick question. "Of course not. I ... ." Landon caught my attention and when I turned I found him forking scrambled eggs onto bread and topping it off with bacon. "I can't believe you would ask that," I said. "All your meals are heaven on pancakes."

"Definitely," Landon agreed around a mouthful of food. He was apparently ravenous after a night spent spying in the woods.

I watched him a moment and then shook my head. "I'll need to start monitoring your calorie intake at some point. Your metabolism won't keep revving forever."

"As long as I have you it will." He kissed my cheek before focusing on his breakfast. "Now, shh. It's quiet time and I'm enjoying a moment with my breakfast."

He was now a lost cause, so I focused on Mom. "I understand what you were trying to do, but it was always going to be a wasted effort. They don't want to know us, and that's okay because we don't want to know them."

"I know that. I do, deep down." Mom flashed a rueful smile. "I just thought if they saw us as a happy family they might want to join us."

She was delusional sometimes. "No, you thought you could impose your will on them. That's where you always make your mistakes. Not everybody will bend to your will just because you want them to. You need to let it go."

"I don't try to bend people to my will."

From his spot next to me, Chief Terry coughed into his napkin. He refused to meet Mom's accusatory gaze as he sipped from his juice, instead focusing on me. "How was your dinner last night?"

"Didn't Aunt Tillie tell you?" I glanced at her empty chair. "Where is she, by the way?"

"She said she had plans for the day," Marnie replied. "She was up before the sun and headed out. She was wearing leggings with firecrackers on them — at least I hope they were firecrackers — and said she had a mission."

"What mission?"

"I don't know, but she had her scooter ... and what looked to be one of those plastic glitter batons. I'm guessing there was more to it than she let on."

Well, great. "Who am I supposed to take with me to question the town perverts now?" I groused.

Multiple heads swung in my direction.

"Why are you questioning the town perverts?" Mom asked. "I mean ... I get it. Wait, no I don't. Isn't your future husband, you know, the guy who is making out with his bacon right now, enough of a pervert for you?"

I glanced at Landon and smiled as he munched his version of a breakfast sandwich. "He's more than enough. I need to find a different pervert." I told them about the conversation I'd had with the girls at the bonfire the previous evening. "If they're right, maybe there's something else going on. Maybe one of the town perverts is responsible for Amelia's disappearance."

Mom made a face. "Wouldn't those girls have told you if they recognized the person who took Amelia?"

"In theory. They're all over the place. I'm not sure I believe the story they're selling."

"That doesn't mean one of the local perverts is responsible. In fact, I would prefer a pervert didn't take her at all."

"I think we all wish that," Landon agreed.

"So you're okay with Bay wandering around talking to perverts?" Mom looked incredulous. "That doesn't sound like you."

"I was only okay with it when I thought she was taking Aunt Tillie," Landon admitted, reaching toward the bacon platter to begin building a second sandwich. "I'm not keen on her going alone, so ... perhaps I will readjust my schedule and go with her."

"We have our own pervert list to run," Chief Terry reminded him.

"And I'm more than capable of taking care of myself," I offered. "I have ghosts who can serve as backup if I need them."

He hesitated and sighed. "Okay. You're in charge of your own life."

It wasn't the reaction I was expecting. "Just like that?"

"Compromise, baby."

I stared at him, hard, and then grinned. "I'm starting to like this compromising thing."

"I'm sure you are."

Noise in the doorway behind me had me turning my head to find Thistle storming through the door like a whirlwind.

"What's for breakfast?" She leaned over Landon's shoulder and stared at the spread. "Looks good. Load me up."

Mom turned her perfectly arched eyebrow in Thistle's direction. "What are you doing here?"

"Where's the love?" Thistle drawled. "I thought there was an open-door policy for breakfast here."

"There is, but ... where is Marcus? Did you abandon him in his time of need?"

Thistle's expression turned dour. "I didn't abandon him, and apparently he's no longer in need ... or that's what he told me this morning when he exploded because he said I was hovering."

I had to swallow a laugh. "Marcus exploded?" I couldn't imagine that. "Did he, like, ... yell?"

"He doesn't yell. He just explained, in no uncertain terms, that I was smothering him and then suggested I go back to work. I don't want to be around Clove and her never-ending 'I'm creating a miracle' talk, so I came here." Her gaze was so intense I was afraid it was going to laser right through me. "I'm back in. What do you have planned for today? The messier the better."

I looked toward Landon and found him smirking. "If I didn't know better, I would think you planned this," I muttered.

He shook his head. "Sometimes the Goddess likes to smile on me too."

. . .

THISTLE AND I STOCKED UP ON COFFEE before heading to the festival. The girls had claimed multiple perverts worked there.

"I don't get what you're hoping to accomplish by this," Thistle admitted. She seemed to be mostly back to her old self. I was grateful for that. Still, she shot the occasional dark look toward the petting zoo as we passed.

I followed her gaze and grinned when I saw Marcus out with the kids. He looked to be having a good time, none the worse for wear, and briefly looked up to mark our progress. He waved — I waved back — and then turned back to his work. "Are you guys fighting?"

"No." Thistle made a sour face. "We don't fight."

"Everybody fights."

"We don't. He's always calm and rational. He never raises his voice ... or swears ... or threatens to make me eat dirt."

"And that's a problem?"

"No." She dragged out the word, as if chewing on it, and then sighed. "I don't think that asking him to take it easy for a few days is the worst thing in the world."

"Definitely not. Obviously he felt differently."

"He was fine the first day. He started chafing the second. After the argument over dinner last night, he got ... annoyed."

She was obviously holding something back. "What did he get annoyed about?"

"You've met Rosemary and Aunt Willa. Who wouldn't get annoyed?"

"He wouldn't. He would just sit there and take it all in."

"I might — and I stress *might* — have protectively thrown myself in front of him at one point when Brian stood up. I thought he was acting aggressively. Turns out he was just going to the bathroom."

That both amused and annoyed me. "I can't believe he's back in town."

"That's another reason I rejoined the mayhem team. I figured you're going to be working overtime to take him down. I want to be there when it happens."

That had my smile widening. "I do want to take him down, but Amelia has to be the priority."

"Which brings us back to my initial question. What do you expect to happen when you start sniffing around the vendors and asking if they're perverts?"

"I didn't think I would attack things quite that way," I said. "I thought we would be more subtle."

"You were going to take Aunt Tillie. How is that subtle?"

I didn't like that she had a point. I threw up my hands, frustrated. "I don't know that we're going to get anywhere. I don't know that it's anything. I just ... need something to do."

"Besides fixate on Brian Kelly and what his union with Rosemary could mean for us as a family, you mean."

Did I mean that? I shook my head. "I mean I want to figure out what he's doing here, but my issues with him have to take a back seat."

"You have to be annoyed that they bought the Lakin house," Thistle pressed. "I know that would drive me crazy. You're going to have a beautiful patio area with a big bonfire pit right on the water. You're going to go out there in the morning with your cup of coffee and a blanket, look across the water ... and see our pig-faced cousin and the world's worst man staring back."

She'd given it more thought than I had. "I don't know what to make of any of it. I would be lying if I said otherwise. Whatever Rosemary and Brian have planned — and I guarantee it's not good — we'll have plenty of time to deal with it once we find Amelia."

"Okay, let's talk about Amelia. Marcus doesn't remember what happened."

"I know. Has the doctor said anything about his memory loss?"

"No. He has no trouble remembering anything else. Just the minutes leading up to the attack are missing."

"Doesn't that seem a little convenient?"

Thistle held out her hands. "If the girls are telling the truth, we already know who we're looking for."

"No, we have a generic sketch. Doesn't it bother you that nobody else saw Amelia taken from a crowded festival?"

She slowed her pace. "I hadn't really thought of that." She glanced around. "Everybody was looking this way." She gestured toward the festival. "The barn is that way, as is the lot. If there was no reason to look, why would they look?"

"And why didn't the girls scream sooner? I mean ... they waited until he was gone in a vehicle with Amelia to scream. Why?"

"Maybe you should have Landon ask them that."

I dragged a hand through my hair and focused on the kissing booth. "Let's check out Todd first. The girls said he tries to lure them into the booth for a good time."

"He's never tried to lure me into the booth."

"He's probably afraid of you."

"And rightfully so."

"And we're older," I pointed out. "Maybe he only likes the younger girls."

"Then he's a sick pig."

"We have to know if he's ever acted on his desires. We don't know that he's a pervert. If he is, we have to do something about it."

TODD LIPSCOMB STOOD OUTSIDE HIS BOOTH, calling out to couples as they passed to entice them inside while yammering on about love and kisses. His voice was neither silky nor sultry. He looked like a man bored with life more than anything else.

"He doesn't look like a pervert," Thistle offered after a few moments of studying him.

"How many perverts actually look like perverts?"

"Harvey Weinstein, Sigmund Freud, Albert Einstein."

I pinned her with a curious stare. "Albert Einstein?"

She bobbed her head. "He wasn't just a genius, he was a perverted genius. He cheated on his wife with his cousin and when his wife found out and complained he actually wrote about how much his wife bothered him. Said she was an employee he couldn't fire."

I had no idea what to make of that. "How do you know all of that?"

"I read about it when I was looking for something else. Then I went down a rabbit hole on Google. You know how that goes."

"Rabbit holes, yes. Albert Einstein rabbit holes? Not so much."

"I'm just saying that sometimes perverts really do look like perverts."

"And other times they don't." I heaved out a sigh and moved in Todd's direction. "Let's not drag this out."

"Just out of curiosity, are you going to open with 'Kidnap any young girls lately?'"

I glared at her.

"Well, I'm just dying to see how this all works out for you."

I pasted a smile on my face and ignored the way my stomach churned as we approached Todd. He looked happy to see us ... until he realized we didn't have Marcus and Landon with us.

"Where are your boyfriends, girls?" he drawled, his smirk obvious. "Not that I'm opposed to letting you two in there together — kissing cousins, eh? You usually have different partners when you visit."

Thistle's mouth dropped open. "I don't go in there with Marcus. I mean ... wait." She glanced at me. "How often do you and Landon go in there?"

I shrugged. "I don't know. He gets all sugared up and drags me in there on a semi-regular basis. I don't know why he's such a fan."

"I provide a special place where love springs eternal," Todd replied, sweeping his hands toward the booth. "I'll give you girls a discount if you want to go in."

"I'll pass," I replied dryly. "We're actually here for a reason."

"Oh?" Todd didn't look worried. "If you want me to advertise in the newspaper, I don't have enough profit margin for that. I don't think it would increase business anyway."

"That's not it."

"What is it, Bay?" Thistle asked in a teasing tone that reminded me of our teenage years and made me want to pull her hair.

"So, we're trying to help the authorities in the search for Amelia Hart," I started. "I'm sure you've heard about her kidnapping."

"I heard. She hangs around with that gaggle of blondes but I'm not sure which one she is. Some pervert probably took her."

I sucked in a breath and glanced at Thistle, who looked beyond amused. "That's the word on the street. You don't happen to know if there are any perverts in town, do you?"

Todd's eyebrows hiked and then he shrugged. "You might want to check out Mike Lintz."

I frowned. "Old Mike Lintz?"

"I don't think that's his official name," Thistle pointed out.

"He puts it on his business cards," Todd countered.

I was baffled. "Why does he have business cards?"

"His son owns the wand shop. He sits out front and complains to anybody who will listen and pretends he's a part of the show. I heard he occasionally likes to show his wand to unsuspecting tourists."

"Seriously?" How had I never heard that? I looked to Thistle for confirmation.

"How should I know?" she challenged. "He knows better than to show his wand to me."

"I've heard some of the girls complain," Todd volunteered. "Of course, I don't always believe what they have to say because they're little flirt monsters themselves. They like to bat their eyelashes and ask for free stuff, but when you call them on their attitude all of a sudden they're frigid little hell beasts."

I frowned. "Have you been flirting with the frigid little hell beasts?"

Todd made a face. "Why would I flirt with them? They're children."

"That doesn't stop some people."

"Well, I have no interest in them. They're a little too young for my taste. I didn't even like kids when I was one. Now, if it was Tillie we were talking about, I might feel differently."

Now I was appalled for a completely different reason. "Aunt Tillie is in her eighties."

"So? I like a mature woman who brings her own alcohol everywhere and doesn't care what others think. She's a firecracker, that one. I would totally take her on."

Thistle's expression of disgust mirrored mine. "You couldn't handle her."

"So she's told me. As for those girls, I don't know what you want to hear. I can't stand them. The feeling is mutual. I reported the one — the tall one with blond hair, but they all have blond hair, so that doesn't really help you — for trying to con one of the jewelry smiths out of a ring. She threatened to tell her father that I was looking at her funny."

That didn't surprise me. "Did her father come talk to you?"

"No, but she's been eyeing me ever since. I think she's plotting something. I run the kissing booth at the festivals and otherwise spend all my time at the Shadow Hills bar. What is she going to do to me?"

"Thanks for your time." I led Thistle away from the kissing booth and considered our next option. "Maybe there aren't any perverts and Paisley just uses that as an excuse to go after people."

Thistle didn't look convinced. "Just because Todd is good at talking himself out of trouble doesn't mean all the people she pegged as perverts are innocent."

"True. I guess we should talk to a few more."

Thistle paused for a moment. "Speaking of losers of the highest order, isn't that Brian Kelly going into Mrs. Little's store?"

I jerked up my head, my stomach twisting. Sure enough, he was indeed walking into the Unicorn Emporium. He didn't look in our direction, which was a blessing, but he was moving fast enough that I had to believe he had specific business on the other side of the door.

"He was at the party circle last night," I said.

"Why?"

"I don't know. Landon had Aunt Tillie cast a storm spell to force the kids to scatter. I thought about spying on him, but I'd already been out there once. I didn't want to get caught ... or shunned."

Thistle rolled her neck. "We could ask him."

"You think he would tell us the truth?"

"No."

"We need to figure out what he's up to before confronting him. That's the only way we're going to be able to get close to him."

"And you believe we'll actually be able to do that?"

"Stranger things have happened." I heaved out a sigh and forced myself to return to the task at hand. "So ... let's track down some more perverts."

"Sounds like a fantastic way to spend the morning."

TWENTY-ONE

We questioned so many purported perverts I'd lost count. Each one pointed us toward another who was supposedly worse. Mike Lintz did indeed show me his wand ... except it really was a wand. He said he liked sitting in the front rocker and threatening kids with curses because he hated all the "snot-nosed little bastards" invading his space. He wasn't exactly a good guy, but he wasn't evil.

"Well, what next?" Thistle asked.

That was a good question. "I was thinking about lunch."

"I could eat." She brightened. "I was just going to head back to the store and check on Clove, but that will involve listening to her go on and on — and on and on and on — about her stupid miracle."

I pinned her with a quelling look. "She's allowed to be excited."

"But does it have to be the only thing she talks about? We used to have other discussions."

"You miss our three-hour breakdowns regarding the dynamics of our family?"

She wrinkled her nose. "We talked about other stuff."

"Like what?"

"Like ... oh, shut up." She scuffed her shoes against the road as we crossed. "I just don't want our entire lives to be about that baby."

"They won't be. I'm getting married."

She rolled her eyes. "Big whoop."

I cast her a sidelong look. "Are you jealous?"

"No."

"Are you sure?"

"I'm perfectly happy with my life."

The fact that she couldn't make eye contact told me otherwise. I wasn't sure if I wanted to press the issue, though. She could be unpredictable. Ultimately, I decided to let it go ... for now. "So ... lunch?"

"Bring it on."

Landon and Chief Terry were at a table when we entered. Another police officer, Hunter Ryan from Shadow Hills, sat next to Chief Terry. The trio appeared to be deep in conversation.

"Should we interrupt them?" Thistle looked as if she could go either way.

"I don't know. If Hunter is here on official business then he doesn't want to hear our nonsense."

As if sensing I was near, Landon lifted his chin and started searching, his gaze falling on me in mere seconds. He smiled and motioned for us to join them.

"I guess they're not having a serious discussion," Thistle noted, cutting in front of me. The five-top provided plenty of space for both of us, and she settled between Hunter and Landon while I plopped down between Landon and Chief Terry.

"How did the pervert hunt go?" Landon asked, his fingers feather light as they brushed my hair from my face.

"It seems we have a lot of perverts in town," I replied. "Every single one of them is willing to point a finger at someone else."

"Perverts?" Hunter cocked an eyebrow. He was attractive in a movie star way, though he seemed oblivious to his good looks. As much as I loved him, Landon was the sort of man who knew he was attractive and liked to use it to his advantage. Hunter was the exact opposite, as far as I could tell. Nothing he did revolved around his looks.

"It's a long story," Chief Terry offered.

"There's a missing girl. We tracked down a bunch of potential perverts in town to see if they might be guilty," Thistle said as she grabbed the pickle off Chief Terry's plate and bit into it.

"Hey." He gave her a dirty look. "I was saving that for dessert."

Thistle graced him with her most impish grin. "Sorry." She swallowed. "Do you want me to buy you another pickle?"

"No, I wanted my pickle."

She tried to hand it back to him, but he brushed her hand away.

"I don't want it now," he groused. "Your germs are all over it."

"Why are you such a gloomy Gus?" Thistle's mood had improved markedly. She didn't even look at the petting zoo to check on Marcus when we did our last round across the festival grounds. It was obvious she was feeling more like herself, which was bad news for Chief Terry, because there was little she loved more than messing with him.

"I'm not a gloomy Gus."

Landon snickered as he draped his arm around my shoulders and pressed a kiss to my forehead. "Hunter is here asking for help with a case."

"That's good." I offered Hunter a grin. I liked him a great deal. Even more, I liked his girlfriend Stormy. She was a new witch just coming into her powers and there was something hinky about her background, something Aunt Tillie knew a little something about but refused to share with us gossipy busybodies. Stormy's great-grandmother was due in town in a few days and Aunt Tillie swore she would be able to shed light on what was going on. I hoped for Stormy's sake that was true.

"It's not a big deal," Hunter supplied. "I just like to touch base with Terry once a week or so. He was busy here, so I made the trip this week." His gaze seemed a little more intense than usual and I had to wonder if Stormy had finally let the witch out of the bag ... so to speak. They had a tempestuous history. She had broken his heart when she left after high school, but had recently returned. She was afraid to tell him the truth.

"We're going to go eat at Two Broomsticks one day soon," Thistle said. She wasn't as familiar with Stormy, but she liked Shadow Hills a great deal and was always open to new food opportunities. "Maybe we'll see you there."

"Maybe." Hunter's smile never wavered. "But get back to the perverts. That sounds interesting."

"Then we're telling it wrong. Hold up." Thistle motioned for me to zip my lips as the waitress approached, then waited until we'd placed our orders to give me the go-ahead motion. It rankled that she fancied herself in charge of the conversation, but given what she'd gone through with Marcus, I decided to let it slide.

"We started with Todd Lipscomb," I explained, keeping my voice low as I glanced around to make sure nobody was listening. The last thing I wanted was for one of the local gossips to hear the conversation and start spreading it around as fact.

"The dude who runs the kissing booth?" Landon's forehead creased. "I don't think he's a pervert. He's kind of obnoxious, but that doesn't make him a pervert."

"He was convincing when we talked to him," I admitted. "He claims that Paisley has been threatening to tell people he's a pervert because he witnessed her trying to shake down one of the artisans at a previous festival for a free ring."

"Yeah, he said she threatened to send her father after him, but I've never known Richard to be all that frightening," Thistle agreed.

"Don't talk with your mouth full," Chief Terry complained as he watched Thistle mow through his pickle. "I know you were taught better manners than that."

Thistle cast him a sidelong look. "Seriously, what is your deal? Did Aunt Winnie shut down access to the love machine?"

Even though I was grossed out — and a little amused — I found myself staring at Chief Terry for answers. "Is she punishing you for wanting to ditch her in town the other day?"

"She's not punishing me." The expression on Chief Terry's face signaled he was likely lying. "She was tired last night ... and this morning ... and she didn't even make French toast like she normally would." His eyes darkened. "I blame you for this."

My eyes went wide. "What did I do?"

"Not you." He flashed a smile for my benefit. "I'm talking about Landon. He started the conversation about ditching her in front of the diner. She overheard and now she's blaming me. I'm innocent."

"I don't particularly remember you being all that innocent that day," Landon argued. "The way I remember it, I was the good one and Bay totally got me in trouble with her mom." He poked my side. "I still owe you for that, by the way."

"You can punish me later," I offered.

"Don't tempt me."

"And don't make me lock you up," Chief Terry warned. "I can only take so much. I'm at the end of my rope here, people."

"Geez, you'd think you'd be able to make it more than a day without sex after you were a lonely bachelor so long," Thistle said.

If looks could kill, Chief Terry would've burned her face off with his blazing eyes. "Stop talking, Thistle," he gritted out.

I had to press my lips together to keep from laughing, and when I averted my gaze I found Hunter watching me. His stare wasn't that of a predator, or even someone interested in a bit of flirting. No, he was digging for something deeper, and it was then that I realized Stormy had likely told him the truth.

Landon redirected the conversation. "What other perverts did you talk to?"

"Well, Todd told us that Old Man Lintz liked to show his wand to people, but it turned out it was really a wand and he just liked to threaten kids with it because he gets off on making them cry."

"I could've told you that," Chief Terry muttered.

"Then Old Man Lintz told us that Chad Torkelson at the post office enjoyed lewdly licking stamps when teenage girls were around," I continued.

"Turns out you haven't had to lick stamps in years," Thistle interjected.

Landon grinned. "Was your whole day chasing dead ends?"

I shrugged. "I don't know. Rumors start for a reason, right? Chad Torkelson said teenagers don't even go into the post office, but they do make eyes at Keith Vick."

"He's the UPS delivery driver," Chief Terry volunteered.

"The dude in the weird little shorts?" Landon made a face. "He could be a pervert. I've never understood those shorts."

"They're part of the summer uniform."

"He wears them in the winter."

"Well ... maybe the truck gets hot." Chief Terry shook his head. "I've never heard anyone complain about him. He doesn't throw packages on the porch in the run-up to Christmas like those jerky drivers you see on television. He's a quiet guy who keeps to himself."

"So was Jeffrey Dahmer," Hunter volunteered, causing me to laugh.

"Don't add to this insanity," Chief Terry warned, though there was a twinkle in his eyes. I was his favorite — I never doubted that — but he had a soft spot for Hunter, who looked at him as a law enforcement god. I wasn't completely up on the situation, but apparently Hunter's father, the former chief of police in Shadow Hills, abused his authority. Hunter refused to work for him, instead joining with Chief Terry to take him down, and now served as one of the few law enforcement figures in town. Chief Terry had great respect for him, which meant I did too.

"Sorry." Hunter held up his hands in surrender, a small smile playing around the corners of his mouth.

"Keith directed us toward Carl Schumer," Thistle explained.

"He makes the stained-glass pieces for the festival," Chief Terry said for Landon's benefit.

"We're pretty sure he's gay," I said.

"Definitely gay," Thistle agreed. "I gave him a clear shot to look down my shirt and he didn't even bother."

"Maybe you're not his type," Landon suggested.

Thistle rolled her eyes. "I'm everybody's type."

He snorted.

"I am," she insisted. "You know you were hot for me the first time you saw me. Don't bother denying it."

Landon's mouth dropped open and he immediately looked to me. "That is not true."

"Of course it's not." I patted his arm and glared at Thistle. "Don't get him worked up. You know he's a bear when you throw him like that."

Thistle was hardly apologetic. "Hey, I have to get my giggles from somewhere. I've been good for two full days. What do you want from me?"

"She has a point," I said to Landon. "Just ignore her. She's annoyed with Marcus because he said she was hovering. She's trying to get her groove back. You can't expect her to be good all day."

Landon sighed. "Is that it? Did you talk to any other perverts?"

"Carl pointed us to Ben Thomas at the ice cream store," I replied. "He looked to be flirting with two teenagers when we came in. He straightened up right away and acted like nothing was going on."

Landon's eyebrows drew together. "Are you talking about the young guy who told me it was sacrilegious to mix Mackinac Island Fudge with Chocolate Chip Cookie Dough that one time?"

"That *is* sacrilegious," Chief Terry said. "Everybody knows you can't mix Mackinac Island Fudge with anything else. What's wrong with you?"

"I like both," Landon replied. "Besides, it's nowhere near as gross as Bay mixing Superman with Blue Moon."

"Hey!" I pinched his flank. "I'm just sitting here being good. You're not supposed to be mean. Was that you paying me back for the thing with Mom? If so, I guess it's okay."

"Your punishment for the thing with your mother will come when we're alone," Landon said. "As for the ice cream, you have the palate of a child. No adult eats Superman ice cream."

"You love it when I have a blue tongue."

His smiled. "That is kind of fun."

"Knock it off!" Chief Terry threw a napkin at Landon's head. "You guys are in heat of late and I can't stand it."

"We're celebrating our engagement," Landon countered. "How can that be bad?"

"Knock it off or I'll knock you in the head."

"I think he's serious," Thistle said as she began rooting around Chief Terry's plate for something to munch. "Why didn't you ask for more pickles?"

"I'm not talking to you." Chief Terry held up his hand and focused on me. "Do you think Ben is a possibility as our kidnapper?"

I didn't have an answer. "I honestly don't know. He could've been flirting with the girls. He's, like, twenty-four, though. He might have just been talking to them."

"We can still question him," Landon said. "It can't hurt to see if he acts nervous around us. Do you want us to check in with any of the other perverts?"

I rolled my shoulders, noncommittal. "I don't know. They all seemed on the up and up. It's hard to tell."

"Yes, perverts never look like perverts," Landon agreed.

"Except Albert Einstein," I said.

Landon's lips curved down. "I don't think Albert Einstein was a pervert."

"Tell him, Thistle," I instructed as I turned my attention to the door when the bell above alerted that somebody was entering. To my surprise, it was Aunt Tillie, and she didn't waste time heading straight for us.

"This doesn't look good," I muttered, sitting straighter in my seat. "Whatever you've done, we're not serving as alibis," I blurted when she reached the side of the table.

"I'm an innocent old lady," Aunt Tillie replied, flashing a sweet smile at Chief Terry, Hunter, and Landon in turn. "I don't appreciate you impugning my reputation."

"I'm pretty sure you do that yourself," Landon muttered.

"Who are you trying to fool?" Thistle challenged. "Everybody here knows you."

Aunt Tillie covered the side of her mouth so Landon couldn't see, but her idea of a whisper would've served as a normal speaking tone for anybody else. "I have to talk in code because of the 'The Man.'" She jabbed her finger in Landon's direction. "He'll arrest me if he gets the chance."

"Oh, geez." Landon rubbed his forehead. "Can you make her stop?" His eyes were imploring when they locked with mine.

"I haven't managed to so far. I don't expect things to change anytime soon." I turned my attention to Aunt Tillie. "What are you doing here?"

"Rallying my posse." She was matter-of-fact. "I've been spying on Margaret all day." She fell silent, her brow furrowing as we waited for her to continue. "I mean I was minding my own business and walking down the sidewalk."

"Just tell us," Landon snapped.

Aunt Tillie pretended she didn't hear him and leaned closer to Thistle. "We're outnumbered by cops. Have you noticed that?"

"Actually, there are three of them and three of us," Thistle noted. "I think we can take them."

"The fed counts as two cops."

"I still think we can take them."

Aunt Tillie straightened. "It doesn't matter how I stumbled across the news. Suffice it to say, Brian Butthead Kelly and Margaret are heading out to the Lakin house. Willa and Rosemary may or may not be meeting them. I had trouble hearing that part. He either said he was getting solar panels for the roof or he was meeting his future wife."

"How are those similar?"

She pretended she didn't hear me. "If you want to figure out what they're doing, now would be a good time. They'll drop their guard by the house. We can listen ... and there are plenty of places to hide bodies out there. I bet some of the holes that they dug when looking for buried treasure are still available."

It seemed a fool's quest, but still ... . I looked at Thistle. "What do you think?"

"I think we should get our food to go." She was already on her feet. "I'm in the mood to kick some butt. That's a foursome who deserves a butt-kicking. What could possibly go wrong?"

22
TWENTY-TWO

I expected Landon to at least force me to promise not to get arrested before I left the diner. Instead, he gave me a kiss and told me to have fun. That was it. No lecture. No demand that I text him. Of course, spying on Mrs. Little rarely ended in a life-threatening situation. Rarely wasn't never, though.

"Do you think Landon is going soft?" I asked when we parked in the woods near the Lakin house. Our entry point had been a debate — Thistle thought we should park on the side of the lake closest to our destination, but Aunt Tillie said we should park at the campground on the opposite side and use magic to power a canoe to get close.

Thistle snorted. "Going soft? What is that even supposed to mean?"

"He used to be more, you know, growly when we were going to spy on people. We had to sneak around. Now he thinks it's fine and dandy and sends me on my way to break the law with a happy wave and kiss."

"You make it sound like that's a bad thing," Thistle argued as she took a step back from the car and slid her gaze to Aunt Tillie. "Shouldn't you hide it or something?"

Aunt Tillie rolled her eyes. "Why don't you hide it?"

"I don't know how to do that sort of magic."

"Then why should I do it?"

"Oh, geez," I muttered. "I'll do it. Give me a break."

AMANDA M. LEE

Aunt Tillie hurried to step in front of me. "I want to do it. I just wanted Thistle to beg a bit."

"I have no intention of begging," Thistle shot back. "This was your idea. You owe us a hidden car."

"I paid for your lunch."

"Bay paid for lunch."

"Chief Terry paid for lunch," I corrected. "It's not a big deal. I can hide the car."

"I said I would do it." The look Aunt Tillie shot me was darker than I expected. "Just because you're the new big witch in town doesn't mean I can't do a simple camouflage spell."

"*Whoo-ee*," Thistle said, her face lighting with amusement. "I think someone has her panties in a bunch because your powers have been expanding, Bay." She looked far too gleeful for my comfort level.

"It's not a big deal," I reassured Aunt Tillie. "Don't worry."

It was the exact wrong thing to say. Aunt Tillie's eyes flared with disgust. "Do I look worried to you?"

"You look ... like my favorite great-aunt, a woman I love dearly."

"Oh, that's not saying anything." Aunt Tillie's lip curled. "Your only other choice is Willa, but a rabid porcupine with syphilis would be preferable to her."

She had a point. Still, it seemed as if I should say something to soothe her, but I had no idea what to say. "Um ... do you want to go spy on Mrs. Little now? She might trip or something. That always makes you happy."

"Stuff it." Aunt Tillie started to stomp away, but she remembered the camouflage for the car at the last minute and threw up an easy glamour to hide it from prying eyes. I was annoyed when I fell into step with Thistle behind her.

"Did you have to bring that up?"

Thistle was seemingly unbothered by Aunt Tillie's mood. "I did. The old loon is no longer the top witch. I freaking love it."

"She's still more powerful than me." I meant it. "I can do a few things she can't, but in the grand scheme of things she's more knowledgeable."

"Or she just wants us to believe that."

"Meaning?"

"Meaning ever since we were three and could understand the nonsense coming out of her mouth she's done nothing but talk up how powerful she is. There's one problem with that. People who are truly powerful never have to go around saying they're powerful. Only people with ego problems tell anybody who will listen that they can turn them into dust with a flick of their wrist."

"I don't remember her using that threat."

"I do. It was Christmas 1997. I wanted a BB gun and she made me watch *A Christmas Story* ten times in a row to show me how things would turn out if I actually got one."

Something niggled in the back of my mind. "I vaguely remember that Christmas."

"Yes, well, she was fighting with Mrs. Little one day and I finally had an idea to get her on my side for the BB gun. I told her that if I received it as a gift, she could use it on Mrs. Little and blame me if there was any fallout. But Mrs. Little heard us talking, and there was a big thing ... and Aunt Tillie said she didn't need a gun because she could just use her wrist."

"I do kind of remember Mom being mad about that now that you bring it up. We were all forbidden from getting BB guns after that."

"Yeah, Aunt Tillie ruined it for everyone."

I smirked and looked ahead on the trail. Aunt Tillie had her head down and seemed to be focused on the ground. "We're going to miss her when she's gone," I reminded Thistle in a low voice. "She's still the most powerful witch in the family, no matter how you like to tease her."

"She's not, but it hardly matters." Thistle increased her pace. "Come on. She's in the sort of mood where she'll level the house rather than find a bush to hide behind. That won't go over well with the new owners."

"No, but I would enjoy it."

She let loose a low chuckle. "It would be kind of fun."

It took us a few seconds to catch up with Aunt Tillie, and by the time we reached the driveway of our destination I was already thinking ahead. "We should head over there." I pointed toward the west side of the house. "There are thick bushes and they won't be able to see us from anywhere but the second story."

"I don't see why we have to hide," Thistle argued. "We can always say we were out for a walk and got turned around."

"They won't believe that."

"It doesn't matter. They'll have to prove malicious intent in front of a judge. The odds of that happening when we've got Aunt Tillie with us seem pretty slim. She can plead diminished capacity because of her age."

"I'm going to plead diminished capacity on your ass if you're not careful," Aunt Tillie warned. "Bay's right. We'll head toward the bushes." She didn't slow her pace, but when she started up the steep incline she began to fall back.

"Hey now." I hurried to catch her. "Where do you think you're going?"

"I can walk by myself." She struggled away from me, tried again, and slid down the same embankment.

"It's your shoes," Thistle offered after a moment's study, her eyes going to Aunt Tillie's boots. "The soles are smooth. Where did you get those things?"

"From an army surplus store."

"A legit one?"

"Of course it's legit. These are the shoes Green Berets wear."

I had my doubts, but this wasn't the time for a sartorial argument. "Let's just get up the hill." I started to push at Aunt Tillie's back. "You climb and we'll push you up."

"I said I could do it!"

"Well, you're not," Thistle argued. "You need to get it together and let us help you. I mean … geez." She joined me in pushing Aunt Tillie up the hill. Unfortunately, the higher Aunt Tillie got, the better look we got at her leggings. With her shirt riding up, we found ourselves staring into the abyss of what was probably a sugar skull at one time but now resembled a two-toothed grin.

"Oh, geez." Thistle put her back into the push but her hands continued slipping. "I'm letting go in a second," she warned.

"Don't you dare," Aunt Tillie hissed. Apparently she was now in favor of us pushing her up the hill. "If I fall I'll break a hip."

"You're only two feet higher than you were," I pointed out, sweat breaking out on my top lip. "Man, what have you been eating? It's like pushing Clove up a hill."

"You're on my list!"

We were so lost in what we were doing — and really, it shouldn't have been so difficult dealing with one elderly lady — that we didn't hear the footsteps behind us until too late. The sound of a clearing throat made me turn … and I found four faces watching us with interest.

"Hello." I racked my brain for an explanation and came up empty. "We're just … ."

"Selling Girl Scout Cookies," Thistle interjected, using her shoulder to balance Aunt Tillie's body weight. "How do you feel about some Thin Mints?"

Rosemary folded her arms across her chest and openly glared. "What are you doing here?"

"I believe we just told you," Thistle replied, doubling down on the lie.

"Help me down," Aunt Tillie barked. "I'll smite them."

I didn't want to deal with the cleanup from that, so I continued to push her up the hill even though my arms were beginning to ache. "We're conducting a survey of the property," I explained. "It's part of an ongoing series I'm doing at the newspaper."

"And it involves a survey of property?" Brian asked. He seemed less amused than the others. Something dark lurked in the depths of his eyes and it made me distinctly uncomfortable.

"Yes." I scrambled. "We thought it would be fun to compare old survey markers with new ones."

"And who is paying for all these surveys?"

"We're doing them ourselves."

"Aunt Tillie is a surveyor in her free time," Thistle added.

"I could do it professionally, full time if I wanted," Aunt Tillie said. "But that would get in the way of my Rapture preparations."

"We're putting together a zombie team," Thistle explained. "We're full up, so none of you will make the cut."

"None," Aunt Tillie readily agreed. "We might let Rosemary temporarily join because she's fresh meat, but I have to warn you, she'll be the first one we shoot to distract the zombies before we make a break for it."

"At least you get to be on the team," Thistle said brightly.

"Knock it off." Brian moved as if he was going to push through Thistle and me to grab Aunt Tillie, but we shook our heads in tandem.

"I wouldn't," Thistle warned.

"She'll chew you up and spit you out," I added.

"Like the shark in *Jaws*," Aunt Tillie agreed before letting loose a hiss that reminded me of a constipated snake.

"Okay, I think we should call the police." Brian dug in his pocket for his phone. "This is a no-trespassing zone."

"Who are you kidding?" Mrs. Little challenged. "Terry will never arrest them, especially this one." She pointed at me. "As for the FBI agent, he'll lie and cover this up. That's what he does."

Intrigue lit Brian's features, making him even uglier. "I don't suppose you have proof of that, do you? I have a few contacts with the state police, and I just bet they'd love a chance to take down a dirty FBI agent."

My heart skipped a beat. "You wouldn't dare."

"Oh, no?" Brian was incredulous. "Your boyfriend stole my birthright and gave it to you. You have no idea how happy paying him back would make me."

I swallowed hard, fear bubbling up. "Is that why you came back? Is this all an elaborate set-up to get payback against us?"

"You'd like to think that, wouldn't you?" Rosemary sneered. "You're incapable of accepting the fact that we're in love and looking to start a new life. You don't think I'm good enough for him."

"Actually, it's the exact opposite." My hands were sweaty and I knew I was about to lose my grip on Aunt Tillie. If we let her down, the magic — and curses — would start flying. I wasn't prepared to deal with the fallout. Things were bad enough. "He's not good enough for you."

"Oh, whatever." Rosemary threw up her hands. "Just get out of here."

She was giving us an escape hatch, and I was more than willing to take it. Brian had other plans.

"No. I want this on record." He was firm, Aunt Willa and Mrs. Little nodding to encourage him. "Even if they don't do anything, they have to file a report. I want that later."

What did he have planned for later? I desperately wanted to ask. "Go ahead and call." At this point, the worst that could happen was a lecture. "We really were surveying the land for a story."

"You're a horrible liar," Brian hissed.

"Let me down." Aunt Tillie started struggling. "I'll handle this. I'll curse that twig in his pants and make it fall off. Even wild animals won't go near it because it will be so foul when I'm done with him."

Brian was full of bravado, but I saw him shift his groin so Aunt Tillie didn't have an open shot. Before I could admonish her to keep her mouth shut, a wailing filled the air and I jerked up my head. The sound caused the hair on the back of my neck to stand on end.

"Now what?" Aunt Willa complained, looking toward the woods. "Is somebody with you? I'll just bet that's Clove. She always did like to whine."

Clove did indeed like to whine, but she wasn't making the noise. It was coming from someone else. Or, rather, something else.

I stopped pushing Aunt Tillie and allowed her to fall back. Thistle, perhaps picking up on my worry, didn't offer a second of argument as we caught Aunt Tillie and dragged her to the ground.

"What is it?" Aunt Tillie was no longer interested in fighting the others. Her expression told me that she understood the rules of the game had changed.

"I think it's the shadow monster," I replied, scanning the woods. The screeching continued.

"You killed the shadow monster," Aunt Tillie argued. "I saw you."

"Unless I didn't. Maybe the ghosts just ripped it apart and it somehow reconstituted itself."

"But ... ." Aunt Tillie didn't get a chance to finish because Brian, jerk that he was, decided to take over the conversation.

"Oh, so now we're dealing with a monster?" He shook his head. "You aren't fooling anybody. Nobody believes this magic nonsense. In fact ... ." His last words were cut off as the shadow monster swooped into the clearing from the woods almost directly behind us and headed straight for him. The creature's eyes flashed with malevolent fury as it knocked him sideways.

What a stupid idiot.

For a moment I thought someone had said the words, but then I realized it wasn't a voice as much as a thought in my head. The sentiment was emanating from the creature, but it hadn't spoken.

"Omigod!" Rosemary's hand flew to her mouth. "What is that?"

I didn't have time to explain, so I did the only thing I could and gave Aunt Willa a terrific shove. "Get in the house!"

Aunt Willa slapped at my hand. "Don't tell me what to do!"

I was at my limit. "Get in the house!" My hair rippled as the magic coursed through me. I couldn't waste time with Aunt Willa. The creature needed to be stopped, and this time I was determined to question it. I would need help.

"*Come,*" I intoned, my voice echoing as I raised my hand to the sky. Energy crackled at the ends of my fingertips and a terrific flash of lightning filled the sky as the ground shook with the rumble of thunder.

"Well, that's new," Thistle said, her eyes going wide as she grabbed Aunt Tillie's shoulder. "Can you do that, old lady?"

"You're going to take up every spot on my list if you're not careful," Aunt Tillie warned, her voice faint over the whipping wind.

"I'm not worried about that as long as these idiots are in town." Thistle gestured toward Aunt Willa and Rosemary, but her eyes never moved from my face. "I hope you know what you're doing."

It was too late to second guess myself. I wouldn't have even if I could.

The ghosts I'd summoned swarmed across the lake, no more than blurs, manic energy driving them. I intended to instruct them to hold the shadow monster, but the creature seemed to understand it was outnumbered. It backed away from Brian, who was a blubbering mess on the ground, and stared at me for what felt like a year encased in a second. Then it was gone, a black blur on the wind as it raced toward the woods. The ghosts gave chase, even as Rosemary threw herself on Brian and declared him her "sweetie-bear" who she couldn't love more because of his bravery.

"It's okay, Bay." Aunt Tillie tentatively tugged on my raised arm and dragged it down. Her face was pale, but she didn't look worried or even surprised by what had happened. "You did a good job."

What was I supposed to say?

"I'm calling the police." Aunt Willa dug in her pocket for her phone. "You'll be arrested for sure this time. I hope you like prison food, because that's all you're going to get for the rest of your life."

23

TWENTY-THREE

Landon's cop face was firmly in place when he arrived with Chief Terry. Brian, standing to the side with Rosemary, started complaining the second they were in earshot.

"I want them arrested for trespassing," he announced.

"And I want you out of this town," Landon replied. "I don't think either of us is going to get what we want." He headed directly for me and hunkered down in front of the log on which I sat. He looked serious. "Are you okay?"

I nodded and forced a smile. "You don't have to worry about me."

"Obviously that's not true." He pressed his hand to my forehead, taking me by surprise. "Why are you so hot?"

I tried for levity. "Oh, that's the sweetest thing you've ever said to me."

He didn't smile. "You feel as if you have a fever."

"I'm fine." That was true. I didn't feel sick as much as shaky. The magic that had flowed through me, however briefly, had dissipated fast and now I felt as if I'd run a marathon.

Landon held my gaze for a beat and then nodded. "We'll talk about it at home." When he stood, his hands were on his hips and his gaze was cool. "Who can tell me what happened here?"

Aunt Tillie's hand shot in the air.

Landon ignored her. "Anybody?"

Aunt Tillie waved her hand to get his attention, and when he sighed, I knew he was resigned to listening to her spin a tale.

"It was like this," Aunt Tillie started. "We were minding our own business selling Girl Scout cookies ... ."

I groaned and buried my face in my hands.

"You were selling Girl Scout cookies?" Chief Terry asked.

"That's a thing," Aunt Tillie snapped. "What don't you people get about that?"

"I thought we agreed we were surveying property?" Thistle challenged. "I know I started the Girl Scout thing, but in hindsight it sounds iffy."

"That was Bay's excuse. The Girl Scout cookie thing is better. I've always thought I would look smashing in one of those uniforms."

"Oh, geez." Landon rubbed his hand over his throat, giving me the brief impression that he was considering giving it a squeeze to knock himself out rather than continue listening. Aunt Tillie took advantage of the momentary lull.

"Anyway, we were minding our own business and these ... people ... showed up out of nowhere and threatened to kill us."

That was an outright lie.

"We said we didn't want to die and then they called you," she continued. "I think it's a bit extreme to threaten to kill people over accidentally wandering onto property while selling cookies but that's just me."

"You can't possibly be falling for this," Aunt Willa interjected. "It's ludicrous. They're traipsing around private property. If you want to know what I think — and you haven't asked because you're giving them special treatment, as usual — they were plotting to hide in the bushes and ambush us when we came out so they could kill us."

"I see ridiculous rhetoric runs in the family," Chief Terry drawled. "Why would they want to kill you?"

"They're upset about us buying this house. We know they wanted it. They plan to buy up the property surrounding the lake and turn it into some Winchester stronghold."

Chief Terry hiked an eyebrow. "Who told you that?"

Aunt Willa worked her jaw in the same manner Aunt Tillie often did, and for the first time I saw a strong familial resemblance. It was jarring. "Margaret might've mentioned it," she hedged.

Mrs. Little stirred. "I said no such thing. What I said was that Bay and Landon bought the property across the lake because they were looking for the treasure, but I didn't say that."

"You did," Aunt Willa challenged.

"I did not."

"You did."

Landon cleared his throat to break up the argument. "I was under the impression that the pirate treasure story was made up."

"It is," Aunt Tillie offered. "I should know. I made it up."

"That's just what she wants us to believe," Mrs. Little argued. "Have you considered that she's only saying that to try to dissuade me from looking? It's something she would do."

"It is something I would do," Aunt Tillie agreed. "The thing is, making up a story about pirate treasure so I can watch you dig holes all through the woods is also something I would do. Oh, wait, it's something I already did."

"I don't believe her." Mrs. Little crossed her arms over her chest, adamant. "She's messing with me."

"I think she's done a wonderful job messing with you," Chief Terry acknowledged. "Out of curiosity, is that the reason you bought this property, Mr. Kelly? Do you think there's pirate treasure here?"

Brian looked exasperated. "Of course not. I'm a big fan of the location and architecture. The fact that Bay and Landon want the property doesn't matter to me in the slightest."

"That's good," Landon supplied. "Because we don't want the property."

Brian stilled. "Why wouldn't you? It's far superior to the property you have over there." He gestured toward the camp, which did look a little dumpy with its sagging buildings and discarded canoes that needed to be rounded up and disposed of.

"It will be at least one year — more likely two — before we start building," Landon said. "We haven't even picked out a design. As for why we prefer that property, it turns out Bay and I met there as children. I visited with my brothers when I was a kid and she happened to be there. We interacted, apparently there was some flirting, and I consider that the place we fell in love."

That was a bit of a stretch. "We were barely teenagers," I reminded him.

"Something happened that day, and it led us to each other as adults. That's what I care about, and that's why we prefer that property."

Brian looked downright depressed. "I thought you wanted a house out here right away."

"Sorry to disappoint you." Landon's smile was benign but there was mirth in his eyes. "We're exactly where we want to be."

"Why does it even matter?" Rosemary challenged as she studied Brian's profile. There was suspicion there, and I was happy to see it. "I thought you said this house was perfect for us and our needs."

Brian recovered quickly. "I did say that, and I meant it. I love the house and the location. I love you." He grinned at her. If I hadn't been suspicious of him before, I would've been tipped over into "he's up to something" territory thanks to that one look.

"None of this is important," Aunt Willa protested. "Who wants the house for what doesn't matter at all. What is important is that they were trespassing."

Landon made a big show of looking around. "Where are the signs?"

"What signs?"

"The ones admonishing people not to trespass."

"I ... we don't need signs."

"This is a wilderness area," Chief Terry interjected. "When hiking in the woods, it's very difficult to tell the border between state land and private property."

"The house is right there!" Brian exploded, pointing for emphasis.

"Yes, but I'm old," Aunt Tillie said. "I don't see as well as I used to. They say one of the first things to go when you hit middle age is your eyesight. On top of that, I have an allergy and my eyes can't take too much oxygen and we're surrounded by oxygen out here."

"Middle age?" Brian was beside himself. "You have one foot already in the grave, you old bat, and I for one can't wait until you have both feet in because you're a hag of the highest order."

Thistle and I both started for him. Aunt Tillie might be a pain — okay, she's definitely a pain — but she's still our great-aunt and there was no way we would let him insult her.

"Hold on." Landon snagged me around the waist before I could throw myself on Brian. "Where do you think you're going?"

"Don't even think about it," Chief Terry warned, extending a finger in Thistle's face. "Do you want to make things worse?

"I want them arrested," Mrs. Little insisted. "All three of them. They're menaces and this town will be better off without them."

"First, you have no say in this," Landon pointed out. "You're not the property owner."

"I am, and I want them arrested," Brian snapped.

Landon ignored him. "Second, this seems to have been a case of errant hiking. They clearly didn't realize they'd strayed so far off state land." The look he shot me said I'd better agree with him.

"We got lost," I seconded.

"And here I thought you were surveying the land," Rosemary said in her snottiest voice.

"We were surveying our property," I said, an idea forming. "Landon and I have been debating where we want to place the house when it comes time to build. Aunt Tillie and Thistle came with me because they're fans of the construction process."

Aunt Tillie agreed. "There's little I love more than hammering things."

"Am I to take it that you're not going to do anything?" Mrs. Little challenged, her gaze on Chief Terry. "I just want to be sure when I file my complaint with the state police."

My heart rolled. It was just like her to pull something like this. "Leave them alone," I ordered. "If you feel you need to file charges, file them against me."

"That's not happening," Landon said. "You were confused. There was no malice intended."

"No malice?" Brian's cheeks had turned a mottled red. I briefly wondered if he might give himself a stroke he was so worked up. "If there was no malice, how do you explain that ... black creature ... that came out of the woods and attacked me?"

Landon's expression never changed. "Black creature?"

"It was some sort of shadow," Rosemary volunteered. "Like in *Peter Pan*. I think one of them turned their shadow into a monster and had it attack us. I heard it. The thing called Brian an idiot."

I snapped my head in her direction, stunned. How could she have heard? The creature didn't speak out loud.

"It didn't say anything," Thistle argued blankly. "It just swooped in from the trees and headed straight for him. I think it has excellent jerk radar."

Landon darted a look at me before turning back to Brian. "Do you really expect me to note in an official report that one of these women somehow harnessed a shadow to attack you?"

"You can play dumb as much as you want, but everybody knows they're freaks," Brian hissed. "That crazy old lady gave me a variety of rashes in my ... private area ... when I lived here before. She bragged about it."

"I would never brag about that." Aunt Tillie was solemn. "That's minor magic. It's not worth bragging about."

"Shh." Chief Terry lightly cuffed the back of her head.

"I'm more than willing to write up a report and present it to the prosecutor," Landon offered, shifting gears. "We'll start with Bay, Thistle, and Aunt

Tillie getting lost in the woods and end with the shadow monster trying to strangle you. That will go over well."

Brian was apoplectic when he took a menacing step toward Landon, his hands clenched into fists at his sides. "I know what you're doing."

"You mean my job? Yes, I'm good at it."

"Whoa, there." Chief Terry moved to intercept Brian. "You don't want to move any closer to him. It could be seen as aggression toward an officer."

"You'd like that, wouldn't you?" Brian shook his head. "I want a report filed. I don't care if you think we're crazy. It's my right and that's what I want."

Chief Terry held up his right hand. "I'll get my notebook and we'll write up your report. Anything to make you happy."

CHIEF TERRY TOOK THE STATEMENTS. The moment there was a lull in the conversation, Landon dragged me toward the woods to ask the obvious question.

"I thought you killed the shadow monster. Why is it back?"

"I don't know." That was only one of a number of questions running through my mind. "It came out of nowhere and immediately went for Brian."

"And it spoke?"

I hesitated and then shook my head. "No. It thought that Brian was an idiot. I thought it spoke too, but it didn't. That was something going through its head, not something spoken."

"Then how did Rosemary hear it?"

That was the question. "I honestly don't know. I mean ... it's possible she has magic in her veins."

"I was under the impression that the magic moved through the females in your family. Your grandmother wasn't Willa's mother, so how does Rosemary have magic?"

Ah, another good question. "I don't know that she does. It's possible she has a little psychic vibe or something. She might not be a full-fledged witch. I just ... don't know."

He leaned in to press a comforting kiss to my forehead. "I'm sorry. I shouldn't be yelling at you. This whole thing is unbelievable."

"It is," I agreed. "I don't know what to say about any of it."

He was quiet for a moment before offering up a small smile. "You weren't supposed to get caught."

"Definitely not," I agreed. "It turns out that Aunt Tillie can't climb a hill in her boots. By the way, those sugar skull leggings are unfortunate when you're looking up at them."

He chuckled. "I'm so used to her that I can't even get upset about the leggings. You know we're going to have to show this report to the prosecutor."

That didn't bother me. "The prosecutor's office hates Mrs. Little because she's constantly filing complaints. As soon as they see her name, they'll ignore the report. When you add the shadow monster, it won't amount to anything."

"That's why I decided to embrace the report. The thing is ... I expect them to file complaints with my office when this is over."

I hadn't considered that, and suddenly my stomach was an endless pit of dread. "I'm so sorry."

"Sweetie, don't." He shook his head. "These are terrible people who like to stir up trouble. My boss is well aware. It won't come to anything, but I might have to head over there for an afternoon to explain what happened."

"And what will you tell him?"

"That you guys got into a fight with relatives and this is all personal. He's met you. More importantly, he's met Aunt Tillie. It'll be okay." He moved his arms around my back and pulled me tight for a hug. "I don't want you worrying about this."

"I don't want you paying for something we did."

"Well ... we're a unit. There's no getting around that. I don't care what Brian Kelly tells my boss, so you can stop worrying about that."

I rested my head on his chest and nodded. "I love you, Landon."

"I love you too."

I absorbed his warmth for a moment longer and then pulled back. "The shadow monster sounded like a teenage girl. That's the inflection it used and the disdain was almost palpable." I barreled forward. "All I can think about is Dani," I said, referring to a local witch I had tried to help but ultimately felt the need to cut loose because she was beyond helping. "Can you make sure she hasn't snuck back into town?"

"I can try. She's smart enough to fly under the radar. I thought you guys stripped her magic. How could she be doing this without magic?"

"We didn't strip her magic. We stripped her ability to use her magic. It's possible she found someone to reverse the spell. It would be difficult but not altogether impossible."

"Okay." He rubbed his thumb against my cheek. "I'll see if I can find her. There's another option that you seem to be overlooking, though. There are a lot of other teenagers in Hemlock Cove — including a missing one. One of them could be providing the magic for this."

I hadn't overlooked that possibility. "I want to rule out Dani. While you're doing that, I'll check out the other teens in this particular circle, because you're absolutely right. One of them could be responsible."

He decided to look on the bright side of things. "At least it's a place to look."

"Yeah. I ... ." The sound of screeching and splashing drew my attention to the lake's edge. Aunt Tillie and Aunt Willa were apparently trying to drown each other in the lake.

"You're the devil," Aunt Willa snapped, throwing herself on Aunt Tillie and causing both of them to tip into the water. "My life would've been so much better if you were never born."

"Oh, no." Aunt Tillie was wet but determined. "I'm the one who would be better off. You're like the wet fart of life. You're noisy, messy, and stinky. I'm so much better than you."

They continued grappling as Chief Terry strode toward them. "Are you going to help?" he barked at Landon.

"Is it wrong that I kind of want to see who wins?" Landon asked me.

I had no doubt who would win. "If Aunt Tillie kills Aunt Willa, you'll have to file more than one report."

"There is that." He sighed. "I'm coming. Don't let them bite each other. Aunt Tillie isn't above it."

"Oh, I know that from personal experience."

I remained in my spot, resigned to letting Landon and Chief Terry sort things out. When I risked a glance at Rosemary, I found her watching me with unreadable eyes. Did she know what she heard? Was she aware she was different? Could she have been faking all this time?

I had many questions and precious few answers.

24

TWENTY-FOUR

L andon walked us back to the hidden car, frowning when we stopped in what he saw as an empty clearing. His eyes went wide when Aunt Tillie dropped the glamour.

"Magic is amazing."

I laughed because he seemed so calm. "I bet you never thought you would end up here two years ago."

He slid his eyes to me, his fingers moving to my cheek. "Bay, I couldn't have dreamed big enough to encompass what you've given me."

I went warm all over and wrapped my fingers around his wrist. "How long are you going to be so romantic? The proposal fuel is going to burn out eventually, right?"

He shrugged. "Given how you respond, maybe I'll stay romantic forever."

"We'll end up with ten kids."

"I don't care."

"That means there will be no more romantic picnic blanket time until we're in our seventies."

He hesitated. "They'll probably steal my bacon, too."

"That's a foregone conclusion."

He smiled and leaned in, lowering his voice. "You've changed my world for the better. I don't want you worrying about whatever Brian is threatening to do."

"You might change your mind if he goes to your boss."

He fervently shook his head. "Nothing will ever change my mind about you. Don't worry about that."

I wasn't worried about his feelings changing. If he lost his job, something he loved, because of me, though, I would never get over the guilt. "Let's just focus on figuring out what's going on with the shadow monster. We can deal with Brian later."

He gave me a soft kiss. "Don't get worked up about this. It'll be fine."

I nodded. "We're going to head back to town. I'll be at the newspaper office. I want to enlist Viola for a job."

His eyebrow hiked. "Looking for a shadow monster?"

"I have to think that this monster has something to do with Amelia's disappearance."

"This whole thing doesn't make sense." Landon's expression shifted, going dark. "The ransom drop is tonight. We're going to talk to the Harts. I'll check on you when we get back to town."

"You don't have to. I can take care of myself."

"That's your mantra," he said. "Checking up on you isn't taking care of you. Believe it or not, I enjoy spending time with you."

"Is that code for you want to take a joint nap on my office couch?"

His grin was devastating. "You know me well."

I DROPPED THISTLE AT HYPNOTIC AND took Aunt Tillie to the newspaper office with me. I was going to suggest she sit in on my chat with Viola, but she had other ideas.

"I'll see you around." She gave me a half-wave before turning in the direction of the Unicorn Emporium.

"Where do you think you're going?" I asked, worrying taking over. "I don't think we need more trouble today."

"How do you know I'm going to get in trouble?"

"Because I've met you."

"That's cold, Bay. I practically raised you."

The comment seemed absurd on the surface but it wasn't entirely untrue. Aunt Tillie had spent oodles of time with us when we were kids. That only increased as we got older and our mothers decided to start their own business.

"You're right." I flashed a smile I didn't feel. "You would never get into trouble. What was I thinking?"

"I have no idea. I'm an angel."

"Just ... make sure you really don't find trouble today. We have enough going on."

"Yeah, yeah, yeah."

I checked the main door to make sure nobody had tampered with it before heading in. I didn't lock it behind me in case any of the advertisers wanted to stop by and instead headed straight for my office. Viola wasn't there, but I knew how to call her, and that's what I did once I settled at my desk and checked my email. She appeared immediately.

"*The Price is Right* is on."

"Isn't it on every day?"

"Yes, but this time both the final showcases look good."

"I'm sorry."

She stared at me for a moment, impatience oozing from her, and then held out her hands. "What?"

"I need a few things from you."

"You know, you always ask for favors of me — or use your magic to force me — but what do you offer me in return?"

"Well ... ." Guilt rolled through my stomach. My necromancer powers had increased my magic base tenfold, but it came at a cost ... and it was one I didn't have to pay. "I don't mean to force you to do things," I said finally. "When I call you it's only because I have no choice."

"I know that." Viola's expression was blank. "But I have a life, too. You think I just sit around and watch television all day, but there's more to me. I spy on people when I'm bored and look out for the town."

"You're definitely a good protector," I agreed.

"I am. I'm awesome."

"I would never say otherwise."

She shook her head. "Okay. You've kissed my ass enough. What do you want?"

"The first thing I need is for you to watch the office carefully. Someone tried to break into the building a few nights ago. Landon installed cameras and increased security, but nothing will keep someone out if they really want to get in."

"I already do that when I'm here."

"I know but ... something feels off." And that was the part I couldn't shake. "Between Amelia Hart going missing and Brian Kelly returning, the ground doesn't feel even."

"Brian?" Viola made a face. "What does he want?"

"I don't know." I'd been thinking about that and I'd come up with a partial answer. "I believe he thinks we stole this place from him, took his legacy. I'm pretty sure he's here for revenge."

"And how does he plan to get it?"

"I don't know. He's not the sort of person who comes at you from the front."

"Definitely not."

"He's sneaky. Whatever he has planned, we won't know until he's already made his move. That's why I want you to keep your eyes open when you're here."

"I'll do that, but he would have to be an idiot to break into this building with all the new cameras. On top of that, your boyfriend will kill him if he gets too close to you. Brian's a coward. He might talk a good game, but he's afraid of his own shadow. He won't do anything that risks Landon going toe-to-toe with him."

"Probably not, but if I've learned anything over the years it's that even cowards can lose their minds. Brian is the sort of person who shrinks in the face of adversity but grows when he feels he's been mistreated. He's the consummate victim."

"I see that. Do you think he broke into the office?"

"I don't know. That makes the best sense, and yet it was a boneheaded move."

"Well, don't worry." Viola squared her shoulders. "I'll totally beat the crap out of him if he shows up."

The declaration made me laugh. "A ghost beating him up will definitely scare him."

"You said there were two things you wanted to talk about," she prodded.

"Right." I bobbed my head. "The second thing is the shadow monster. It has appeared several times. I thought we destroyed it at Hollow Creek the other day, but obviously I was wrong."

"I'm not familiar with shadow monsters."

"Neither am I. I don't know if the creature that looked to be destroyed at the creek is the same one that attacked this morning. I don't know if someone is creating them, if they're sentient, or if they're simply empty puppets being controlled. Keep your ear to the ground. If you see anything, hear anything, find me right away."

"I can do that. Do you think this thing is dangerous to me?"

"It flees whenever it sees ghosts. It seems to recognize that it's outmatched. It only appears to be dangerous to humans."

"Then I'll definitely take it on." Viola beamed. "We're kind of like a magical crime-fighting team, aren't we?"

She seemed so happy at the prospect all I could do was nod. "We're definitely a team."

"And we have to keep Hemlock Cove safe."

"We do."

"Then you can count on me."

Her giving nature touched me. "Thank you."

"Hey, I love this town. Even the people I hate, I love to hate them."

"We'll figure it out." That was the only thing I was certain of. The alternative was too terrible to consider.

I WORKED ON MY COMPUTER FOR A FULL two hours before getting up to stretch. My back was killing me. I hadn't done much desk work the past few weeks — not that I ever did — and I was feeling the muscle fatigue.

Viola had taken off to look for the shadow monster. As much as I liked her — and I did — she wasn't conducive to a quiet working environment. I didn't expect to find anyone in the lobby when I crossed on my way to the lunchroom, so I was understandably taken aback when I found Brian sitting behind the empty desk near the front door, his feet propped up.

"I wondered if you would ever come out," he said.

I halted, my eyes darting to the door, which was shut. "What are you doing here?"

"I came to talk to you."

"You could've rung the bell." I inclined my head toward the bell sitting on the desk. "That's what most visitors do when they stop in."

"I'm not a normal visitor," he pointed out, his gaze sharp. "This is my building."

"Actually, it's my building. I bought it."

"You mean you stole it."

I should've been worried, but he was such a bombastic imbecile I couldn't work up the fear he clearly wanted me to feel. But I was leery. If he made a move, I would handle it.

"Is this about this morning?" I drifted to the front of the desk, placing the door to my back for an easy escape route.

"This morning was fun." He flashed a predatory smile. "I guess I should've known you guys would head out there. You can't help yourselves from poking your noses into other people's business."

"We don't make a habit of that, but you're a special case."

Brian beamed. "I do love being considered special."

"I'm sure that's true. You have a fragile ego, so even negative attention is welcome because you can't handle the thought of anyone not seeing you as important."

"Is that what you really think?"

"It's what I know."

"Well, that's disappointing." He made a tsking sound with his tongue. "I thought you were a student of human emotion. You clearly don't read people well."

I recognized what he was trying to do ... and he was horrible at it. "Right now you're upset that I've pegged you. The real problem is that you don't want to admit your shortcomings to yourself. Everybody has them. It's those who acknowledge them who have a chance to succeed. You pretend you're perfect, so you'll always be a failure for that fact alone."

His gaze darkened. "You want to be very careful what you say about me."

"Is that a threat?"

"It's a promise." He shifted in his chair, placing his feet on the ground and resting his elbows on the desk. He was no longer interested in pretending he was relaxed. Now he wanted to appear intimidating. That was fine with me. There was little I loved more than taking down a bully.

"I'm not afraid of you." My voice was clear and firm. "You don't frighten me. You can't. You don't even rank on the list of things I've faced."

"Like, that ... thing ... that you conjured to come after me this morning?"

He had lived in town long enough to know there was something different about my family, even if he didn't want to acknowledge it. The fact that he was placing it out there so easily made me suspicious, enough so that I reached out with my mind to nudge at him, looking for ... something. I wasn't sure what I was searching for until I found it. In his right hand, which he tried to keep hidden under his untucked shirt, he clutched his phone, which meant he was likely recording our conversation. Well, two could play at that game.

"You think I conjured something to come after you?" I let loose a hollow laugh. "That is ... really weird."

"I was there," he snapped. "I was almost strangled."

"That thing was weird," I agreed, appropriating a wide-eyed stare that I knew the phone couldn't pick up but would infuriate him all the same. "What do you think that was?"

"How should I know?"

"It went after you. I've never seen anything like it."

"I very much doubt that. You are the witch, after all."

My smile never wavered. "Everyone in Hemlock Cove is a witch. That's why I love this town. There's a real sense of camaraderie."

His eyes narrowed. "What are you doing?"

I ignored the question. "I think that's what you didn't understand when you took over the newspaper," I continued. "You looked at it as a business that could give you something. It was all about what The Whistler could do for you. You never once considered what you could give to the community. That's why you were never fully accepted."

"Is that a fact?" His voice was dangerously iced.

I let him see the amusement in my eyes, how I enjoyed playing with him. "You come from a big city. Things are different in a small community like this."

"I know what you're doing."

"What I want to know is what you're doing in my building. If you're not here to conduct business, why are you here?"

"To tell you my plans." Slowly, he got to his feet. His motions were exaggerated to the point he looked like a cartoon bad guy. I refused to cede my ground to him because I knew that's what he wanted. No, actually that's what he needed to feed his ego. Instead, I remained rooted to my spot.

"You have plans, do you? I'm shocked. I thought you getting engaged to my cousin was some sort of weird coincidence. At least we're finally getting close to the truth."

"I love Rosemary." He could play the game too, and he wanted me to know it. "She's the love of my life."

"I'm happy for you. I think that's another thing you were lacking when you were here before. The love of a good person can't be underestimated. It can change lives. There are plenty of good people around and many of them have found love. That doesn't always translate into contentment. When you find the right person, however, everything becomes clear. If Rosemary gives that to you, I couldn't be happier."

His scowl was pronounced. "Stop messing with me. I want to know what that thing was out at the house."

"How am I supposed to know?"

"You're a witch."

"Everybody in town plays at being witches. Maybe you should ask one of them, because I legitimately don't know."

"No one buys your innocent act."

"It's not an act. That thing went after you. Perhaps you're the one with the answers. You were the target."

"Because you targeted me." He took a step in my direction, his arms flexing.

I remained calm, but my heartbeat picked up a notch. "I have no interest in being around you." The sound of the door opening behind me really jumpstarted my heart rate, but only because I knew who was joining the party. I felt him the moment he moved into my space.

"What's going on here?" Landon asked as he took up position next to me. When I risked a glance in his direction, I found him glaring at Brian, his jaw clenched.

"Bay and I were just having a discussion about the newspaper," Brian replied, instantly deflating. Viola was right, I thought. He was terrified of Landon ... and rightly so. I could hurt him more, but he didn't realize it.

"You have nothing to do with this newspaper," Landon shot back. "It's her property. You don't belong here."

"We really shouldn't start arguing about people trespassing after this morning, should we?"

Tentatively, I reached out and touched Landon's arm. He patted my hand to tell me everything was okay, never looking away from Brian.

"Stay away from Bay." Landon's tone left no room for argument. "Don't look at her. Don't talk to her. Just ... don't even think about her."

"I've thought of little else but her since she stole my inheritance," Brian said, making a point of skirting around the opposite side of the desk to avoid Landon. "That's why I stopped in for a quick visit. I wanted her to know that I intend to reclaim what's mine."

Landon's lips curved. "Bay bought this business fair and square. If you move on her, I'll move on you."

"I don't think an FBI agent is supposed to threaten civilians."

"It wasn't a threat. You're in her private space trying to intimidate her. If you want to discuss what you believe is a threat, I suggest we take a trip to Traverse City. You can sit down with my boss and lay out your concerns."

Brian, clearly recognizing the challenge in Landon's eyes, shrank back. "I don't think that will be necessary."

"It's up to you. What's not up to you is Bay's safety. If I find you in here trying to terrorize her again, I will take you into custody."

"I'm not trying to terrorize her. We were just having a conversation."

"You're done having conversations." Landon started herding him toward the door. "If you come in here again, you'll be arrested. You've been warned."

"You can't arrest me for just walking into a building."

"Watch me. The owner of this establishment doesn't feel safe in your presence. You have no business here. Stay away."

"And what if I don't want to?"

"Then I guess you're going to have a rude awakening in your future."

"Maybe you're going to have the rude awakening."

"Maybe, but I doubt it."

Brian hung by the door a moment longer and then left. Landon locked it as soon as he was gone, and when he turned to me I thought there would be a lecture in my future. Instead, he grinned and held out his hand.

"That was fun! It got my testosterone going. What do you say to some vigorous ... snuggling ... and then a nap?"

Was that what he really wanted? "Seriously?"

"I'm feeling a little wound up. I need some Bay time."

Oddly enough, that sounded good. "I could use a nap. He's creepy."

"He's going to be trouble. He's not our problem today, though. We'll tackle him tomorrow. Right now, I just want to tackle you."

"I can live with that."

"That's why we're such a good fit."

25
TWENTY-FIVE

I woke from our nap before Landon. The first thing I saw were our clothes heaped on the floor. Months before, he'd talked me into hanging a warm blanket over the back of the couch so we had something to burrow under, especially during winter. Now it was bunched around us.

I saw our reflection in the window on the back wall and it caused me to smile. It didn't matter that my hair looked as if birds had been trying to build a nest in it. It didn't matter that he had a self-satisfied smile on his face as he slept. All that mattered was the way he curled around me, as if we fit.

I sensed he was going to stir the moment before he exhaled.

"What are you doing?" he murmured before kissing my bare shoulder. "Go back to sleep."

It was a nice but impractical thought. "It's after four."

His eyes snapped open and he looked to the clock on the wall for confirmation before swearing under his breath. "Man, Terry is going to be mad. I bet he's tried calling ten times. I told him I would be here two hours max."

"He'll be okay." I patted the hand tugging me closer to him. He seemed to be in no mood to jump to his feet and start scrambling. "You can blame me."

"Oh, I will." He chuckled and gave me a tickle as I squirmed. "You shouldn't have let me sleep so long."

I wanted to point out that he obviously needed the rest, but it was unnecessary. "I just woke up too."

"What woke you? Are you worried about Brian? I'll lock him up before he comes near you again."

"That's not why I woke up."

He propped himself on his elbow. "What were you thinking about when I first opened my eyes? You had a serious look on your face."

"I was thinking about sex."

"Oh, well ... ." His lips moved to my neck and I had to elbow him before he settled into another round.

"I was thinking about sex in a philosophical manner," I corrected.

"That doesn't sound nearly as fun."

"Probably not. It's just ... two years ago you weren't in my life. Two years isn't a long time in the grand scheme of things. It's ... nothing. Everything is different, though."

"Better, right?"

"Yeah." It wasn't even a question. "You changed everything, made it better, and here we are having nooners in my office, in a business I own because of you."

"Nooners?" He barked out a laugh. "Oh, I love you and your prudish tendencies." He snuggled me close. "I wouldn't really call this a nooner. It was well after noon when I came in here."

"You know what I mean."

He was quiet for a moment. "We changed each other's lives, Bay. I don't know if I believed in destiny before you, but now I know I was always meant to end up here."

"That's kind of sweet."

"I'm a sweet guy."

I turned in his arms to face him. "I wish we could stay here all night, lock out the rest of the world and just ... be."

"That would be nice," he agreed, pushing my hair from my face. "But I don't think it's possible."

"No, definitely not."

He cupped the back of my head and gave me a kiss. "How about we take an entire day just for us when this is over? We can hide in bed — or on this couch, I'm not picky — and lock the rest of the world out. We'll have food delivered and pretend the rest of the world — especially your family — doesn't exist."

I wanted to agree, but we had more than one problem to solve. "And what about Brian and Rosemary?"

"I'll throw them in jail for a day. They won't be an issue."

"They have a plan, Landon." I kept my voice soft. "Brian thinks we wronged him. He wants revenge."

"I'm well aware. I won't let him hurt you."

"What if ... ." I trailed off, uncertain.

"Tell me," he prodded.

"What if Brian is somehow involved in what happened to Amelia? What if the shadow monster went at him as some sort of ploy? Maybe he's behind all of this?"

Landon's mouth fell open but he didn't immediately respond.

"You think I'm being ridiculous," I surmised.

"I don't think you're being ridiculous. I just ... I can't figure out how a teenager going missing benefits his plan to get the newspaper back. By the way, he can't. I don't want you making yourself sick with 'what ifs,' because it's not possible. You own this paper. It's yours. He will never take it from you."

He was so insistent I had to smile. "I'm not worried about losing The Whistler."

"Then what are you worried about?"

"That we're missing something. None of this makes sense, Landon. It's all ... a mess. From the other teenagers and how they're acting to what happened to Marcus to the shadow monster. It seems as if there should be a common thread, but if there is it's invisible."

"We'll figure it out. We always do."

"You sound really sure of yourself."

"I'm sure of you." He leaned close and pressed his forehead against mine. "Bay, you can do anything you set your mind to. You're smart ... and strong ... and loyal. I'm not going to pretend that there's not a missing piece to all of this, but when we find it it will make sense."

I let him hold me close for so long I thought he might've fallen asleep again. Then I heard the rumble of his stomach and had to laugh. "You're hungry too."

"I'm starving."

"What do you say to carnival food for dinner? We can sit at a table and watch our suspects. If one of them is maneuvering us into a certain place to collect a ransom tonight, we might be able to figure it out before the big event happens."

"Sounds like a fantastic idea."

. . .

"OKAY, I GOT HOT DOGS, HAMBURGERS, shawarma, something green, fries, onion rings, and those fried mushrooms you go gaga over."

Landon unloaded a huge box of food on the picnic table, making my eyes go wide. "This is enough food for eight people."

"You say that like it's a bad thing."

"We'll get fat."

He shook his head, clearly unbothered by the prospect. "If we put on a few pounds, we'll just take more naps in your office. We burn a lot of calories that way."

I could only shake my head. "I love that in your mind there are always two solutions to every problem," I said as I grabbed the container of fried mushrooms. He wasn't lying; I absolutely loved them. "Sex and food. You think they can solve any problem."

He sat across from me, planted both his feet on either side of mine, and squeezed my legs between his before handing me an iced tea. "Name one problem that can't be fixed with food or sex."

"Um ... government misspending."

"If they had better food they wouldn't want to misspend funds."

I could see where this was going. "That's not a real solution."

"It's always a solution in my book." He surveyed the food and went for one of the hamburgers. "Your problem is that you like to chew on something so long it loses all taste. You dwell and dwell and dwell until there's a misshapen hunk of food that could've been a delicious steak or disgusting tofu at some point, but there's no telling what it is now."

I popped a mushroom into my mouth and methodically chewed and swallowed before speaking again. "Have you ever noticed that every conversation we have comes back to food?"

"I'm a simple man, Bay. You could lock me in a cabin in the middle of nowhere with no wi-fi or electricity for the rest of my life. As long as I had you and good food, I'd be the most contented man in the world."

That was sweet ... and also a bunch of crap. "Really? You're going to be fine with no sports to watch on television?"

"I can play sports with you."

"No video games. No music."

He stilled. "I didn't really think about the music."

"That's right. You'll just have my voice yammering in your ear twenty-four-seven forever."

He held my gaze. "I think I would be okay with it."

Ugh. He was being too sweet for even me to stomach. "You should be done with the overly romantic stuff for a few days."

"Too far?" He grinned before biting into his hamburger.

"Just a little." I turned my attention to the crowd. I struggled to believe a kidnapper would have time to hang out at a festival before a ransom drop, but it would make a pretty good alibi.

The first face I saw belonged to Todd Lipscomb. He stood outside the kissing booth trying to entice couples to venture inside. He looked bored with his job and yet resigned because his livelihood depended on it.

"How hard do you think it is to make a living running the kissing booth?" I asked, reaching for one of the hotdogs.

Landon helped me by sliding it closer and grabbing the small container of onions included in the paper bin. He focused on Todd. "I'm guessing it's not easy."

He shoved some fries in his mouth and eyed me. "What's going on inside that busy brain of yours?"

That was a very good question. "What if Todd has been inappropriately flirting with the girls to the point he started a relationship with one?"

Landon made a face. "You think a teenager willingly started a relationship with that guy?"

I shrugged. "Stranger things have happened. Someone married Aunt Tillie."

"You've got me there." He grinned and winked and then went back to watching Todd. "Is he married?"

"He was married back when I was in high school. Her name was Sandra, or maybe Sandy. She wasn't local and reportedly hated how small Walkerville was."

"He doesn't look like the sort of guy who would be able to entice a teenager."

That was an odd statement. "What do you mean?"

"Well, for starters, it's not unheard of for teenagers to convince themselves they're in love with an adult. Amelia is seventeen. She'll be eighteen in three months. It's not illegal in the state of Michigan for an adult to have a relationship with her."

I made a face. "It's frowned upon."

"It is, and I'm one of those people who would do the frowning. The thing is ... teenage girls are lured in a variety of different ways. One is through a position of power. That's how high school teachers, principals, and guidance counselors manage it. The girl thinks they have power over her and acquiesces out of fear."

I pursed my lips. "That doesn't describe Todd."

"Not even a little," he agreed. "There's also the money factor. Older men who have money sometimes shower teenagers with gifts and attention to draw them in. Girls who can be bought, even if they don't realize it, often go that route."

"Okay. That makes sense. But it also doesn't apply to Todd."

"No. The third type are generally younger men who went to school with the girls. Say the man would've been a senior when the girl was a freshman or still in middle school. There's a mystique factor. These men were very popular boys and they managed to garner crushes from a lot of girls. The crushes tend to be holdovers, even if the boys in question never grew into successful men."

What he said made sense, but it blew my theory out of the water. "You're saying there's no way it's Todd."

"I can't say that with any degree of certainty," he countered, searching through the food until he found the other hot dog. "If the kids think he's a pervert, there's usually something behind that."

"The problem is, I don't trust this particular group of teenagers," I said.

"They're unreliable, to say the least. They also might be trying to manipulate us. I get that feeling, especially from Paisley."

"She might be trying to manipulate you because she thinks you're hot."

"Maybe, but this feels darker." He handed me a fry. "Todd doesn't fit the description the girls gave us."

"But what if they're lying about that?"

"That's a heckuva risk. If one of them slips up, it's all over."

"If only Marcus could remember what happened," I muttered, shoving the fry into my mouth and turning my attention to another table. "And then there's those jerks."

Landon followed my gaze, frowning when he saw, about three tables over, Brian sitting with Rosemary, Aunt Willa, and Mrs. Little. They appeared to be engaged in lively conversation, but I didn't miss the sly looks Brian kept shooting in our direction.

"I really don't think he has anything to do with this, Bay," Landon said. "There's nothing I would like more than to have a legitimate reason to drag him in, but I don't think it's going to be this."

He was right. I knew it deep down. Still, something was off about the entire situation. Er, well, something more than the obvious. "He was hanging out in the woods behind the Dragonfly that night."

"That's true." Landon stroked his chin, considering, and then did something I wasn't expecting. "Hey, Kelly, I have a question," he barked out.

If Brian was surprised to be called out in such a manner, he didn't show it. "You can call me Brian," he drawled, his smarmy nature on full display.

"Great." Landon's expression never changed. "Bay and I were discussing this case I'm working on and you might be able to answer a question for me."

Brian's eyebrows migrated up his forehead. "You think I can help you with a case?" It was obvious he believed Landon was trying to trick him into saying something. He also was attracted to the idea of looking important in front of those gathered around us.

"I don't know about help, but you're the only one who can tell me what you were doing hanging out with a bunch of teenagers behind the Dragonfly the other night," Landon replied. "There were about thirty kids out, more girls than boys. You would've been the only adult mixing with them."

Brian worked his jaw, his eyes kindling with fury. While rage seemed to be the primary emotion fueling him, there was fear, too. And embarrassment, if the pink of his cheeks was an indication. "What makes you think I was hanging out in the woods behind the Dragonfly? I mean ... come on."

"It's probably because you're a pervert," a female voice rang out from the crowd, causing me to snap my head to the left. I couldn't be sure who had said it, but Paisley, Sophia, and Emma were all in attendance.

Now that all eyes were upon him, Brian's face reddened. "If you're accusing me of something," he started.

"Accusing isn't the right word," Landon countered. "It's more that I'm curious. We have a missing teenager and you were sneaking out into the woods to hang with a bunch of teenagers the other night. I want to know why."

"I was not hanging out with a bunch of teenagers," Brian snapped, his eyes immediately going to Rosemary. "I wasn't. Don't listen to him."

"Before you deny being out there, you should know that I was watching," Landon said. He didn't come right out and say he'd seen Brian.

"You were watching?" Brian's eyes bulged.

"I'm looking for a missing teenager. Teenagers have been partying in the woods out there for weeks. I wanted to hear what was being said."

"So you were spying on teenagers?"

"If you like."

"Well, that's just ... gross and disgusting." Brian's gaze bounced to a few tables as he searched for support. "Do you like that an FBI agent is spying on your children?"

"It's a lot more disgusting to party with teenagers than it is to eavesdrop in case they know something about a missing kid," Mike Lintz called from his place in the food line. I hadn't even seen him approach. "Only a pervert hangs around with teenagers."

"Totally," Paisley intoned, drawing my eyes to her. She seemed amused by Brian's discomfort. "This town is full of perverts. He's just one of them. I thought we'd gotten rid of him, but he just had to come back."

"Do I even know you?" Brian challenged.

"Think really hard," Paisley drawled, rolling her eyes.

I opened my mouth, the intention to say something to diffuse the situation on the tip of my tongue, and then I felt it. Magic. It was zipping through the air.

I turned quickly, my eyes scanning the trees at my back. I didn't see anything, but then the clouds opened up out of nowhere. A flash of lightning split the sky and I saw a figure in the woods.

The sighting was brief, and I wasn't even certain what I saw, but the thunder that followed sounded like a freight train. When the lightning flashed again, the figure was still there, and I saw it more clearly this time. It was a female, and she had delicate curves ... like a teenager.

Then another terrific rumble of thunder hit and those gathered at the tables scrambled as people farther inside the festival grounds began screaming. It was utter bedlam, and the storm raged harder.

26
TWENTY-SIX

I had one thought and went with it, hopping up from the table and bolting toward the woods. Landon, who had been trying to save our food, dropped everything he was carrying and gave chase.

"Bay!"

I didn't turn around. I couldn't. I could only think that someone was in the woods controlling the storm. That someone was likely responsible for kidnapping Amelia, or at least knew what had happened to her.

The rain poured down in sheets. Even ducking under the wide boughs of the trees did little to help. I scanned the woods for movement. I couldn't see anyone and yet I felt someone ... and he or she was close.

"Bay." Landon growled as he caught up. When I risked a glance at him, I found he was bewildered more than annoyed. "What are you doing?"

"Someone is here." I gripped my hands into fists at my sides as I searched the trees. "Someone started the storm."

"Aunt Tillie?"

Under normal circumstances, that would've been a possibility. The form I'd seen had been taller than her. Thinner. "I think it's a teenager."

He didn't look convinced. "Who?"

That was a very good question. "I didn't see a face."

"What did you see?" His shoulder-length hair clung to the sides of his face, but he made no move to brush it away. His attention was only for me.

"I saw ... someone."

"Tell me exactly what you saw." He was calm and rational. There was no judgement in his tone. It rankled all the same.

"I don't know what I saw." Annoyance bubbled up and grabbed me by the throat. "I just ... saw something."

He studied my face and then nodded. "Okay. Let's do this."

And just like that, he gave me everything I ever could've needed and more. I squeezed his hand in appreciation and then let it go. If there was a magical being out here, I would need to be quick to protect us. "This way." I inclined my head toward the area at which I'd been staring.

He didn't draw his gun. I thought he might — he was big on being a protective force — but he understood this was my show. He would help if he could, but I would have to take down whatever enemy we found. He rested his hand on my back so I knew he was close and allowed me to take the lead.

The wooded area near the festival grounds was small, without many places to hide. I picked my way from tree to tree, carefully peering around them before moving forward. When we got to the spot where I thought I'd seen the movement, it was empty. The frustration I'd been bottling up threatened to explode.

"I swear I saw her right here." My eyes were pleading when I turned them to Landon. "She was definitely right here."

He held my gaze and nodded. "I believe you, Bay. She's not here now, though."

"But ... she was here. Are there footprints?"

He studied the ground, frowning as he knelt closer to the tree. "I think someone was standing here," he said finally. "Actually, I think two people were standing here."

"I only saw one silhouette."

He looked up at me, a question in his eyes.

"It wasn't the shadow monster," I reassured him. "This was different. Maybe the shadow monster was with her, but I definitely saw a human female."

"Describe her."

"I only saw her through the lightning. She was thin, not a lot up here." I moved my hands in front of my chest and thought hard. "Narrow hips. Long hair. It moved when she did."

"What color was her hair?"

"I couldn't see that. I'm sorry."

"Don't be sorry, Bay." He was solemn. "There's no reason to be sorry. I just want to know what we're dealing with." He continued to study the area before shaking his head. "Whoever it was went that way." He pointed in the direction of the parking lot.

"Maybe we should check over there," I suggested.

He forced a smile. "Regardless, we should get out of the rain." He moved his arm around my waist as he stood. We were both sopping wet. "Do you think it was one of our teenagers?"

"They were eating at the picnic tables," I reminded him.

"Yeah. They were giving Kelly hell." He managed a smile. "That was kind of fun."

The picnic table area was empty when we got there. Everybody had scattered, and the feast Landon had so lovingly collected was obviously ruined. "Let's pick this up and head to the inn. They'll have food. And we both need to change." He didn't sound happy about the prospect, but we had few options.

"I'm sorry." I couldn't stop myself from apologizing. "I really am sorry. I just ... I had to look."

He met my gaze, the storm raging around us, and leaned forward to kiss my forehead. "I need you not to apologize for stuff like this," he said. "You did what you thought was right. I'll never be angry because you followed your instincts."

I cocked a challenging eyebrow. "You've been angry about me following my instincts before."

"Okay, maybe a few times," he conceded. "That was before I fully understood what you could do. I have faith in you. That's never going to change."

"I'm still sorry."

He extended a warning finger. "Don't make me spank you for unnecessary apologies." He was obviously trying to lighten the mood.

"Maybe we can play that game later, when this is over and it's just the two of us."

He nodded. "I think that's a fabulous idea."

Once we cleaned up the remnants of our food — and everybody else's — we headed for the parking lot. There were a multitude of cars still there, filled with people perhaps trying to wait out the storm in case a night at the festival could be salvaged. I studied the faces as we passed.

"Sophia and Emma are in that car." I nodded with my chin as we hurried toward his Explorer. "Paisley isn't with them."

"Paisley was near us when the storm started. I think we would've seen her run to the woods."

I rubbed my chin. "So where did she go?"

"I don't know." He hit the fob on the Explorer and opened my door for me first. "Get in. I'll hit the heat so we can dry off a little."

I extended my hands in front of the vents the second the engine roared to life. He messed with the temperature controls and then searched the back seat.

"What are you looking for?" I asked as I rubbed my cheeks. I was glad I hadn't bothered with makeup today because it would've been pooling beneath my eyes right about now.

"I thought maybe there was a towel or blanket back here." He turned back to me. "I think I tossed that blanket we had the other day into the washing machine."

I wiped my nose. "We look pretty wrecked."

He snickered. "We'll head home first to shower and then hit the dining room at the inn."

"That sounds like a plan."

"Just do me one favor first."

"I'm not having sex with you right now." I was firm on that. "I might be able to get out of these clothes but there will be no getting back into them. And I don't want to risk someone seeing us driving through town naked."

"I'm not an animal."

I was understandably dubious.

"I'm not," he insisted when I didn't say anything. "I just want to go home and get changed. We'll save the romance for later."

"Then what do you want me to do?"

"Check the cars." He turned serious. "Tell me who is present. Call out the names."

"Why?"

"I just want to know."

Not fully understanding but knowing he wouldn't ask if he didn't feel it was important, I did as he requested. "Mrs. Little is hiding under the eaves of her store with Connie Halstead. Mike Lintz is watching the show in front of the cauldron shop. Sophia and Emma are in that car over there."

I had to squint to study a few more vehicles. "Rosemary and Aunt Willa are in that blue car about ten spots over."

Landon sat up straighter. "Is Brian with them?"

"No, but he's definitely not the person I saw in the woods."

"He could be the owner of the second set of footprints, though. We don't know that he didn't head into the woods to help whoever was there escape."

"And what would be his motive?"

"We don't have a motive. That's what makes things so difficult."

I pressed my lips together and checked a few more vehicles. "The Robsons are over there. They have small children with them. I think that burgundy SUV belongs to Leona and Patrick Sturgess. They're older, and I guarantee they weren't running around the woods."

He nodded and prodded me to continue.

"Um ... huh." I craned my neck and wiped my hand over the foggy inside of the Explorer window. "That's Todd's truck, but it's empty." I flicked my eyes to the kissing booth. "Where did he go?"

"I don't know." Landon used his hands to wring out my hair. "Anyone else?"

"I think that's it."

"So we definitely know that Kelly, Paisley, and Todd are unaccounted for."

I had trouble grasping what he was getting at. "So?"

"So, I'm curious if this storm is a distraction for the ransom demand. We need to dry off and get to the inn. Terry is there. He should have more information by the time we arrive."

Realization dawned. "You think multiple people are involved in this."

"I think that when we finally get our answers we're going to be shocked at how many people knew a little something about this."

"Brian?"

"I don't know. I think all the girls know something more than they're saying." He clenched his jaw as we passed the vehicle where Emma and Sophia waited. They stared hard at us as we rolled by. "Let me ask you something. Is it possible these girls created their own coven?"

"I don't know. Anything is possible, I guess. Why?"

"I'm starting to think that they're all involved ... and that includes Amelia. I think they made up the kidnapping, and that Marcus' memory loss is magical in origin. We have a shadow monster running around. We have four teenagers acting weird. We have a lot of accusations of people being perverts. I think there's truth in there somewhere, but not for everybody."

"The girls are working with a pervert?"

"Or they're calling everyone perverts to distract us."

I hadn't considered that. "I guess it sort of makes sense."

"We'll break it down after dinner. We need to get out of these wet clothes first."

. . .

THE ENTIRE FAMILY WAS IN THE DINING ROOM. They seemed surprised by our sudden appearance.

"I thought you were eating in town tonight," Mom snapped, her tone full of accusation, as if we'd somehow decided that someone else was the best cook in the Midwest and had abandoned her accordingly.

"We got rained out," Landon replied as he herded me toward our regular spots. "Where are the guests?"

"We only have a handful until tomorrow," Marnie replied. "Then we're completely booked for the weekend. The two couples we have staying with us headed down to the festival."

"Then they got rained out," I said, rubbing my hands together when I saw the food. "Tacos. Yay."

"We thought they were festive," Mom agreed. "But you're late. I'm not sure we should feed you."

"Don't give us grief," Landon complained as he reached for some shells. "We've had a bear of a night."

"What happened?" Chief Terry asked, passing me the diced tomatoes. He knew they were my favorite.

Landon launched into the tale, leaving nothing out. He even touched on Brian's visit to my office earlier in the day. When he finished, he looked ready to go to war. "I think one of the purported perverts is helping the girls. I don't think there ever was a kidnapping."

Thistle stirred at the end of the table. "What about Marcus? The girls couldn't have done that."

I thought back to his stint in the hospital, my forehead creasing. "The doctor said he thought Marcus was struck with a heavy object. I explained what the girls said and he kind of brushed it off because we had bigger things to worry about, but what if he was right?"

"You think the girls knocked me out?" Marcus asked, confusion evident. "But ... why?"

"Social proof," Landon replied grimly. "They needed to sell a kidnapping. They must've felt they needed an injured individual to sell it properly. Because the area behind the barn is isolated, I think you were a victim of opportunity."

"It never made any sense that someone managed to get Amelia in a vehicle without anybody noticing," I offered. "The odds of no one seeing a teenager being dragged away from a festival are astronomical."

"But why?" Clove challenged. "What do they have to gain?"

"The ransom," Chief Terry volunteered. "They want money."

"Do you have the specifics of the exchange?" Landon asked.

Chief Terry nodded. "They want us at Hollow Creek in two hours."

"Why Hollow Creek?" Mom asked.

"It makes things easier for them," I said, my mind working overtime. "We were just down there, Aunt Tillie and me. There are still magical fragments there." I shifted on my chair. "What if that's the answer?"

"What's the answer?" Landon prodded.

"You asked if it was possible for four seemingly normal girls to suddenly create their own coven. I thought it was difficult, maybe impossible, but there's magic at Hollow Creek. What if they somehow discovered that and used the magic to their advantage?"

"Is that possible?" Landon directed the question to Aunt Tillie.

Aunt Tillie hesitated — she was serious for a change — and then held up her hands. "Normally I would say no. What you're suggesting would take a lot of work. These girls have access to books that could tell them how to do the work. This isn't a normal town, and the magic still floating around Hollow Creek was provided by powerful witches."

"They're using our own magic against us," Thistle mused. "Does that mean we could've created the shadow monster?"

"I don't know what sort of spell they used, but it's possible," Aunt Tillie replied, her expression grave as she focused on Landon and Chief Terry. "You realize if you take that ransom to Hollow Creek that you'll be attacked by a shadow monster."

Landon nodded. "I figured that out."

"You're not going alone." I was adamant. "You need me with you. I can call ghosts to take on the shadow monster."

"And then what?" Aunt Tillie leaned back in her chair. "You'll have four young witches down there with access to magic."

"Our magic," Thistle said. "You'll need extra help if you expect to take them out."

She was right, but I didn't want to ask. "Well ... ."

"We need four witches in case we have to call to the four corners," Aunt Tillie decided. "Clove is obviously out."

"I'll do it," Mom volunteered. "We should have more than enough power with you, me, Bay, and Thistle."

Aunt Tillie nodded in agreement, but Chief Terry was already shaking his head.

"I don't want you in danger, Winnie," he protested.

"I don't see that we have much choice in the matter." Mom was matter-of-fact. "Terry, you and Landon have to go because there's always a chance we're wrong and Amelia is in danger."

"Except she's the enemy," Chief Terry argued.

"Most likely," I agreed. "We can't be sure until we get there. You need us with you."

"But ... ." Chief Terry sputtered and turned to Landon. "You can't possibly think this is a good idea."

"On the contrary." Landon had made a monster taco and was about to bite into it. "I don't think we can do it without them."

"But ... they'll be in danger."

"They will. So will we." Landon blew out a sigh and looked to me. "We're a family. All of us. We have to do what's right for everybody in this family. You and I can't take on four teenage witches and a shadow monster alone. We need help."

"From me," Aunt Tillie volunteered, grinning evilly. "You need my help, which means I'm going to be owed a favor somewhere down the line."

"I don't think we agreed to that," Landon countered.

"And yet that's what's going to happen." She rubbed her hands together, gleeful. "This is going to be a fun night after all."

She was likely the only one who thought that, but it didn't mean she was wrong.

"We need to come up with a plan," I interjected before we could go off on a tangent. "Those girls might be using leftover fragments of our magic, but they're at a distinct disadvantage. They don't have Aunt Tillie ... or our knowledge base."

"Oh, don't make her head bigger than it already is," Thistle groused. "She's a bear to deal with on a normal day."

"Keep it up, Mouth," Aunt Tillie warned. "I'll show you what a real bear looks like if you're not careful."

"We'll diagram it out," Landon said. "As far as those girls are concerned, Terry and I will deliver the ransom. You guys can hide a vehicle. I've seen you do it. That's how you'll slip in and serve as our backup."

"Sounds like a plan to me." Mom's smile was serene. "Everybody needs to eat first. I don't want anybody going into a magic fight without proper nourishment."

There was really nothing more Winchester than that statement.

27

TWENTY-SEVEN

We went in first, using Mom's SUV because it was easily capable of handling the muddy roads to Hollow Creek. Aunt Tillie glamoured the vehicle so it was not only invisible but also silent. Our biggest problem was the lights. We couldn't use them. No matter how Aunt Tillie tried, she couldn't hide the light beams. That meant the person most familiar with the road leading into Hollow Creek had to drive.

"Hold on!" Aunt Tillie shrieked. She didn't slow as she pulled from the paved highway onto the dirt road that led to the creek. She was dressed for battle, her combat helmet at an angle on her head. As I held the handle above the window, I couldn't help but wonder if we would survive long enough to reach our destination.

"Slow down," Mom ordered from the back seat. I was still debating why I had sat in the front.

"I've got it," Aunt Tillie insisted.

I contorted myself in the seat to look through the rear window. Chief Terry and Landon were supposed to be behind us by a few minutes. I was anxious to see them, if only to reassure myself we were still on the road.

The vehicle lurched as Aunt Tillie drove over something hard, causing Thistle to viciously swear. When I glanced at Mom I found her eyes closed, a serene expression on her face, as if meditating.

"I think she's passed into another world," Thistle offered. "We won't be far behind because we're all going to die thanks to this crazy old bat's driving."

"Stop being a kvetch," Aunt Tillie ordered, her eyes on the windshield. "I've got this. I meant to do that."

"Whatever."

Somehow, and it could only be divine intervention from the Goddess as far as I was concerned, we finally reached the parking area near the creek. I recognized the fallen log Aunt Tillie parked next to and let out a pent-up breath. We'd made it.

"Should we get out now?" Aunt Tillie asked, her attention on me.

I shook my head. "We have to wait for Landon and Chief Terry." She'd been there when we laid out the plan. "It will only be a few minutes."

"I think we should head out there," she insisted. "We could end all of them before the men even get here. No muss, no fuss."

"No." I was firm. "We agreed to a plan. I won't put them at risk."

"How would my plan put them at risk?"

"They could get hurt by errant magic. I said no."

"You're such a killjoy." Aunt Tillie worked her jaw as she turned her attention to the woods. "Do you see them?"

I shook my head. "I'm sure they're close."

"Here comes Landon and Terry," Mom said from behind me. She sounded grim. At least she'd emerged from her catatonic state.

"Remember, we can't show ourselves until all the girls show themselves."

"What if someone else is with them?" Thistle asked. "We haven't ruled out the possibility that there's an adult guiding them."

"We haven't." I nodded. "We'll just have to play it by ear."

"Lower the windows," Mom instructed. "We need to listen to what's being said."

Aunt Tillie lowered all four windows and we watched as Landon and Chief Terry exited the Explorer and moved to the front of the vehicle. They'd left the headlights on to illuminate the area.

It was quiet for what felt like a really long time. I sensed movement before I saw it.

We'd been right. All four girls were there, including the supposedly kidnapped Amelia. They looked triumphant, as if they'd managed to pull off something amazing. Their blond heads almost glowed thanks to the illumination provided by the Explorer and their smug expressions caused my stomach to twist.

"Hello." Paisley beamed at the men. "I'll bet you didn't expect to find us."

Landon shifted the briefcase he carried to his left hand and regarded her with cold eyes. "Actually, you'd be surprised at what we've figured out."

Paisley exchanged an amused look with her friends. "Oh, really? What is it you think you know?"

"We know that the four of you planned Amelia's supposed kidnapping for money. We know that you've been using the magic fragments from the creek and somehow managed to create a shadow monster to do your bidding. We know that you've been trying to direct our attention to others. We also know there's an adult helping you. I think that about sums it up."

Paisley's forehead furrowed. "I ... you ... ." She looked genuinely perplexed.

"I don't like this," Emma announced. "This isn't going like you said it would."

"You said they would be surprised," Sophia insisted. "They don't look surprised."

"They're just acting," Paisley insisted, although she didn't look altogether convinced herself. "They didn't know it was us."

"That's where you're wrong." Landon's voice was calm and strong. I could tell he wanted to look in our direction. He refrained. We still had the upper hand. "None of the details of the kidnapping ever made sense." His gazed at Amelia. "You should've picked a less crowded spot if you really wanted us to believe the story you were trying to sell."

"You should've worked on your acting skills, too," Chief Terry offered.

"Our acting skills were spot-on," Paisley argued. "You totally fell for the story we told you. I mean ... how can you deny it? I saw you called in the state police to look for the kidnapper. If you didn't believe us, why did you do that?"

"We didn't have a choice in the matter. And, to be fair, we had no reason not to believe you that first night. It's only been in the days since that we grew suspicious."

"But ... no." Paisley simply couldn't believe that her plan hadn't worked to perfection. "We covered everything."

"Not even close." Now it was Landon's turn to look smug. "The doctor said Marcus was struck with something. You left that out of your story."

"I told you," Sophia hissed. "We should've said the kidnapper used the board to hit him. That was a loose end. The television shows always have people being caught because of stuff like this."

"We're not caught," Paisley insisted.

"You're beyond caught," Landon said. "You are in so much trouble. What was the plan? Were you going to take the money and start a new life on some sandy beach?"

"We were thinking Hawaii," Amelia volunteered. She didn't look as worried as the other girls.

"And how did you think that was going to work? You can't check into a hotel without identification and a credit card. No hotel is going to allow four teenagers without parents to squat in rooms just because they're cute."

"Money talks," Amelia shot back. "Now we have a million dollars. We can do whatever we want. As for an adult ... you were right about that earlier. We have an adult."

I willed Landon to ask the obvious question.

"Todd Lipscomb?" Landon prodded. "Really, ladies, did you think that the guy who runs the kissing booth going missing wouldn't be suspicious?"

Emma gasped. The others exchanged terrified looks. For the first time, they appeared to realize that they were nowhere near as sly as they thought.

"How can you possibly know that?" Paisley demanded. "I mean ... we pointed you to him because we knew that you would immediately discard him. We even pretended we were horrified about Amelia being missing when your girlfriend was eavesdropping in front of the Unicorn Emporium. We thought of everything."

"Like I said, you're not very good actresses," Chief Terry said. "Everything you did was suspect. Amelia's actual kidnapping was suspect. Marcus's convenient memory loss was suspect. You didn't do anything right."

"I told you we should've killed him," Amelia growled, her gaze on Paisley. "You said it wasn't necessary, and now look."

"It wasn't necessary." Paisley was adamant. "We don't need to kill people."

"We're going to have to kill these guys." Amelia jerked her thumb toward Chief Terry. "They know too much."

"We can just make them forget." Paisley refused to back down. "I don't want to kill people. If we disappear with the money and they end up dead, we can't risk that."

"They already know we're guilty," Amelia snapped. "We have no choice but to end them here and now."

I reached for the door handle, prepared to draw the girls' attention, but Aunt Tillie extended a hand to still me. "Not yet," she whispered.

It took everything I had to remain in the vehicle and ignore the sweat running down the back of my neck.

"I agree that you're going to have to kill us," Landon said, causing my stomach to shrivel. "But you won't get away with it. As for money ... ." He opened the briefcase and let them see that it was empty. "Did you really think we were going to bring a pile of cash out here when we knew who was behind this?"

The rage rolling off Amelia was palpable. The wind responded to her mood and the tree leaves started rustling. I reached for the door handle again.

"Bay, knock it off," Aunt Tillie hissed. "You said we have to wait for this to play out. It's your plan. Now we have to stick to it."

I hated — absolutely *hated* — having my words thrown back in my face.

"Where's the money," Amelia demanded.

"There was never any money," Chief Terry said. "We don't have endless funds and your parents don't have the money to cover a ransom."

"But ... the government is supposed to pay," Amelia insisted. "I saw it on television. The government pays for ransoms in situations like this."

"I don't know what you were watching but it wasn't factual. It's the government's policy not to negotiate with terrorists, which you are."

"But ... ." Amelia was incensed and the wind picked up in accordance with her mood.

"She's doing it," I said, leaning forward to study the trees. "She's the most powerful one."

"She's the one controlling the shadow," Thistle agreed. "The others are just idiots playing at magic. She's the one with the power."

"Then we have to stop her now." I was insistent as I met Aunt Tillie's gaze. "We have to end this."

"We have to wait for the signal." Aunt Tillie refused to give in to my demand, which was beyond frustrating. "It won't be long."

"You need to go back and get us our money," Paisley insisted. "We need that money. We're all packed and ready to go."

"With your kissing booth friend?" Landon sneered. "How do you think that's going to work?"

"He's not going with us." Paisley rolled her eyes. "We just used him to get what we want. He's hiding in the woods. He thinks we're going to share the ransom with him. He's a moron, just like everybody else."

"He's also afraid of what we can do," Amelia said with an evil grin. "We don't have to worry about him saying anything because he'll be implicating himself if he does. We've got everything under control. All of it."

"Except the money." Landon could do smug better than most and it was on full display as he folded his arms over his chest. "You have nowhere to go and no money. This is over."

"It's nowhere near over," Amelia countered. "We're in charge. We're ... powerful. We can get whatever we want."

THE WITCH IS BACK

"You're not real witches," Chief Terry said. "You're using borrowed magic."

"It's not even good borrowed magic," Landon said. "It's remnants of good magic left over from actual witches, but most of the power has already been spent. What's left over is ... weak."

"Oh, listen to this guy." Paisley made a disparaging gesture toward Landon. "He acts as if he actually knows things."

I was done waiting. We wouldn't get a better opening than this. "You would be surprised what he knows," I announced as I climbed out of the vehicle and moved beyond the glamour.

Shock registered on all four faces as they absorbed my appearance.

"You," Paisley said. "I should've known you were a part of this."

"You should've," I agreed, closing the distance between myself and Landon. I wanted to be close when the shadow monster arrived. I knew it was only a matter of time.

"People say you're real witches," Amelia noted. I could feel the ripples of fear moving through her. Nothing was going according to plan. They began improvising. "Your family, I mean."

"People say a lot of things about my family," I agreed.

"You're here because of him." She inclined her head toward Landon. "He involved you in this."

"We're family," I replied. "When a member of your family needs help, it's not a question of if you'll answer the call but how."

Amelia narrowed her eyes. "We're not asking for the world. We just want enough money to get out of here. We'll never be a bother again."

"If you want money, earn it. Don't fake a kidnapping."

"This place is the worst," Amelia insisted. "We don't want to stay here."

"Then find other means to leave. What you're doing is wrong. People have been hurt. As for that shadow you've created ... ." I shook my head. "It's an interesting piece of magic. I've been thinking about it. You enhanced a poppet."

Behind Paisley and Amelia, who were clearly the ringleaders, Sophia and Emma started whispering.

"How can she know that?"

"I don't like this."

I decided to take advantage of their fear. "If you don't like this, may I suggest moving away from them and climbing in the back seat of the Explorer? That's the only way you're going to get out of this unscathed."

"Your cooperation will be taken into account," Landon said. "You might not even do any jail time, unlike your friends."

Amelia let loose a hollow laugh. "Who are you trying to frighten? They know I'm more powerful than your blond witch here. Everybody knows the old lady is the real power in the Winchester family."

"What old lady?" Aunt Tillie asked, appearing out of the gloom. She'd exited the vehicle when I wasn't looking and appeared to be amused by the entire scene.

Amelia jerked when she registered the new voice, her eyes flying to Aunt Tillie. When Thistle and Mom joined the party, it was obvious Sophia and Emma were ready to surrender.

"We'll just ... go to the Explorer," Sophia murmured, ducking her head to avoid eye contact with Amelia and hurrying away from the other girls.

"We're really sorry," Emma offered me as she passed. "We just ... wanted a different life."

"I think you're going to get your wish," I said. "Wait in the SUV."

Emma didn't look over her shoulder. She'd severed ties with Paisley and Amelia, even if she wasn't ready to acknowledge it.

"And then there were two," Mom intoned.

Amelia's eyes blazed. "Do you really think it's going to be that easy? We're not just going to climb into your truck and say we've been bad girls and accept our punishment. We have a plan. We made a pact."

"Then you'll go down harder," I supplied.

Amelia growled. "We're not afraid of you."

Paisley didn't look as if she agreed, but she stood with Amelia.

"Then you're dumber than you look," Aunt Tillie said. "It doesn't matter. It's time to end this."

Paisley turned shrill. "Are we going to throw magic at each other until someone is dead?"

"We don't need to kill you," I said. "Our magic is stronger. Yours is temporary. Our magic is in our blood. You borrowed fragments you found out here.

"Do you know where those fragments came from?" I continued. "They're left over from previous battles. We thought we'd cleaned it up, but obviously we were wrong. You stumbled across it — I'm guessing you were out here to party or plot against your enemies — and thought you'd opened up a whole new world."

"You think you know everything," Paisley grumbled.

"I do know everything," Aunt Tillie said. "I also know that this magic you think is going to make everything easier is already waning. You didn't have much to start with. It dissipates a little more every day."

"I started a storm," Amelia shouted. "I created a shadow to serve us."

"Where is the shadow now?" I asked, looking toward the woods. It was the shadow that worried me most now. "It's probably best if you call it. We need to undo the magic you've wrought."

"You want to face it, do you?" Amelia looked practically tickled. "Well, then have your wish." She snapped her fingers, as if calling a dog. "Kill the witches," she ordered.

I watched the trees for signs of movement and wasn't disappointed when the shadow emerged, eyes flashing as it registered us as enemies. "I'll handle this," I said, briefly pressing my eyes shut. I didn't snap my fingers or raise my arm into the air this time. The plea I sent out was quieter, and the ghosts who'd responded the first time in this location stirred again.

"You find a lot of trouble," Carter noted as he floated toward the incoming shadow, Carol trailing disinterestedly behind. "Why is this thing back?"

"Just end it again," I instructed. "Do the same thing you did before. She won't be able to bring it back after this."

Panic licked Amelia's features. "Who are you talking to?"

"You're powerful," I said. "Shouldn't you already know?"

"I ... ."

The ghosts chased the shadow into the woods. Amelia might not have been able to see what I'd conjured to fight her monster, but she couldn't miss the way the shadow turned tail and raced back into the woods.

"Come back!" she ordered. "Come back right now! I mean it!"

The shadow didn't return. I knew it wouldn't be seen again.

"While a nifty bit of magic, your shadow can't stand up to the ghosts I can call," I explained. "I think we're finished here."

"We're nowhere near finished." Fire built on a foundation of hatred kindled in Amelia's eyes. "We're nowhere near done." She waved her hands, reminding me of a bird, and her fingers managed to ignite in faint light. "I'll end you all."

I pushed forward until I was directly in front of her. I grabbed her wrists, fire exploding around my fingers as I locked her in. "You're done," I insisted. "Just ... let it go."

"No!" Tears formed in Amelia's eyes. "We had a plan. You're ruining everything."

Aunt Tillie slid behind me and extended a warning finger in Paisley's direction when it looked as if the girl might run. "Don't make me hurt you."

"She doesn't like to run," Thistle called out. "She'll make a huge pile of dog crap or something for you to trip into if you're not careful. It's best to just surrender."

Paisley briefly glanced toward the woods, as if calculating the odds of being able to make an escape.

"Don't," Aunt Tillie repeated. "It's over."

"It is," Landon agreed, moving closer to me. He looked hesitant as he took in my glowing fingers and the fierce expression on my face. "I need to take her into custody, Bay."

He was right, but we weren't quite done. "We need to bind them so they can never use magic, and modify their memories."

He looked taken aback. "What?"

"If they start talking about magic and shades once they're in custody you could get in trouble," I insisted. "We have to modify their memories."

He didn't look convinced. "Can you do that?"

"I can't without a little help." I slid my eyes to Aunt Tillie. "Thankfully, I know someone who can help."

"I'm good at it," Aunt Tillie reassured Landon. "I've got everything under control. Trust me."

"Oh, you have no idea how much I hate those words coming out of your mouth," Landon groused. "They're the absolute worst."

"It's going to be fine, you big baby." She slapped him on the shoulder. Hard. "This was an easy takedown compared to the others we've faced lately. You should be happy."

His eyes drifted to me and he flashed a smile. "I am happy. But we still have a few things to deal with."

He was right. The night was nowhere near over.

28
TWENTY-EIGHT

Landon and Chief Terry left Paisley and Amelia for us to watch and headed into the woods in search of Todd. They weren't gone long, and when they returned, they were dragging the man against his will.

"Where did you find him?" I asked.

"He was cowering behind some bushes," Landon replied, directing Todd to sit on the ground with the girls. "He claims the girls made him help them."

"They did," Todd insisted, his eyes wide. "They have magic. They're conjurers. I didn't want anything to do with this. They forced me."

Part of me wanted to smack him across the face, but I managed to refrain for Landon's sake.

Aunt Tillie didn't struggle with the same need to behave. "You're a turd," she announced, slapping her hand against his cheek as hard as she could. I think she might've put a little magic behind it, because she left a visible print on his face.

"Ow." Todd sank lower and hid his face between his knees.

"The other two are still in the Explorer," Thistle announced as she joined us. Her expression was hard to read. "Do you want to do them first?"

I considered the question and then shook my head. "I think we need to handle Amelia and Paisley first." I lowered myself to the tree trunk closest to me, using it as a bench, and studied them in turn. Paisley looked legitimately worried, but Amelia appeared ready to strike out and try to escape at any moment. "Do you have questions?"

"Questions?" Amelia's eyebrow arched like a soap opera villain on the make. "Are you kidding me? You plan to mess with my memory."

"That's no worse than what you did to Marcus," Thistle pointed out.

"We didn't hurt him," Paisley insisted. "I made sure he was okay. I did the right thing."

"I'm pretty sure you don't understand what 'the right thing' is," I countered, my voice measured. "It doesn't matter. We have to protect our family. That means silencing you."

"I'll come back," Amelia warned. "I'll make you pay."

"I have a feeling you're going to make a lot of people pay for trusting you before it's all said and done," I said. "There's not much I can do but watch you."

"Watch me? I'm not afraid of you."

"You should be." I raised my hands to touch them to her temples and she jerked away, her eyes wild. "Is this what you did to Dani?"

I faltered, surprised. "What do you know about Dani?"

"I know that one minute she was here and the next she wasn't. People said her mother and brother moved away without her, but I never believed that. Did you make them all forget too?"

"Not that it's any of your business, but the mother and brother voluntarily moved away because Dani was dangerous," Landon volunteered. "As for the girl herself ... ." His gaze landed on me and he held out his hands, unsure what to say.

"Dani was a born witch," I explained, opting for the truth. They wouldn't remember, so it didn't matter. "She had legitimate magic and she was much more powerful than you. She didn't want to be good. She was drawn to the darkness, willingly embraced it. She also wanted her freedom. As a compromise, we made sure she couldn't use her magic, and she left of her own volition. I have no idea where she is now."

Amelia didn't look convinced. "You're lying."

"From where you're sitting, it really doesn't matter." I raised my hands again. Amelia jerked so far back she almost fell over.

"Wait." Amelia was desperate, and I understood why. "I know what that dude Brian Kelly is doing here. I heard him talking to that old lady in the unicorn store. I know what he wants."

I stared at her for a long moment, debating, and then shook my head. "So do I. He wants revenge because he believes we took the newspaper from him.

He believes it to be his legacy, even though he clearly doesn't understand what that word means.

"I believe he's using Rosemary to further his revenge," I continued. "She'll end up hurt in this mess, but she's here to screw with us anyway, so it could be considered karmic retribution. We'll handle them when the time is right."

Landon flashed a soft smile and grabbed Amelia by the shoulders, pushing her upright. "Bay is right. We'll handle Rosemary and Brian. You don't have to worry about it."

"Please." Amelia's voice cracked. "I don't want to forget."

"You won't forget everything," I promised. "You'll remember who you are, and your parents. As for your plan to take off ... you'll forget that. You won't remember what happened to you when you were gone. Some memories will be shifted, others removed. In the end, you won't remember the magic."

"I don't want to forget." Amelia was desperate. "There's more in this world than I ever dreamed. I don't want to forget that."

"Unfortunately, you can't be trusted to use your knowledge in a good way," I said, casting a heavy look to Aunt Tillie to see if she was ready to help me reset their minds. "Until you figure out how to be a good person, it's best you don't remember any of this."

Hatred flashed hot and hard in her eyes. "Somehow I'll remember and come back. I'll make you pay."

"And that right there is why you can't be trusted with this knowledge. Now, close your eyes. This won't hurt. It might itch a little, though."

HOURS LATER, I FOUND LANDON DRAWING a bath for us in the guesthouse. He'd been quiet since he got home — he and Chief Terry had to drop the girls with their parents and come up with a lie to cover all of us — and he appeared thoughtful now.

"Are you okay?" I moved my hands to his shoulders and rubbed, causing him to groan.

"If you keep doing that for the next hour I'll play whatever dirty game you want tonight."

I cracked a smile. "How about I do it because you've had a long night and leave it at that?"

He slid his eyes up to me and smiled. "I think you've had a longer night. Maybe I should massage you."

"We could take turns."

"I'm up for that." He grabbed my hand and drew me closer. "This bath is for both of us. I thought we could soak a bit and then go to bed early."

"Is that code for something?"

He tried for a flirty grin ... and failed. "I just want to hold you tonight. I really am tired."

Because the truth of that statement was reflected in the depths of his eyes, I nodded and took a step back. "A bath sounds good." I kicked off my shoes. "You haven't talked about the Harts. How did they take Amelia's return?"

He tugged his shirt over his head before answering. "They were relieved to see her. We explained that when we showed up for the ransom drop all the girls were there, dazed, and we had no idea what to make of it. We tried questioning them but they couldn't answer."

"Maybe leaving so many unanswered questions was a mistake," I mused as I pulled my own shirt over my head. "It seemed like a good idea at the time, but it could come back to bite us."

"It was a good idea," Landon reassured me, pulling me to him. His skin was warm as I rested my head against his chest, his fingers gentle as they combed through my hair. "It's easier for us to feign ignorance than try to come up with a lie to cover all of this. I think it's the only option we had."

"Still ... ."

"Still," he agreed, pressing a kiss to my forehead and then pulling back. "I don't think I told you earlier, but I'm really proud. You held it together and modified five memories. You put in a lot of work. I could tell it was wearing on you by the end."

"I don't know that putting Todd back in the populace was a good idea."

"He'll likely screw up again," Landon said. "We'll be watching more closely."

"I guess."

"We couldn't risk arresting him, not with what happened and so much at stake."

What he said made sense. I was starting to think I was simply too fatigued to absorb it. "So, that's it."

"That's it for the girls, for now at least," he confirmed as he dropped his pants. "We'll have to make additional attempts to question them to make it look good."

"Right. I didn't think of that."

"You can't think of everything." He climbed into the tub and motioned for me to join him once he settled.

The water was the perfect temperature. I groaned as I rested my back against his chest, smiling as he wrapped his arms around me and sank lower in the water.

"This is nice," I murmured, sleep threatening to catch up to me.

"It is." His lips were close to my ear. "That thing you said about Kelly earlier, you don't have to worry. We'll figure out a way to get him out of town."

That was far down my list of worries right now. "Can we talk about that tomorrow? I don't want him to be a distraction tonight. I want it to be just the two of us."

"That's my perfect combination."

"Mine too."

He exhaled heavily and closed his eyes. "I really am proud of you, Bay."

"Thank you."

He waited a beat. "Aren't you proud of me?"

"What for?"

"We're in a bathtub and I'm not trying to cop a feel."

I laughed, as he'd intended. He felt he needed to lighten the mood so I wouldn't dwell on everything that had occurred and have nightmares. "I'm proud of you too."

"We're quite the team."

"We are."

"Do you want to start talking about honeymoon destinations tomorrow? That kind of fell by the wayside when Amelia went missing."

"That sounds like a perfect day. We can stay in bed and talk about wedding plans."

"What about breakfast?"

"We'll sucker Mom into bringing it down to us."

"You just described my perfect day, Bay."

"And it's just the first day of the rest of our lives."

"And that right there is something to look forward to."

I agreed wholeheartedly.